Shep

The Firefighters of Station #8

S. R. Wyatt

LOVE ENDURES

THE FIREFIGHTERS OF STATION #8

Mike (Book 1)
Shep (Book 2)
Jared (Book 3)

DEDICATION

To all firefighters around the world, true American heroes who put their lives in jeopardy every day. Thank you for your bravery and dedication. Although it may seem you are taken for granted, you are greatly appreciated, valued, respected and this world is blessed to have devoted souls like you. I have first-hand knowledge in a life altering experience. My own home was burned to the ground. While many made comments on the destruction, my thoughts were solely on the safety of the men who came to my aid.

I would also like to thank and give recognition to my inspiration guys who allowed me to interview them for my books. Who willingly answered my questions with enthusiasm and even allowed me into their bay and climb in their big fire trucks. So many wonderful, fun men who were so nice to a stranger. I did not model any character after a certain individual. Since the guys were being respectful, I had to use my imagination for the personal aspects. I combined what I learned with my own ideas and created each firefighter with his own charisma.

ACKNOWLEDGEMENTS

As always, I'd like to thank my husband who has been my main support and encouraged me every step of the way.
I'd like to thank my editor, and my cover artist who does wonderful covers.
For everyone who loves a little romance and a Hot Firefighter.
Keep the Spirit!
Samanthya

Contents

CHAPTER 1

The *Pitt Stop* sign glowed above the brightly-lit building centered in the middle of a huge parking lot. Shep shoved the gearshift into park and shut off the headlights. After the day he'd had, a cold beer sounded mighty fine.

There were too many unanswered questions. An unexplained explosion weighed heavy on his conscience. The fire investigator had not found any leads and his squad, the men he was responsible for, had gone back to the training site on their own. If his profession didn't kill him, worry would. Yep, he needed just one hour free of his current problems.

An hour wouldn't make much difference in solving a conundrum when you didn't know where to begin, but it could offer a moment's reprieve, keep him from brain overload. Damn, he hated feeling powerless. Maybe a break would give him the breather he needed to look at the incident with a new perspective.

He climbed out of his vehicle and waited for Mike before punching the remote to the door locks.

"Smell that?" Mike, one of the firefighters in his squad, puffed his big chest out as he inhaled. The smell of charcoaled beef drifted through the door at the front entrance. "Aren't you glad you agreed?"

Yep. Shep's taste buds tingled, but right now he wanted a cold drink more than food. He gave a nod and followed Mike into the noisy bar. Loud voices, laughter, and the jukebox blaring a country song made him glad for the loud commotion. Even though the *Pitt Stop* had great food, it was better known for music and dancing. Bands played every weekend and when they didn't, the jukebox stayed operational, making the place lively.

"Hi Mike. Shep. Two beers coming right up."

Since he and Mike were regulars, Sam, the bartender, knew what they wanted without question. Shep didn't drink a lot, but he frequented the place as much as anyone. Not to mention, the firefighters were well known and always welcome.

"Thanks, Sam. Put it on his tab." Shep nodded toward Mike as he picked up one of the bottles.

"Guess that's only fair since I talked you into coming."

"Sure thing." Sam grinned and moved down the bar to take another man's order.

Shep leaned a hip against the bar while he surveyed the crowded room and twirling bodies. Been a while since he'd been on the dance floor, but he was one of the few men who actually liked to dance. Women were partial to a man that could boogie, but then they got other ideas in their heads. So, most of the time, he just watched.

"Well, I'll be damned."

Shep turned at the sound of Mike's voice, seeing a huge grin on his face. "What's up?"

"I see someone I know."

Shep searched the room looking for the person responsible for putting that expression on Mike's face.

"Cassie and her friend," Mike said before Shep saw them.

"The school teachers?"

"Yep. Right over there." Mike gestured with the bottle in his hand.

Shep saw a blonde and a redhead, giggling like a couple of teenagers. He recognized them from the Mexican restaurant the team had gone to after the training exercise. Mike had been keeping the blonde company and seemed to be getting attached.

"From the Mexican restaurant?" Shep asked, even though he already knew.

"They're the ones."

"I seem to remember Jared taking a fancy to the redhead." Shep had noticed her right off. The woman had an inviting smile and her eyes had sparkled while she'd flirted with Jared, another member of his squad the team called *Pretty Boy*. He had the looks and the personality to warrant the nickname.

Jared had seen the women first. Being his normal, cocky self, he'd swaggered over to their table and moved right in. For the first time in years, Shep had almost felt the pang of jealousy.

"Naw," Mike said. "Jared said he didn't take her flirting seriously. I think she was just having fun. Not trying to pick him up."

"Hmmm."

"Come on. They look a little too chipper. Let's see what they're up to."

Again, Shep followed Mike. He weaved his way through the dancers toward the booth. Mike leaned against a post at one side, so Shep stood alongside the opposite one. The blonde took a huge bite of her burger and closed her eyes.

"Mmm mmm. Heaven." Damn if she didn't look like a woman having an orgasm. She opened her eyes and froze, her gaze fixed on Mike.

"Heaven?" Mike teased in a sensual tone.

Shep knew his buddy had had the same thought. Now, the woman looked like she might choke. Mike let her stew for a few seconds, but Shep knew he wanted to laugh.

"This is Shep," Mike said to both women. "Shep, this is Tammy. And this"—Mike angled his beer at the blonde—"is Cassie."

Her face turned red and she dropped her burger.

"It's a pleasure, ladies." Shep glanced to the blonde, then the redhead, who was staring back at him, her beautiful green eyes blazing with devilment.

"Hello, Shep. You a big strong firefighter, too?" Tammy asked with a hint of innuendo. She'd propped her chin in her palm, resting her elbow on the tabletop. He wondered if her provocative behavior had been prompted by the margarita glass sitting in front of her. Even so, she was too cute for words.

"Why, yes ma'am. I am."

"Well, come on over here, fire-hero, and tell me all about yourself."

Chuckling, he slipped into the booth beside her. She acted all silly and cuddled right up next to him, causing his gaze to drop to the fabric straining across her full breasts. Mike had warned him about her flirting, but Shep figured the alcohol was a contributor tonight. Typically, he did not engage with women who drank a lot of alcohol, but she was Cassie's friend, and Cassie was Mike's girl. Besides, she seemed harmless. And he couldn't help playing along.

"When Mike mentioned coming to this place, I almost suggested going somewhere else," Shep told her. "At the time, it didn't make any difference to me. Now I'm glad we came here."

"Is that so?" Tammy's glassy eyes peered up at him, drawing him into their charming depths. That's when he noticed a brownish tint in one. And freckles sprinkled over a cute nose.

"Yes, ma'am."

"Please don't call me ma'am," she said, rolling out her lip in a sexy pout.

"My mother taught me manners."

She perked right up. "I can appreciate that."

He couldn't help but add, "Thought tonight would be boring. Not so, now."

"Really? How come?" Her breath tickled his cheek.

"Because I met you."

"I've met you before. Well, not actually met," she said, waving her hand. "But I remember you from El Puerto's."

Tammy remembered him? She'd been flirting with Jared.

"The whole fire department showed up there," she said with some awe. "Cassie and I thought we'd hit the jackpot."

The jackpot?

"We had training that week," Shep began, explaining why the guys were there. "Several County units gathered for drills and preparation exercises. That day, we went out for some dinner." He didn't add the reason. An explosion at the training site had shaken the men. Station Nine had been in charge so Shep, being the Captain at Station Eight, had stayed at the firehouse. After he'd heard everyone's versions of what happened, the men had decided to go out to eat. Dumb luck, they'd ended up at the same restaurant.

"You men in your blue uniforms caused quite a stir." Tammy leaned closer to him and smiled in adoration. He recognized the look. He'd seen it enough. Still, he didn't move. He kind of liked the attention.

"We get that a lot."

"I love a man in uniform."

Blue T-shirts weren't exactly uniforms, but they were standard issue. He chuckled, wondering how much she'd had to drink.

"Here ya go, gals." A waitress placed two shot glasses of dark liquid on their table. "You said keep 'em coming."

Now he understood. *Shots.*

The sexy waitress propped a hand on her hip. "What can I get for you boys?"

"What's that?" Mike said, pointing to the drinks.

"B52 bombers."

"Sounds good to me," Shep said, thinking why not. The girls were having fun. They must be celebrating. He didn't mind keeping an eye on the lovely Tammy. He was sure Mike felt the same way about Cassie. "Two more."

Mike raised his brows. Mike knew Shep didn't drink hard liquor. And he wasn't exactly planning on starting now.

"Are you ladies celebrating?"

A cloud of darkness screwed up Tammy's face and he wished he could take back his question. Cassie quickly filled the silence.

"We, uh, received some troubling news."

Shit.

"And we're here to forget." Tammy lifted one of the shot glasses. "Bottoms up." She stared at Cassie as if daring her. Shep wondered what kind of shit storm he'd opened up.

"Why don't you take mine?" Cassie slid her glass across the table to Shep.

"Oh, no. I couldn't take yours." He shoved it back. For one thing, he didn't want it. For another, if these girls were trying to forget bad news, what better way than drowning out their problems. For the moment, anyway.

"Bottoms up," Shep echoed Tammy.

"We agreed ..." Tammy stared across the table, then flung back her head and the contents of the shot-glass disappeared. She gasped as if the liquor had stolen her breath. He lifted his beer and offered it to her. He didn't expect her to take it but she grabbed it and gulped, her creamy white throat rolling as she swallowed.

His belly tightened. Amazing, the reaction the woman had on him.

"What the hell." Cassie shrugged, tilted her own glass, and drained it.

Shep grinned and saw Mike's shoulders shake. Just then, the waitress placed more shots on the table. Unable to resist, Shep held up his fingers. "Two more."

"How you doing on beers?"

"Another round, please. And two more burgers." He needed food.

The *Pitt Stop* served man-sized burgers. Damned if he wasn't hungry. Looked like he might be here a spell.

"Oh, yeah." Cassie stared at her burger as if she'd forgotten it was there. Then she picked it up and took a huge bite. He just smiled.

"I love a woman with a good appetite," Mike said.

"Scc? I told ya," Tammy shouted.

"Told her what?" Shep asked, leaning closer to Tammy.

"She was worried about eating a juicy burger in front of a hunk like him." Tammy pointed directly at Mike.

Cassie made choking sounds. Mike patted her on the back. It would seem Tammy had let some cat out of a bag that her friend would rather not be made public.

Time for some space.

Shep lightly grabbed Tammy's hand. "Can you two-step?"

Her eyes flew wide as he tugged her from the booth. Once his idea registered, she quickly scooted to her feet and skipped along beside him. In a smooth motion, he slid his arm around her back. Tammy packed some pretty sexy curves. She didn't resist when he tugged her close. Instead, she just gave him another one of her beaming smiles as he led her around the dance floor. Her adoring gaze gave him a funny feeling in his chest. He liked her looking at him as if he was the greatest thing since chocolate. Like maybe she wanted to take a bite.

Before his reaction could cause a stirring below his belt, he spun her in a circle. Damn if her arousing laugh didn't do the very thing he'd tried to avoid. Ignoring the sensation, he stepped faster to the Dierks Bently tune.

Tammy was fun and lively and laughed like a tinkling bell. Her face was getting flushed and he wondered if it was from him spinning her around. Her plump lips had his head doing some spinning of its own. The song ended and Tammy fanned her red cheeks. He followed her bouncing backside to their table thinking the woman was a ball of fire.

"This guy knows how to dance," Tammy told Mike and Cassie as she skidded into the booth. Shep slid right in behind her.

"I grew up in a house with four brothers," he explained. "My mom believed we were made for dancing and took great pleasure in torturing us."

"Torture?"

He faced Tammy, lowered his voice and directed his words to her. "That's what we thought about prancing around until we found out that girls liked boys who danced. A girl will pick a guy that can dance over the best-looking guy in any place."

"Like you have anything to worry about." Tammy walked her fingers right up his chest.

Christ. He might as well give up on trying to control his arousal. He doubted Tammy would notice anyway. The woman was well on her way to getting tanked. He'd never take advantage either. He slowed his breathing, attempting to calm things down and ignore the heat from her fingers scorching his chest.

Getting her to eat was a bigger chore than he'd anticipated. So, when his burger came, he coaxed her to take a few bites of his. Damn, Tammy was sexy. She crooned and nibbled, at least she swallowed something other than alcohol. She was bound to have regrets in the morning.

He thought about that. Guess he should feel guilty. He didn't. Whatever the bad news had been, she deserved to have a minute—or a night—of tranquility. A moment where she didn't have to worry about her problems. Let the women have their fun.

After all, he'd come to the *Pitt Stop* with Mike looking for a distraction.

The evening passed without him realizing how much time had gone by. Tammy kept him entertained and as time went on, he noticed she was not the flirt he had first thought her to be. He was sure the alcohol had made her bold, but the woman showed her intelligence discussing several issues. She'd spent more time talking and less trying to entice him. He glanced at his watch. *Hell.* Three hours? He chuckled in amazement. He'd gotten his hour and more.

"What do you think?" Mike asked.

Shep glanced between the two women. "I think it's time to take these girls home. Which one of you ladies has keys?"

Tammy pointed across the table.

"I do." Cassie giggled and dug into her purse. "I'm not sure I should drive."

Hell no, she shouldn't drive. Mike would see to that. Tammy snuggled into Shep's side, where she'd been plastered pretty much all evening. He'd had women throw themselves at him, their intent abundantly clear. Not Tammy. Her actions were entirely innocent. This woman was an open book. He'd bet she didn't behave like this on a regular basis, if ever.

"I want my big handsome"—hiccup—"fire guy …" She hiccupped again.

"Come on, sweetheart," he said, pulling her from the booth. He kept one arm around her, since she wasn't too steady on her feet, and tried not to think about her plush curves against his chest. Or how good she felt.

"You taking me home?" Her sparkling green eyes peered up at him. He was glad she'd eaten something. He hoped she didn't puke in his truck.

Since Tammy was all wobbly, he had to help her into his SUV. The woman might carry a few extra curves, but he lifted her easily. The problem was, she kept clinging to him and he couldn't untangle himself quick enough to get the damn door shut. Finally, he clicked the seatbelt, closed the door, and turned to find Mike standing behind him.

"Woman's got more arms than a squid," he said.

"Cassie's already asleep." Mike nodded toward her car.

Shep chuckled again. He hadn't laughed this much since … He couldn't remember when.

"You aided and abetted."

Shep wrinkled up his forehead.

"Bottoms up," Mike mimicked.

"Don't worry. They won't remember a thing in the morning." He still didn't feel guilty ordering more shots for the girls. "I'll take Tammy home, put her in bed and leave. I won't even undress her. She's a school teacher." He said the last part as if he needed to remind himself.

Shep glanced at the woman in his truck blowing him kisses. Damn, his face might crack from this constant grinning. "I figured if the girls wanted to cut loose, let them. Better with us than some other guys that could have happened along. At least with us, they're safe."

"The distressing news was Tammy's."

He raised a brow. "You know what happened?"

"Yeah. Her ex. Cassie said she needs a good lawyer. Said she needed to get drunk."

"Well, she managed that."

"With your help."

Shep chuckled again. This was a habit he could get used to.

***

Somewhere down a deep tunnel, a peeling noise shrieked. It grew louder. A weight sat on Tammy's head then started thumping like a hammer. She struggled to consciousness, willing the offending noise to go away. It continued. She pulled the pillow over her head and groaned with a new flash of pain.

The damn ringing. If it was her ex, she'd gladly kill him. Thinking it might be the kids, she rolled over, reaching for the phone. She slammed out a hand and ended up smacking the headpiece to the floor. *Great.* Now she had to lean over to get the damn thing.

She rolled to her side and grabbed the curly cord and pulled, hand over hand, until she clasped the receiver.

"Hello," she said, her voice coming out as a croak

"You sound as bad as I feel."

"Oh, Cassie," Tammy breathed a sigh of relief, glad it wasn't her husband. "I've died and gone to hell."

"Tell me about it. When I woke, I wanted someone to shoot me."

"Spartacus raced his chariots from one temple to the other, continuously back and forth inside my head," Tammy grumbled. "Now Thor is swinging his mighty hammer."

"Tammy, are you okay?"

"Are you deaf?" Tammy croaked, then groaned as pain thumped her skull. "I just told you—"

"Are you alone?" Cassie interrupted.

Tammy wasn't sure she'd heard correctly. Why wouldn't she be alone? Except for the boys.

"What? Oh … your sister still has the boys. I don't think I'm up to getting them just yet."

"Don't worry about the boys. There're fine."

Thank God. The way she felt, another two hours of sleep would be greatly appreciated. Especially when twin boys at the age of six were constantly on full throttle.

"So, um … you're not alone?"

Cassie sounded weird. It looked like Tammy would need her wits for this phone conversation. "Hold on a minute."

Even at the protest from her head, she forced herself to stand up. So far so good. She glanced down at her apparel. Bra and panties. She must have been too tired to put on her nightgown. The throb at her temples drove her teeth together, causing an ache in her jaw. She avoided looking in the mirror and turned the water on to wash her face. Her head hurt, her mouth tasted like cotton. After a quick facial scrub and gargle of mouthwash, she grabbed a bottle of aspirin, swallowed three and washed them down with water. Then, she padded back to the bed and picked up the receiver.

"Okay. What's up? Why did you call?"

"Took you long enough," Cassie snapped. "Did you forget I was on the phone?"

"I took some aspirin. With two boys, you learn to bounce back quick. Even after a night of unplanned drunkenness. What was I thinking?"

Oh yeah. I was trying not to think.

That's why she had downed so many shots. The fear of losing her children had driven her near panic. She'd had to do something. Alcohol might not have been the best choice but ...

"Is anyone with you?" Cassie sounded like she was shouting in a whispering voice.

Confusion made Tammy wrinkle her brow. "No, I'm by myself. Who would be with me?" Cassie knew the boys were with her sister. "What's with the questions?"

"I just wanted to make sure you got home okay."

Whoa. What— Her head hurt enough without adding the strain of trying to remember last night.

"Didn't you bring me home?"

"Um, about that ..."

"Please don't tell me something I don't want to hear," Tammy groaned. *Shit.* She couldn't remember and her head still pounded. "Good Lord. What happened?"

"Mike brought me home. Shep took you home."

Tammy held the phone from her ear, staring at the earpiece as though it was an alien. With a Martian on the other end. Speaking in a foreign tongue.

Shep?

"Did you hear me? Tammy?"

"I heard you. *Shep* brought me home? Were you with us?"

"No. I don't think so."

"You don't think? What the hell do you mean, you don't think?" she shrilled, the headache forgotten. An uneasy feeling crawled down Tammy's spine. A lot like the feeling she'd had yesterday evening. At the school. Before they'd gone to the *Pitt Stop*.

Panic.

"I don't remember." Cassie sounded miserable, but at the moment, Tammy couldn't feel sorry for her.

"We both were out of it. Mike told me."

"Mike? When did ... is he there now?"

"Yes." No wonder Cassie was whispering.

"Damn. Why couldn't I get that lucky? Why are you on the phone with me? Oh, I get it. You called to see if Shep was still here." Tammy glanced at the bed to be sure. If he'd stayed, surely she would remember. "Well, I'll be damned. A chance at a fireman and I blew it. Drunk. Just my luck. How will I ever live that down?"

What Shep must have thought of me.

Embarrassment heated her cheeks.

"Well, you had a good reason."

As soon as the principal had told Tammy her ex called the school, she'd been bewildered. When he told her Steve had mentioned relocating her sons to another school, she'd gone into orbit. Cassie had gotten her sister to babysit, then had taken Tammy out for drinks. Since she couldn't strangle her ex, she'd drunk herself stupid.

"Don't remind me that Steve is up to something."

"Maybe you'd rather think about being rescued by two hot firefighters."

"If only I could remember. Oh, noooo," Tammy wailed. "What if I got sick? Oh God, Cassie."

"Don't beat yourself up. It's over now. We did what we did."

"Easy for you to say. You have your man."

"You really don't remember?"

"Do you?" Tammy countered.

"If Mike hadn't been here, I'd be at a total loss. I have no memory of leaving the place or how we got home."

Tammy tried recalling last evening and didn't remember much. Other than Shep and Mike joining them, dancing—that was about it. He brought her home?

"Shep didn't bother to hang around, so I must have repelled him," Tammy mumbled, the thought impossible to bear.

"Don't even think that. Mike said Shep was a gentleman. The kind of guy who would deposit you home properly and leave without taking advantage."

"Just what I need. A good Samaritan," she huffed.

"You've got more spirit than that. Once you feel better, things will be clearer. You'll bounce right back to your bubbly self."

Only if she pretended the entire night never happened. Except the part of them dancing. She wanted to remember that.

"You're right," she told Cassie. "I don't like pity parties. Thanks for the info dump. I'm going to take a shower and rejoin the living. I'll call later when my head is clear. Or you can call me after your man leaves."

She hung up before Cassie could say any more. Tammy really shouldn't feel sorry for herself. She didn't have time. Her boys would be returning soon.

She stood and headed to the bathroom. There, lying on her sitting chair, were the clothes she'd worn the night before, neatly folded. That didn't make sense. In her condition, it seemed more likely she would have flung them about, not caring where they landed.

Oh hell.

Had Shep undressed her? Had he put her to bed? She closed her eyes, refusing to trod down the road to humiliation.

Not yet. There'd be plenty of time for that later.

Chapter 2

The chilly air smelled fresh and brisk. The morning sun's glow promised another beautiful day. Shep would never tire of stepping onto his back porch and watching the scenic view on the horizon.

He propped his bare feet on the wooden railing of the deck he'd built with his own two hands. Huge logs defined every section, from the A structured ends with oak framed windows large enough to walk through, to the A designed middle. Slated rock from the riverbed, housed in cement, formed the pillars on the front porch. The same rock he'd used to build the fireplace inside. Pride filled his chest as he gazed at the pastures and the forest of trees. He'd replanted some of the smaller ones that currently surrounded his house. The structure had turned out a bit larger than he'd planned, but the inside he'd designed to suit himself, making it a cozy home. It all belonged to him, as far as he could see and beyond.

Little by little he'd scrimped and saved, accumulating a few acres here, a few more there. Today, he presently owned eighty-three acres, with his house sitting smack dab in the middle. He took a sip of coffee, relishing the gratification that knowledge brought.

Guess if he had a woman, he wouldn't have his land. A woman liked to fritter money. He had everything he needed. Not a big spender, he bought what was necessary. He didn't splurge on frivolous things, items he deemed worthless. He didn't do without, but he saw no reason to throw money away. In his opinion, that's what a lot of people did. And they didn't have the sight that greeted him every morning.

On days like today, his day off, he was lucky enough to sit and linger. Soaking up the sounds of the wind blowing in the trees and the birds flying overhead. He might hear the occasional cry of an animal. Then there were the silent creatures that treaded quietly. Like the deer that came to the edge of the woods around dawn. Fifteen, he'd counted this morning.

He took another sip of coffee and dropped a hand to scratch his dog's head. An Alaskan Malamute, he'd been the runt of the litter and had taken to Shep right away. Hutch had grown like a bear cub. No one would mistake him for a runt now. They'd been together four years. Shep sucked a lung full of fresh country air, taking comfort in his surroundings. Just him and his dog.

The rumble of an engine echoed in the trees, drifting around the side of his house. Someone was coming up the lane. Then he heard a truck door slam. Hutch took off like a bullet. If Shep hadn't already expected Mike, he'd know the visitor was a friend by way of no warning from his dog.

Mike strode around the corner, looking fresh as new money.

"Figured you'd be along." Shep greeted Mike.

"Oh yeah? Why's that?"

"Checking up on your girlfriend's cohort."

"That's one way to put it." Mike climbed the steps; Hutch padded over and curled up beside Shep.

"Want a cup of coffee, help yourself."

"Nah. Had mine already. You sleep in?"

Mike knew him better than that. He was fishing. Still, Shep took a sip of his brew before he answered. "That your subtle way of asking what time I got home?"

"The thought crossed my mind."

"Hmm." Shep stared back over the landscape.

"You're being deliberately evasive."

He wanted to tell Mike to mind his own business. Or laugh. His prying was not getting the desired effect. Mike crossed his arms and leaned back against a post. A twelve-inch pillar matching the ones out front. Shep supposed he might as well put the guy out of his misery. Mike was probably snooping for Cassie anyway.

"I took Tammy home, put her to bed, and left."

Mike stared as if he expected more. "Short and simple."

Shep dropped his feet and placed his mug on a small table to the side of his chair. "Nothing simple about it." He gave Hutch another scratch and stared out into the pasture beside the barn. His empty barn.

He'd love to fill it with horses, watch them graze in his meadow. Horses needed care. From one day to the next, his life could change. With his schedule and his well-being not a surety, he'd decided to wait until his circumstances changed.

Most men desired a family, the kind that included a wife and kids. He was no different. His parents were gone, but he had siblings. They were pretty close. His brothers had children. Maybe it wasn't in the cards for him. He'd been alone a long time.

Tammy had boys. Twins.

"Tammy is something else." He spoke out loud the name of the woman occupying his mind.

"Think I'll get that cup of coffee." Mike shoved from the post and went inside.

Shep shrugged and propped his feet back on the railing. Logs made up most of his house. It had been backbreaking work when he started. Of course, he had been much younger then. Younger than the members of his team. Except for maybe Cooper. That boy had spunk and grit Shep didn't remember having at that age.

"So," Mike said coming out the back door. "Tammy got your attention."

"She's pretty. And fun." Shep shook his head. "When she forgets about that asshole husband of hers."

"Ex," Mike corrected.

"I'd like to make him an ex ... as in *extinct*."

"She talk to you about him?"

"On the ride home. After what you told me last night, her actions make sense."

"Cassie said he's been giving Tammy some trouble. The latest is why they were in the bar drinking themselves stupid."

Picturing Tammy all soft and smiling, Shep lifted his lips in a grin. He seemed to be doing a lot of that. He took another gulp of his coffee. "I don't cotton with a man using kids to scare their mother."

"She must have been pretty shaken up."

"Yeah. She talked a lot on the way to her place. A regular chatterbox." He'd liked looking at her, too. She was damned easy on the eyes.

"Alcohol will do that," Mike snickered.

Shep grinned again, recalling the chatty female. Almost non-stop. "She talked about her boys. Sounds like a great mom."

"Cassie said those boys are her life."

"I got that impression." He gazed at the mountains, not focusing on anything particular. His mind drifted to the woman and whether or not Tammy might like his place.

"Are you going to tell me or not?" Mike barked.

Shep knew what Mike was asking. "Not." He could feel Mike's heated stare.

"So, that's the way it's going to be?"

Shep didn't get riled up over nothing. He had enough apprehension dealing with serious matters at the station. That's why he enjoyed his free time as he could, sitting on his back porch drinking in nature.

"Are you asking for your girlfriend?"

Mike's silence confirmed what Shep already suspected. Mike thought because of his profession as a firefighter, he couldn't have a girlfriend, let alone a wife. One of these days he'd figure it out.

"One of the first things Cassie asked when she woke up was how Tammy got home."

"No need asking you the same question you asked me."

"Yes, I stayed the night. I slept on her couch. I gave her a tonic when she woke up."

Shep laughed. *Good God.* "Your hellish hangover drink?" He didn't know who had invented that stuff, but he was glad he didn't have a drinking problem. He never wanted to take that so-called *cure.*

"Don't knock it. It works."

"I'll take your word for it." He glanced down into his mug, wondering if he should put on another pot. Must be about empty. "I'm sure Cassie has called Tammy by now. If I know women, she called first chance she got. Either you were asleep, or the minute you gave her some space."

"You think Tammy remembers last night? Cassie didn't remember much."

"Those girls were pretty bombed."

"It didn't help you kept ordering more drinks."

"The waitress said the women told her to 'keep 'em coming'." Shep shrugged. "Looked like they needed it. Besides, we were there."

"Thank, God."

Shep let out a long heavy sigh. "I will admit. I kind of liked the way Tammy clung to me. Felt good."

When Mike turned in his seat with his mouth hanging open, Shep ignored him.

"Didn't have to help with her clothes much. Not sure she was aware of what she was doing. When Tammy got down to her skivvies, I put her in bed and pulled the covers to her chin." He let a chuckle escape, thinking back to her scrambling around in the bed trying to shuck the covers. If she hadn't been drunk as a skunk he might have given up and let nature take its course. The woman had a body. All plush and curves. Provocative as sin. He'd had a hell of a time trying not to notice.

"And then, like the gentleman you are, you left," Mike teased.

"Of course, I left. Don't need a remorseful mamma out for blood." Who knew what her thoughts might be the next morning. At the time, he figured with her red hair, he'd be lucky to escape with his life.

"So? What do you think?"

Shep glanced at Mike. "Of what?"

"Haven't seen you this interested in a woman before."

"Who says I'm interested?"

Mike glared at him. Shep placed his mug on the solid oak table, another thing he'd built with his hands from his own timber. He dropped a hand on Hutch's head. Scratching his dog brought him comfort. Silence stretched between him and Mike. Finally, he murmured the words he'd been thinking.

"She's got something. A zest for life. A kind nature. I hate to think of her menacing hus—*ex*—bullying her."

"Did you know her ex threatened taking the boys out of her school? Cassie tried to get Tammy's mind off a possible custody threat. That's why the girls got hammered." Mike crossed his boots over at his ankles.

"She rambled her suspicions." Shep paused. "You know, I might be able to help her with that."

Mike choked on his coffee. "How?"

"My brother. I think I'll give Eddie a call. Maybe do some checking into this ... ex of hers." If there was a way to help Tammy, he'd find it. And if there was dirt on her ex, Eddie would find that.

"Sounds good to me. I don't think Tammy has a lawyer. Cassie didn't mention one."

"I'll call Eddie anyway."

"You know, if you help get her a lawyer, it might get you into her good graces," Mike jabbed. "Especially if she gets pissed about last night."

Shep cringed. What if Tammy was pissed? What would she do? His chances with her would be shot to hell. But then, why was he worrying about a chance with a woman he barely knew?

"Women. And their damn sensibilities. She doesn't have anything to get mad about. She didn't molest me, no matter how much I wished she had."

Mike grinned. "The woman doesn't give me the impression she's timid."

Shep laughed in spite of himself. "No. She's outgoing, no mistake about that. You're right. I haven't had that much fun, real fun, since I can remember." Hutch raised his head and Shep ruffled the dog's fur. "Do you know her ex's name? Any other information you can give me?"

"I'll ask Cassie."

"Enough data to make sure I have the right guy. I'll have Eddie do a thorough search on him. See if the man has anything to hide."

And if the shit gives Tammy any trouble, I'll be there to kick his ass.

***

Life started early in the country. Some days Shep beat the sun up. Usually had his shower before the birds started chirping. Then, he'd set on his back porch with a mug in his hand and watch the sunrise. A great way to begin the day and today was no different.

With a nip in the air, he grabbed a jacket and shrugged it on. He gave a last glance to Hutch and headed out the door. An hour from now, the temperature would be ten degrees higher. He drove his Land Rover onto the back parking lot at the firehouse, noticing each of the bay doors were closed, just like they should be. Station Eight was one of the few firehouses that had bay entry doors in the front and the rear so the rigs could pull straight through without someone needing to back up or block the street while turning around. Shift changed at seven and, out of habit, he came in at six. He liked arriving early, checking on the night's activities, and just being there if he was needed.

Not a sound could be heard as he unlocked the door and stepped inside. Although, as he got closer to the stairway, the buzz of a radio echoed down to him. Someone was up. One never knew what he might find upon arrival at the firehouse. A 911 call, trucks gone out on a fire or an accident, or the men could be returning from an emergency. At the moment, things seemed calm. He could smell diesel, so the trucks had been used. Anyone that was lucky enough to catch some sleep might still be in bed.

The men and women coming on duty for the day had to be at work ready to go by six forty-five so they could step in for the shift coming off duty. The new crew had to be ready to roll out right at seven on the dot if need be.

If not, the crew knew the routine. Their first task of the day—going over each rig, checking to make sure all the necessary equipment was working. Some would grab breakfast or head to the in-house gym for a quick workout—the guys had thanked him numerous times for managing to get them that extravagance. Then they'd get started on their daily chores. Shep ran a tight ship. Cleaning bathrooms, mopping floors—everyone took their turn.

Whether it was reviewing pediatric and obstetrics procedures, practicing tying knots for rope rescue scenarios or going through a mock water rescue, each department had stringent training requirements. And that was if the morning remained quiet. Some days the station would get their first call before the men even had a chance to think about their daily schedule. One minute it could be quiet and the next, a call could come in, throwing a firefighter into a life-altering position.

That was his life. And he wouldn't trade it for anything.

He headed up the steps toward his office, thinking he might take a peek in the lounging room to see who was in there. He was surprised to see Laredo stretched out on the couch with his feet propped on a low table.

"What are you doing here this early?"

Laredo dropped his feet to the floor and stood. "Hi, Cap. Damn neighbors at it again. Then their dog started howling and I couldn't get back to sleep. Had to come in here to get some peace and quiet."

"Does their dog usually keep you awake?"

"Naw. I like dogs, you know that. The mutt had the same problem I did. His owners got him all *irritado*."

"How long have you been here?"

Laredo glanced at his watch. "Three hours."

As far as sleep, some nights the guys got less. "Why aren't you in a bunk?"

"I slept a bit before the dog started howling. Figured I'd just rest my eyes here on the sofa."

"As long as you don't fall asleep on shift."

Laredo spread his arms and flashed that wide grin he was so famous for. "You know me, Cap. I'm always ready to go."

Shep shook his head. Laredo bore charm as a second skin. "Anyone else around?"

"Pete's somewhere downstairs, the rest are in bed. Had a house fire. Came back two hours ago. They'll be getting up anytime, I imagine."

"I'll be in my office." He turned on his heel and sauntered down the walkway. After one more glance about, he closed the door to his office and settled down to a mound of paperwork. One of his least favorite duties. Lately, more so. The training day explosion kept him from concentrating.

He leaned back and stared at a calendar on the wall. Four weeks and Hooley hadn't told them a damn thing. He was a tight-lipped son-of-a-gun during his investigations. As a fire detective, guess he had to be.

Still, Shep was apprehensive. From everything he'd been told, the explosion had to be deliberate. Someone had intentionally sabotaged the fire department's training. Men had been hurt. Troubling to think an individual had consciously and calculatedly timed that house to blow up, knowing men would be in danger. Firefighters. *His* men. The pain in his jaw shot up to his temple, letting him know he was grinding his teeth.

He wasn't a violent man, but if he came face to face with the bastard, it would be damn hard not to break his neck.

CHAPTER 3

A trickle of sweat rolled down the back of Tammy's neck. Her big breasts screamed in protest of being so confined in this heat.

No-brainer the air conditioning was not working. A freaky hot day in autumn, the county had already changed their boilers to heat. Even if they hadn't, the air-conditioning rarely worked. Maybe the hot coffee had something to do with her body temperature. More than likely it was the image of a panty-melting smile that had hiked her temperature more than the normal ninety-eight-point-six. Taunting bright eyes teased her mercilessly. The bits of gray at his temples only made her want to run her fingers through his hair, maybe even grip it while they had wild—

My God.

Her breathing came out in gasps. All she'd done was fantasize about the man. Shep stuck in her head like lyrics of a favorite song, over and over, again and again.

"Maybe you should go to the lounge and get a wet rag and mop up your face."

Tammy's gaze jerked to the doorway, finding her best friend looking much too put-together. "How come you don't look like it's a hundred and eighty degrees in here."

"Believe me, I'm hot." Cassie grasped the front of her shirt and pulled in a flapping motion.

"Does that work?"

"Not really. Something tells me you're hot for a different reason."

Smoldering hot body, mile-long legs … Tammy couldn't help but wonder if that meant another part of Shep's anatomy was long.

"If your face is anything to go by, I'm right."

Good Lord.

What had come over her? She'd never had a man affect her so.

"What's your special today?" Cassie asked.

"Library. Linda even came and picked up my class so I wouldn't have to walk down there. I feel like I've been to the Sahara Desert without a camel." Tammy smoothed the hair from her face.

"My kids are in music. Joan had a fan aimed toward the stage. I almost stayed."

"Why didn't you?"

"I talked to Mike. I think he was fishing for Shep."

That got her attention. "Shep?" Why bother acting all coy when she'd been dying to hear from him. "What did Mike say?"

"That Shep was a real gentleman. He wanted to know if you were mad about him taking you home."

"Mad? The only thing I'm mad about is that I was in no shape to enjoy my time with him. I'm mad at myself."

"You don't need to be. You had fun, didn't you?"

"From what I remember. It's the blank spots that worry me."

"Anyway, Mike said you have nothing to worry about. Shep wants to know if he can call you."

What? Tammy's heart pounded. "He said that? What exactly did he say?"

Cassie scrunched her forehead. "I believe his words were, Shep wondered if he should call."

"That's it?" Tammy chewed the end of her fingernail while she paced. "Why would he call? Should I apologize? Does he want to check up on me?"

"I suppose there could be a number of reasons, but I'll bet he's interested."

"Oh my God. Do you think he likes me? After the way I behaved?"

"Beside the fact we were inebriated, we didn't do anything bad. You have nothing to apologize for. You were funny. You danced. Of course he likes you."

"Do you know he actually folded my clothes and hung them on a chair?" At least she suspected he had.

Cassie choked on the water she'd just sipped.

"Are you okay?"

"You left that part out," Cassie croaked.

"My clothes?"

"You didn't tell me you took them off." Cassie hiked her eyebrow. "Those are deets you need to share."

"Do you share what you do with Mike?"

"You mean ... you did not—"

"Close your fly trap. I'm sure we didn't do anything. But my shirt and jeans were on the chair. I must have taken them off. I still had on my underwear. Get back to Mike. He say anything else?"

"Yeah. Lots. But that's personal."

"About *Shep*."

"No. But he was fishing, so I think Shep will be giving you a call."

Really? She remembered having fun. Laughing a lot. Leaning against a hard chest. He had the kindest smile. She guessed she couldn't have behaved but so bad. It would be great to see him again.

"I hope so," she said.

"Tammy. Are you interested in Shep?"

"Who wouldn't be?"

"You were flirting hard with Jared that first night we saw the guys, and when I asked you about him you said you were just flirting. You were doing the same thing with Shep."

Yeah. She'd flirted to keep her nerves from pouncing and the liquor had helped her to unwind. Shep was more her speed. But the man was hot. Why would he be interested in her?

"Shit, Cassie. I'm a mother. But I can't stop thinking about getting naked with Shep. I'm acting like a silly girl." She plopped down on a chair and fanned her face with a folder.

"You won't be getting any cooler with those thoughts."

"Don't make jokes. I remember not too long ago you had the same problem. At least you got your man."

"It's a work in progress. But we're talking about you."

"Do you think Shep was, you know, just flirting?"

"I think if that was all, Mike wouldn't have mentioned him."

"I really like Shep. I mean, what's not to like? He's solid. Has a smile that melts me to my toes. He's fun. He can dance. A little gray at a man's temples has got to be the sexiest thing there is."

"I don't know about that," Cassie mumbled. Of course, she wouldn't agree. She had her own hot man. Tall, handsome, and built like a tank.

"Anyway, you think he might call?" Tammy hoped so, but she needed to hear Cassie's reassurance.

"Yes, I—"

Several students walked into the classroom, single file, alerting them both that specials were over.

Time to get back to teaching.

Tammy glanced at the clock. The end of the day couldn't come soon enough.

Would he call?

***

A warm breeze fluttered over Tammy's face as she grabbed her cart of school books and lugged it up the driveway to the side door. The rubber hose stretched around the corner to the backyard, reminding her of how the boys loved romping in water. It was too darned hot. After dinner, she should let them play outside so they could burn off some of their hyper energy before bed.

Ever since they'd spent the night at Cassie's sister's, Christopher and David kept asking for movie night. Jennifer had given the boys the Ninja Turtle costumes they'd worn at her house. Tammy didn't mind movie night, but the boys' insistence on costumes matching each movie ranged outside her budget. After visiting a thrift store, she'd found some old clothes that she'd ripped apart and altered into outfits. Amazing how a single strip of cloth could be used for Batman and Superman. Tress up a few boxes and Transformers could be created. The boys were great at pretending.

She stepped inside and parked her crate beside the kitchen door, then breathed a sigh of relief to be in her air-conditioned house. She kicked off her shoes and curled her toes on the cold linoleum floor. She headed to the refrigerator, grabbed a bottle of water and took a few swallows. Then her eyes landed on the shelf her father-in-law had made. He'd given it to *her,* so after the divorce, she kept it. She liked the man. It was probably a good thing he died before he could see what a mockery his son had made of their marriage.

When she'd first discovered Steve cheating, she'd been furious. She'd gone through the motions—disbelief, hurt. Shame that she'd been so stupid. She'd been happy thinking their family was picture-perfect. She had a home, twins, her dream job of teaching kids. Life was complete, or so she'd thought.

To keep her family together, she'd given Steve a second chance. The two of them had gone back to a normal routine. She played the dutiful wife but stayed vigilant, keeping her eye on his comings and goings and late nights at the office.

Blindly trust her cheating husband?

She wasn't that dumb. Her father raised his daughters to be smart. If it happened once, of course it could happen again. And it had. So, she divorced him. She and her children were better off.

For the last two years, she'd made a home for her and her boys. She'd done a pretty good job of it too.

And now he wanted to take it all away.

The bastard.

She slammed the bottle down and braced her arms on the counter. She'd given him everything while they were married. *Everything.*

Well, not anymore. No way in hell Steve would take her boys.

Sucking air into her lungs, she fought for control. She mentally went over the list of things she needed to do before the boys got home. Thank God for Scouts. It gave her an hour or two to collect her thoughts. Get herself together. Prepare for the battle she suspected was coming.

She had no time to be weak. No time to fall apart. There was no one to put her back together if she did. No. She needed to be strong for her boys. There were lessons to plan. Bills to pay. She should do laundry. That would occupy her mind.

What was she going to do?

Her lip trembled. She fell onto a chair at the kitchen table, rested her head on her arms and cried.

CHAPTER 4

Shep reclined in soft leather while a cute redhead did a two-step in his mind. Tammy was one fine woman. Even if she had been a little tipsy the other night. Tipsy, hell. She'd been zonkered. His chest rumbled with laughter. Damn, that felt good. She'd felt good. He spent the last few days trying to forget how good. He'd better forget. Tammy had needed a distraction. He had happily volunteered to give her one. When she sobered up, the thing she'd tried to forget would still be there. So, he would go back to his boring existence of living alone. Except for his dog, of course. He and Hutch got along just fine.

But he hated the thought of Tammy's dickhead husband taking advantage of her.

Shep picked up his cell phone and punched in some numbers. His brother kept late hours, but he should have left the office by now. His wife, Laura, wanted him home before she put the kids to bed.

"Hello."

Laura.

"Hey, doll. Are you ready to leave that no-account husband and run away with me?"

"Is now soon enough?" she shot back.

Shep laughed, as he always did when they picked on Eddie. "Is he home?"

"Sure thing. Hold on and I'll get him."

"Thanks." Shep turned the volume down on the TV while he waited. Laura was a good woman, and good for Eddie.

"Are you propositioning my wife again? You can't have her." His brother's mocking voice came across the line.

"Sounding possessive, as usual."

"What's up?"

Shep scratched at the stubble on his face. "How's your workload?"

"Are you in trouble?" Anxious concern filled his brother's voice.

"No. Not me," he assured his brother. Mom had raised her children with a lot of love, making the kids share most everything. Losing both parents had brought him and his brothers even closer. They were quick to take up for each other, offering help at the drop of a dime. "I know someone. Her ex-husband is giving her a bit of trouble."

"Hang on." A door closed and Eddie was back on the line.

"Okay. Who is this someone?"

He knew his brother would ask. Keep it light and simple. *Yeah, right.* The hound dog in Eddie would turn pit bull if Shep gave any inkling Tammy was more than a simple acquaintance.

"Mike's girlfriend—"

"Mike has a girlfriend? When did that happen?" Eddie sighed and Shep could imagine him leaning back in his own leather chair. Probably propped his feet on his desk, too.

"Some of the guys went to a Mexican restaurant after training a month ago. He met her there."

"Sounds interesting. Did you meet anyone?"

He knew it. Eddie and Laura were too damn concerned with Shep's love life. Which was nonexistent.

"Look. I called to see if you were free to help a friend."

"Don't get your hackles standing on your neck. So, Mike's girlfriend was married? What's her name?"

"Her name is Cassie. And no, it's not her. It's her friend, Tammy." Saying her name plastered her face right in the middle of his vision. Her laughing face. Cute dimples on each side of her mouth. Glowing, clearwater eyes. One misty green and the other with a hint of amber. Reminding him of a kitten his mom had. One brown eye and one green.

"Tammy is the friend of Mike's girlfriend?"

"Yeah. Evidently, she's been divorced a year or two. I'm not sure."

"Have you met this woman?"

Oh yeah. He'd met her. Drank with her. Laughed with her. Took her home and put her to bed. But he sure as hell couldn't tell his brother. The conversation would take on a whole different direction. One he didn't want.

"Yep. She's a good woman. Has two kids."

If Eddie had any ideas of matchmaking, this latest bit of information should derail his objective.

"Two kids." Eddie whistled through his teeth. "That's tough."

"From what I gather, he had a woman on the side. Maybe more than one. He left, she has the kids."

"Did he give her custody?"

"That's the thing. He remarried and is threatening a custody suit."

"Threatening? So, he hasn't actually filed the papers?"

Shep frowned, trying to recall if that detail had been mentioned. "I'm not sure. Cassie said he'd contacted the kids' school. Both women are teachers, by the way."

"I'm assuming the kids go to the same school as the mom?"

"Yeah. All I know is what came up in mixed conversation. Then what Mike told me, which isn't a lot."

"Like what?" Eddie asked.

"Like what a good mom she is and how her ex is an asshole."

Eddie laughed. "Sounds like you already have an opinion of the man."

"I sure do." He'd like to take the guy around the corner and slam him up against a brick wall. Repeatedly.

Realizing he was squeezing the TV remote so tight his fingers cramped, he tossed the thing on the table. Pressing his feet against the footrest, he shoved the recliner upright.

"I have a pretty heavy caseload right now," Eddie said. "It would be good to know if her ex is just trying to intimidate her."

"I'm sure he is. But she's pretty upset."

Silence.

Did his brother hear the concern in his voice? Or the anxiousness in his breathing?

"Shep? How important is this to you?"

Damn. He raked a hand over the top of his head.

"I think she needs a lawyer."

Another bout of silence. Shep knew his brother was weighing more than whether or not Tammy needed a lawyer. Eddie was trying to guess the connection. Then Shep heard the sound of paper being shuffled.

"I'm looking at my calendar. It would be better if I met with her."

Shep released the air he'd been holding in his lungs. Thank God, Eddie hadn't asked any more questions.

"Why don't you give her my phone number and I'll tell my secretary to expect her call."

"Great. Thanks, bro," Shep replied, relief flowing through his chest. Even his shoulders relaxed.

"What's her full name?"

"Tammy Michael."

"Got it. Anything else I should know?"

Shep decided to ignore the possibility that his brother might be digging in his private life. "Nope, that's it."

"Then Laura and I expect you for dinner. Soon."

"You got it, buddy. When Laura makes fried chicken, you better let me know."

"I'll put in your order. See you this weekend?"

"Sure thing. Give the kids a hug for me."

"Will do. Night."

Shep pressed the red button on his cell and stared at the glowing lights. Now, should he be the one to call Tammy, or let Mike handle that?

Shep smiled. She might not be too eager to talk to him after the other night. Liquored up, Tammy had still behaved like a woman. No slutty wiles. No loudmouthed comments. Just a hell of a lot of fun. Even so, she might be embarrassed.

The more Shep thought about it, the more his chest squeezed. Hell, he was not a nervous man. The idea of calling Tammy, hearing her voice, wondering if she'd want to skewer him, had him reexamining his actions.

He'd had fun. She had too. But how much did she remember, and did she have regrets? Maybe he'd better call Mike first.

Shep punched in the number.

"Shep? What's up?"

"There's no emergency and we're not on call, so relax."

"Habit," Mike explained.

"I just talked to my brother. Eddie."

"The lawyer?"

"Yes. I mentioned Tammy's ex. He's going to help her out."

"That's great."

Shep figured Mike could pass the information on. "Thought you should know so you can tell her."

"What do you mean?"

"Well, you can tell Tammy about Eddie, and she can give him a call at the office."

"Why don't you tell her?"

Shit. He hadn't expected Mike to right out ask. "I'm not too sure of the reception I might get."

"Did something happen? Or you still worried about when you took her home?"

"No. I already told you nothing happened."

"Then what's the problem?"

How did he get himself into this? "You know how women are. They get these things in their heads."

"What things?"

How was he supposed to know what things? Women were funny creatures. "How's Cassie?"

"What's she got to do with it? And don't change the subject."

"Not changing the subject. Just saying, maybe she said something." Women told each other everything. Maybe Cassie had said something to Mike.

"Who, Cassie? What would she have to say?"

"Whether or not her friend freaked when she found out I was the one who took her home."

"You haven't talked to Tammy?"

"Nope."

He heard Mike's sigh come across the line.

"You're usually not so dense. Or chicken. Give the woman a call."

"If she's embarrassed, she won't want to talk to me. But, if she wants me to call, and I don't ..." Shep shrugged, then realized Mike couldn't see him. "You see what I mean? You never know with a female."

Mike laughed. "I don't believe this."

Shep cringed. He feared nothing. But Mike was sure to tell the squad how Shep shied away from a conversation with a woman. Then he'd get a ton of ribbing at the station.

"Believe what? That I'm considering her reaction before I put my neck in a noose? Save a lot of trouble if Tammy doesn't want to see me again." That was just being reasonable.

"I've already been snooping for you. Cassie made it sound like you should call Tammy. What am I supposed to tell her when she finds out you haven't done it yet?"

Damn it. He didn't believe in going around the barn to get to the front door. The only way to get the facts was to go to the source. As a captain in the fire department, he knew how to take charge. Assess a situation and quickly arrive on a decisive plan. Tammy had him floundering around like a fish out of water. And this conversation was going downhill fast.

"Might be a good idea," he muttered. It seemed like a good idea ten minutes ago. Hutch nuzzled Shep's hand. The dog sensed his unease.

"Tell you what," Mike said. "I'll talk with Cassie and get the lay of the land. If everything seems okay, I'll let you know and this time you better give Tammy a call."

"Be nice to know if a woman is gunning for ya." He hesitated only a moment before he asked, "Cassie didn't say anything else?"

"Wait till the guys get a load of this."

"If you know what's good for you, you'll keep your mouth shut."

"Come on, Cap. All's fair, you know?"

The team picked on each other all the time, and he'd done his fair share. He had his hands full keeping the guys from getting out of control. Being the butt of a joke, he didn't mind. His personal life was another matter entirely. He had a tough hide, but he might not be able to handle his crew poking fun at Tammy.

"Bad enough to have a woman steamed at me," he told Mike. "I don't need the team sticking their nose where it don't belong."

"Why don't you give the woman a call now and put an end to your misery?"

"Misery? Who said I was miserable? No hardship thinking about her. She gets a man distracted."

Shit. Why didn't he just come out and tell Mike his feelings?

Feelings? Did he have feelings for Tammy?

"Distracted, huh? I call it good ole lust."

Shep's gut clenched. Been a while since he'd been with a woman. "Yep. That too. But I need to know which way the wind is blowing. Is she mad or does she want to see me again?"

"Something did happen, didn't it?"

"Nope."

"So ... what's the deal?"

"She's fun. Plain ole fun. Down to earth. When she laughs, she doesn't snicker or act coy or none of that snooty, high and mighty stuff. She's easy to talk with. Hard not to like her." He barely knew the woman, but he sure would like to. "Who's to say we'll be anything more than friends?"

"You aim to be friends with her?"

"At least that. If my brother takes her case, we'll have a reason to see each other."

"You sly dog," Mike said in an accusing tone. Mike was one of the few men Shep gave the freedom to speak his mind. They'd known each other going on twelve years. More than good friends, they were like brothers. Shep already had four of those. But he confided things to Mike he didn't share with his blood.

"We'll cross that bridge when we come to it. She's a mom. With two boys, she has to present a proper image. Tammy is a lady and needs to be treated like one. But she's still a healthy young woman with needs of her own. Who knows? She may want a fling. Or she may want to get back at that dickhead husband of hers."

"Ex," Mike reminded Shep, as if he needed reminding. His blood boiled every time he thought about the SOB wounding Tammy.

"If I have my way, it will be ex-dad. Asshole doesn't deserve kids if he can't be faithful to his wife. Or at least civil. Filing for custody and not having the balls to notify her, he's asking for a boot up his ass. Eddie's the one to give it to him."

I'm the one to give it to him. I'll shove it so far up—

"You planning on giving a relationship a chance?"

Mike's voice drew his attention back where it was supposed to be.

Relationship?

"Well, now. There's different levels of involvement in relationships. You know that, Mike. You won't let a woman get but so close."

Mike had been hurt by his mother leaving when he was just a kid. It had taken him a long time to let a woman in his heart. Cassie was perfect for him.

"We're not talking about me. What are you going to do about Tammy?"

"Take it one day at a time, my friend."

"I'll talk to Cassie. Let you know what I find out."

"See you in the morning." Shep thumbed the red button and glanced down at Hutch, curled up on the rug. Just him and his dog.

Might be nice to have someone else to talk to besides his dog.

CHAPTER 5

After spending an hour dissecting Hooley's report, Shep had more questions than answers. He couldn't blame the guys for going back to the Wimer property to scout around. But if there was anything to find, Hooley would discover it. Shep tried tackling some paperwork, but today must be the day for distractions.

Images of a cute redhead with short bouncy hair and flirty bangs filled his mind, keeping him from getting anything done. Giving up, he tossed a pen onto his desk and leaned back in his chair. A smile tugged the corner of his mouth as he remembered her flitting about the bedroom, plucking at her clothes. A chatterbox, that one. But real. So real. Down to earth. Nothing fake about that woman. And nothing fake about her chest.

He knew the real thing when he saw it. Silicone didn't jiggle like that. Large pillows of flesh tempting any man to bury himself in them. Tammy had a body made for sin. Only she didn't know it. That was kind of cute, too.

The phone rang, interrupting his thoughts.

"Shepherd speaking."

"My name is Daniel Williams. I'd like to speak with the captain, please."

"I'm captain of Station Eight Firehouse. May I help you?"

"Hello, Mr. *Shepherd*, did you say?"

"That's correct."

"I believe one of your firemen met my son at Mercy hospital last week."

"Is there a problem, Mr. Williams?"

"I'm not sure. That is, I want to be sure there is no problem."

The hairs stood on the back of Shep's neck.

"Do you have a fireman by the name of Mike?"

"Yes. Mike is a firefighter at Station Eight." Mike was an upstanding guy. No way he'd done anything. What was going on?

"Todd, my son, has been asking to come to the fire department. It seems this Mike mentioned something to my son about coming to the firehouse. My son is very astute, Mr. Shepherd, and I've never known him to lie. He knows the respect one earns from telling the truth. But he seems to have gotten the impression from your firefighter that it's all right for him to come to the firehouse."

Tension rolled from Shep's shoulders.

"Mr. Williams, I'm glad you called. Let me ease your mind. Todd is not mistaken. We often have children visit the firehouse. Mike is an esteemed individual as well as a valued firefighter. Your son must have made an impression on Mike if he personally invited him here."

"That's what I'm trying to resolve. That my son was invited and he did not misinterpret Mike's words. We would not want to intrude or interrupt the functioning of the fire department."

"I assure you, Mr. Williams—"

"Please call me Daniel. Mr. Williams seems so formal."

"Daniel, I can assure you the invitation was real. I'd be happy to speak with Mike and have him call you if you like?"

"That's not necessary. I would hate to interrupt his busy schedule."

"He won't mind."

"Then yes, I would like to speak with him. Todd received a nasty gash to his leg when he landed on a saw. One which he knew not to leave lying on the ground. According to my wife, Mike had Todd seen quickly. They'd been sitting in the waiting room for quite a while and when your firefighter saw the wound was still bleeding, he approached a nurse and she took my son back right away. I'd like to thank him."

"That sounds like Mike."

"He made quite an impression on my son. I wouldn't mind meeting him and coming to the station myself. My job keeps me busy and I'm out of town more than I'd like. Mike told Todd to remember Station Eight. I think the kid repeats it in his sleep."

Shep heard the smile in the man's voice. Earlier, he had expected this conversation to go quite different.

"Mister, uh, Daniel, you have nothing to worry about. Todd is welcome and so are you. Of course, you never know when we might get an emergency. You could show up and we would be gone. But that's not something to worry about. Plans change, get interrupted. But we still make them. You're welcome anytime. I'll have Mike call you."

"Thank you, Mr. Shepherd."

"Call me Shep."

"Thank you, Shep. Do you have a pen? I'll give you my number."

Shep glanced at the one he'd tossed earlier. "I've got one."

Daniel rattled off his number. "There's no hurry. Although once I tell Todd he can go, he'll be worse than he is now."

Shep laughed. He didn't have kids. He'd like some.

"Mike will call you."

"Thanks, Shep. It's been a pleasure speaking with you."

Shep ended the call and shook his head. Calling the fire station to be sure it was okay for his kid to visit. Daniel hadn't mentioned the kid's age, but the boy had to be old enough to understand the value of telling the truth.

Shep tapped in the code to page Mike. A few minutes later, two sharp raps echoed on his office door just before it opened. Mike's impressive size filled the doorway.

"You looking for me, Cap?"

"Come in and close the door."

Mike's size intimidated many, but it amused Shep that Mike could be daunted by him.

"I just got a call from a Mr. Williams."

"Who's he?"

"Apparently, the father of a boy you met at Mercy."

Mike's brow arched in confusion. "Todd?"

"Todd Williams. The boy who fell on a saw in his backyard."

"Well, yeah," Mike rubbed a hand over the back of his neck. "The boy was waiting in ER. Blood oozing down his leg. He hadn't been seen and I asked Tracey to look at him."

"Tracey," Shep repeated.

"Yeah. I know most of the nurses there. She recognized me and took him in to be examined. Is this because I carried the boy to the examining room?"

"Why'd you do that?"

"Hell, Cap. He hadn't been seen yet. The place was full. He was bleeding like a stuck pig."

"Doesn't explain why you carried him. How old is he?"

"Ten, I guess. And it was faster. By the time Tracey had to go looking for a wheelchair, I had him on the table."

"I see." No wonder the kid had hero worship. A big firefighter carrying him with a room full of people watching. Shep could picture it. The entire ER must have been in awe. Probably posted it on *Facebook*.

"His father mad 'cause I touched his kid?"

"No." Shep gave a slight shake of his head. "Evidently the boy is singing your praises."

"He's a sharp kid," Mike said with a grin.

Shep arched his brow.

"What I meant was, the kid is intelligent. He talks like an adult. He's tough. Not squeamish. Hell, he had a gash in his leg. Didn't even cry. His mom said he came walking in the house with blood running down his leg. I think she was about to have a heart attack."

By Mr. Williams' tone, his wife considered Mike a hero, too. "His mother the one who brought him to the hospital?"

"Yeah. And I remember her telling the kid, 'wait till your father gets home' Made me wonder what kind of man his dad was."

Shep leveled his stare on Mike. "Would you like to hear why Mr. Williams called?"

"Yes, sir."

"Like I said, it appears the boy, Todd, has been pestering his dad to come to the firehouse. Station eight. He was very specific about that."

"Told ya. The kid's sharp."

"Mr. Williams wanted to make sure it was all right for his son to pay us a visit. He said his son doesn't lie. But since Mr. Williams was not part of the conversation between the two of you, he wanted to know our policy on children coming to the fire station, or if it was even allowed."

"That's it?"

"What did you think? He was suing you for manhandling his son?"

"Well..." Mike shrugged. "You never know."

"Seems you made an impression on the kid. His father's work takes him out of town a lot. He can bring the boy by next week. I explained we might get a call, or if there was an emergency you'd be gone. Mr. Williams said they'd work that out."

"That's great, Cap. Wait till you meet this kid. You'll see what I mean." Evidently, the kid had also made an impression on Mike.

Shep could talk with Mike all day, but he had to get this form filled out. "Budget cuts. I've got to get these figures to the chief."

"Guess there's no chance of us getting new equipment. Not only the lives we save but our own lives depend on our gear working properly."

"That's the same sermon I preach every quarter."

"It's a touchy subject. I'll let you get back to it."

As Mike closed the door, Shep noticed Cooper standing outside. Arms crossed, grin on his face, ready to razz on Mike about something. The newest member of the team, Cooper fit right in. At first, Shep thought the kid might be a hothead. Gun ho. Quick to act without thinking. He'd proved Shep and every other member at the station wrong. True, he was young, eager to please. But the young man listened and followed orders. That went a hell of a long way in Shep's book. Cooper had even earned the respect of the team. They picked on him and he took it in stride, giving back as good as he got.

Shep didn't have time to wonder or care what pranks were about to transpire. The men knew their duties and their limits. At the moment, he needed to concentrate on figures.

And not the busty one of a certain redhead.

***

I'm just one big ray of crappy sunshine.

Chin propped on one hand, Tammy stared at the cup in front of her, chewing on her bottom lip. She should be more concerned about her ex and what his plans were than stressing about the hot firefighter who brought her home and tucked her into bed. Why couldn't she remember? Had Shep been there when she'd done a strip tease? Had he helped her remove her clothes?

"Hey Mom, can we have some cookies?" David had slipped into the kitchen without her knowing.

She straightened at the voice of her little trooper. What would she do if Steve tried to take him away?

Christopher came running around the corner, plowing into his brother.

"Whoa, Tiger. Where's the fire?" Good grief. Even the words coming out of her mouth were related to the man.

"I want cookies too."

"Sure thing, champ." She scooted from the high barstool and opened the freezer door. Most days, she baked from scratch, but the school had promoted a fundraiser and the teachers bought most of the products. Baked goods—everything from pizza to cookies and cakes. She and Cassie had gone a little crazy ordering from the fundraiser. Teachers received the profits to purchase items for their classrooms, so the money was considered well spent. With the items being frozen, the stuff would last throughout the year. Except at her house. She liked to bake, but frozen cookie dough made them too available, and the boys loved cookies.

She grabbed a tub of chocolate chunk.

"Fifteen minutes, guys. You know the drill."

The boys rushed out of the room with excited squeals, back to watch *Sponge Bob*, their favorite cartoon. She turned on the oven, pulled out a tray and opened the frozen container.

"What the heck is this?" It looked like—she studied it closer—chili.

A few weeks ago, Cassie brought over two containers for the boys. She'd started another diet and wanted temptation out of reach. She thought the twins were the perfect place to unload the sweets and gain their devotion, as if they didn't already adore her. Tammy went to the freezer and pulled out the second one, then popped the lid.

"Whew." She spooned chunks on the cookie sheet and put them in the oven. Then picked up her cell phone and tapped in Cassie's number.

"Hello?"

"Hey Cassie, it's me."

"Hi Tammy."

"You sound out of breath. Your hot man there?"

"No, but he'll be here later. I was carrying in groceries."

"Speaking of food, do you have a minute or you still have groceries in the car?"

"No. I'm done." By the sounds coming from the other end, Tammy figured Cassie was putting things away. "What's up?"

"You remember the containers of cookie dough you gave me?"

"Of course. I was glad to get them out of my house. They're too tempting."

"Well, I'm glad I had a spare, or two little boys would have been disappointed."

"What do you mean?"

Tammy glanced again at the bowl of chili that should have contained chocolate chunk cookie dough.

"*Joe Corbi's* made one whopping mistake with their packaging. I could swear this is chili."

By the sound of Cassie's laughter, Tammy pictured her doubling over clutching her stomach. "Guess you're not surprised."

"Oh my God. My mother."

"Your mother?"

"Yeah. I keep the empty containers for her. You know her chili is the best. She makes it and saves some for me using those containers. You better check the other one. It might be chicken and dumplings."

That was just too funny. Tammy had to laugh. "I did. It's cookie dough."

"Keep the chili for supper."

"I will. I plan on being home. Where will you be?"

"If I play my cards right, I'll be here with candlelight and wine."

"Hmph. You don't have anything to worry about. That strapping man is hooked." If she'd ever seen two people made for each other, they were Cassie and Mike. The guy was huge, but he was a big old teddy bear with Cassie.

"I hope so. I really like Mike. What about you? Have you talked to Shep?"

"Not since the other night. Cassie, I'm worried."

"About what?" Cassie's voice turned serious.

"Did I make an ass out of myself?"

"No more than I did. Mike says Shep is a really nice guy. From what I do remember, he was having fun. And he seemed to be into you."

"You think so?"

The oven beeped, signaling the cookies were done. "Gotta go. The twins know what that bell means."

Sure enough, the sound of thundering feet stormed into the kitchen.

"Back up guys. The oven is hot, so the cookies are hot."

"Can we watch you put them on the rack?" David asked as he climbed onto the high stool.

Christopher crawled up to the bar right beside his brother. The two boys did everything together. "Yeah, Mom. Can we help you put them on the rack?"

"I'll do that part."

The boys waited eagerly while she grabbed the iron cooling rack and transferred the cookies.

"They smell good." Christopher's eyes were as big as his little face. Her heart would just break if she couldn't do this with them as often as she did now.

Steve had left them. Left her. Two stinking years. That SOB—

It wouldn't do her any good to get worked up over a worthless man. She would spend every minute with her kids and not waste a moment on her ex.

CHAPTER 6

Should she call him? She'd been putting this off all week. She couldn't put it off any longer. By the time Tammy got the boys bathed and in bed, she was a bundle of worn out nerves. She paced the kitchen floor in anxiety, waiting for the kids to go to sleep. After another fifteen minutes, she checked their bedroom and found them both snoozing away.

She tiptoed back to the living room and clutched her cell, her fingers trembling as she punched in the numbers.

"What do you want?"

"Hello to you too." *Asshole.*

"It's late, Tammy. What do you want?" Just like Steve to make her feel like shit.

"Since when do you consider nine p.m. late? Or are you and your current wife getting busy?"

"None of your business. What the hell do you want?"

"Don't shout at me!" Then she remembered to lower her voice so the boys wouldn't hear. She marched to her bedroom and closed the door. "Let me tell you what is my business. You want to explain to me why you called the school principal?"

"He shouldn't have told you that. It's confidential."

"How are my children confidential? What are you planning, Steve?"

"They're my children too."

"Funny, you didn't remember that when you were screwing your bimbo."

"I'm not going to listen to you—"

"Just stop it," she hissed. Steve never wanted to listen. That had always been their problem. "Why did you call the school?"

"I have a right to see how my kids are doing in school. You are not the only parent."

The only one who'd been interested in them until now.

"Why the sudden interest?"

"They are my children," he said slowly as if she was an imbecile. "I have rights. I want to know—"

"Know what? Their grades? Their curriculum? Do you even look at their report cards? I've shared them with you." She'd tried to share a lot more but he was always too busy. The excuses multiplied. He had a meeting. He couldn't take them this weekend. He'd be out of town.

"You have too much control, Tammy. You only give me what you want me to see."

"If you showed any interest in *your children* then maybe you would learn more."

"I'm not having this fucking conversation with you."

"How dare you talk to me like that," she shouted, forgetting to keep quiet. She heard his heavy sigh on the other end.

"You bring out the worst in me."

What happened to the last eight years?

Her temples pounded. She rubbed her thumb and forefinger over them. "Look Steve. If something is up, I want to know."

"Marlene and I have a nice home and we've decided we want kids."

"So have them." He didn't want the ones he'd conceived with *her*. Would he be any different if he had more with the new wife?

"I want the boys to get to know Marlene. She's their step-mom."

Tammy bit her tongue before she said something she would regret.

Stepmom. Hussy.

"You don't take them as often as you could, now. You expect me to believe you're going to do better? Why the change of heart?"

"Get off your high horse, Tammy." She heard shuffling in the background. Marlene must be listening to every word. "You always did like to make mountains out of molehills."

Counting to ten had aided her in the past when she and Steve argued. It kept her from screaming. At the moment, she didn't give a shit. She glanced at her bedroom door to make sure it was closed.

"Are you going to tell me or not? I know you're up to something."

"You'll just have to wait and find out."

The line went dead. The son-of-a-bitch had hung up on her.

She hurled her phone across the room. Then cried, because she didn't have the money to get another one if it broke. She threw herself down on the bed, sobs racking her body. She hugged a pillow to her chest and buried her face, muffling the sound.

As grueling as the conversation had been, the knot in her throat had lifted. Of course, she felt no better now than before she called. But she'd vented some of her frustration. Steve was a difficult man. Demanding, irritating, exasperating, all those things and more. She'd suffered his exacting standards for years, pressuring her, exhausting her, nearly crippling her. Making her think the fault lay with her.

Her father had disciplined his children with a powerful constitution. She and her sisters were strong. She hadn't realized what Steve had done in their marriage, because little by little he'd asserted his domineering ability. Over time, he'd become the authoritarian, oppressing her. Thank God, she'd found her backbone before it was too late.

When she caught Steve cheating, she'd gone ballistic. Now she had a calmer head. No more succumbing. Defeat was not in her vocabulary. She was pissed. All those years wasted, except for the two bright, beautiful darlings who stemmed from their union. If Steve thought he'd take her children, he'd have one hell of a fight on his hands.

Too bad her father was gone. If he were still alive, there'd be no place for Steve to hide.

***

Shep was not one to procrastinate. If something needed to be done, he did it. Without delay. All day he'd planned to call Tammy, but he'd been stalling. He'd kept busy giving orders, assigning tasks and in general, pacing the floor.

Not like him at all.

He headed to the lounge for a Coke.

"Hey Cap."

Hearing Laredo, he stopped.

"I just spent an hour over at county arguing with Campbell. Asshole tried to tell me I'm not to drive the quint down Main Street. Not my fault that *baboso* didn't stop. Had to hear the sirens. Dude's eyes bugged out of his head when I laid on the horn."

"He still managed to enter the intersection."

"Taking on a forty-ton truck? Pecker won't be doing that again. Campbell acts like it's my fault."

"Campbell had a run in with Wilson and lost. Still carries a grudge. Since Campbell was elected into office, he's been throwing his weight around."

"Well, he can't tell me what to do. I'm gonna—"

"Don't get into a pissing contest with Campbell. Let me handle him." Shep had had to deal with the man before. If Campbell wanted to measure dicks, Shep would cut him down to size.

"Yes sir, Cap."

"Besides, it was caught on film. A bystander recorded you on his cell when he heard the sirens and it clearly shows the car running through the intersection. The eyewitness turned it into the TV station. I just got the heads up. It will be on the six o'clock news."

"No shit."

"Quick thinking, Laredo. You avoided an accident."

"Thanks, Cap. It was a close one."

Damned people. What was wrong with them? Of course, the guy had heard the sirens. He had plenty of time to stop, but instead, the dumbass tried to beat the fire truck through an intersection. Some people had no sense. Or respect. As for Campbell, Shep wouldn't mind handing the man's ass to him.

"Now that you're back, go show the new guy how to tie knots. I've scheduled a scenario for tomorrow with a mock water rescue."

"On it, Cap."

Though he trusted his crew, Shep followed through on his responsibilities inspecting the bathrooms, the gear, the rigs and found each man had done their job to his high standards of satisfaction. He didn't need to crack a whip. The men knew the procedures and what was expected. Doing every job right, no matter how trivial, meant a firefighter could be trusted to perform his role in the field. A slothful firefighter could get a man killed.

The rest of the evening remained fairly quiet. After dinner, he left Mike and Cooper to clean up. As was his habit, he took a stroll across the bay and tested the back door to make sure it was locked. He checked his watch. Nine fifteen.

Is it too late to call?

He shook his head. He couldn't put it off any longer.

While he trudged up the stairs, the rest of the squad watched TV in the big room. Better do it now, before it got any later. The chair behind his desk squeaked with his weight. Since it was a personal call, he used his cell.

She answered on the first ring.

"Hello!"

Whoa. She sounded pissed. Maybe it was too late.

"Tammy? This is Shep." He swallowed, waiting for her to let him have it.

Silence. Then he heard her mumbling.

"I'm so sorry," she said.

"I think I should be the one apologizing. I'm sorry I called so late."

"Oh. It's not that late. My mind was ... somewhere else when I answered. I didn't mean to snap."

He released a sigh and silently thanked the man upstairs. Whoever Tammy had been mad at, at least it wasn't him.

"I, uh, don't want to bother you. If you have a minute, I'd like to talk to you. If you're busy—"

"No! I mean, no. I'm not busy. The boys are sleeping."

Shit. Had he woken them up? "I hope the phone didn't wake them."

"No. You called my cell number."

"Oh." That's the number she'd given him.

"When the house phone rings, I figure it's solicitors or the doctor's office, so I rarely answer it anyway."

"I see." He had a landline too. It was there for emergencies, and like Tammy, he let the answering machine pick up the calls. Anyone important knew his cell number.

"I, um, well, the last person I talked to was my ex, so I was in the same frame of mind when I answered your call. I'm sorry."

That explained a lot.

"Nothing to be sorry for," he assured her. Now to see if he was in the doghouse. "I think maybe I should apologize to you. I assure you nothing happened last week." *He should have called sooner.*

There was a moment of silence before she spoke. "I'm so embarrassed." At least she wasn't yelling at him. He could imagine her face turning red.

"Don't be. You were delightful." Beautiful. Funny. Sexy as hell.

"Delightful? There's something you don't normally hear associated with inebriation." She talked so fast he had to catch up. He was used to his own slow drawl.

"I wanted to set your mind at ease. Mike took Cassie home and I volunteered to take you home. I had fun. I figured you needed a little safeguarding and I was more than willing to do the job." He leaned back and propped his feet on his desk. "My mama raised me to be a gentleman. She'd tan my hide if I was anything other than protective."

"Wow. Chivalry. I thought it was dead."

"No, ma'am. Not with me."

"Please don't call me ma'am."

He heard a shuffle and wondered where she was. In the kitchen? In the living room? In the bedroom?

"I know I behaved badly."

"Now how would you know that?"

"For one thing, I don't remember much. So, that right there shows I drank way too much."

"I heard it was for a good cause." *Her asshole husband.*

"Oh. Yeah." Her voice sounded sad, cutting him. Right then he could have kicked his own ass. He wanted to make her feel better, not worse.

"I had a good time. You were a lot of fun." He meant every word.

"I remember dancing." She sounded better.

"You do a mean two-step."

"I had an excellent partner."

He smiled. "Thought you couldn't remember."

"I remember everything up until I don't," she said mischievously. Shep laughed out loud. "Thanks for bringing me home."

"My pleasure."

"That's the part I don't remember much about."

"Don't worry your pretty head. I took you to your bedroom and helped you to the bed." He left out the part about her dancing around, removing her clothes. And the part where he'd watched her hungrily. "Anything that happened after that, I was gone. I'm supposing you fell on the bed and went to sleep."

"I was afraid I'd embarrassed myself."

"You didn't do any such thing. I'm glad I was there to keep an eye out for you. Wouldn't want anyone taking advantage."

"I seem to remember you ordering shots."

Uh oh.

"However, I don't remember you drinking any," she added.

"I don't drink much. A beer now and again."

"God, I must have looked like a lush."

A very beautiful lush.

"How could you stand me?"

Very easily.

"I enjoyed every minute," he told her. "Sometimes a body just needs to cut loose. Cassie trusted Mike. Since I was with him, I guess she trusted me."

"I'm glad you were there. I don't normally get like that. I had received some distressing news."

When she hesitated, Shep figured he better get to the second reason why he'd called. Then he thought better of the notion. He didn't want Tammy to get the idea they were talking about her behind her back. She'd mentioned her ex, but still ... maybe he should let her tell him in her own way. If he disclosed that he'd talked to his brother, she might take this call the wrong way and think he pitied her.

Nothing could be further from the truth.

Tammy had a feisty charm that seized more than his interest. Like flowers in a garden, the attraction for the lovely redhead had sprouted and grew. Of course, he'd nurtured the image, fed it, allowed it to flourish. Now every time he thought of her, a certain ambiance would come out and play. Dancing with her at the *Pitt Stop* had been icing on a longed-for cake.

"I'm a good listener if you'd like to tell me about it."

She took a deep breath as if she needed strength to spit out whatever she wanted to say. "That rat. He's barely paid attention to the boys for two years and all of a sudden he's nosing around at the school. I'm not sure what he's up to, but knowing Steve, he is definitely up to something. He's calculative and manipulative. He doesn't do anything without a reason."

Sounded like a man who needed his ass kicked.

Another silence. Then, "I don't want to bother you."

"Bother me." The words were out of his mouth before he realized the double entendre. His breathing had grown heavy. His voice had deepened. He liked the idea of Tammy bothering him, in more ways than one.

The woman was beautiful with a spirit to match. She had a rocking body, plump and full and delectable. Perfect for him. His hands itched to roam those enchanting curves.

"If you're sure."

His tongue too big for his throat, he could only nod. She continued without him needing to say anything.

"Steve, my ex, called the school asking for the boys' records. Then mentioned they'd be moving to another school. Principal March called me into his office to let me know. I was flummoxed."

"Can he do that? Take the boys out of the school without telling you?"

"I have physical custody, but he's so arrogant he thinks he can do anything. I called him tonight hoping he'd admit what he's up to, but he hung up on me. That's when you called."

The son-of-a-bitch. No wonder Tammy answered the way she had.

"I'm sorry, Tammy. I'd like to help."

"That's sweet. There's nothing you can do."

Except rip your ex's tongue out. He hated the sound of defeat in her voice.

Can I come over? Let me hold you.

Shit.

"Well, maybe not me"—Shep cleared his throat—"but my brother is a lawyer."

"A lawyer?"

"Yeah. Eddie practices law. Do you have a lawyer?"

"I had one for the divorce. If I need to, I guess I can use him again."

"Why don't you let me call my brother?" It wasn't like he was lying to her. There was no need to mention he already had. He would call again. There.

"Shep, you've been so nice to me. I don't know."

"Tell you what. I'll mention you and see if he has time to speak with you. I'm sure he will. You don't have to do anything now, but it might be a good idea to ask questions. Eddie can give you an idea of what to expect. If nothing else, talk with him to ease your mind."

"Shep, you're wonderful."

His chest swelled at her words.

"I mean, that sounds wonderful. I'd like that."

Yeah. Tammy was getting under his skin.

Chapter 7

Another confrontation with Steve. Only this time, he made Tammy doubt herself. Just like when they were married. She thought she'd fixed that. Built her self-confidence to a point where he no longer threatened her.

Her hands shook. From anger. Not doubt. She refused to fall back into the pitiful shell she'd lived in before the divorce. Not that she had cowered like a pathetic, frightened creature. But she'd not been happy. Nor had she been the self-assured woman her father raised her to be. Steve had made her dependent on him. Thank God, she'd come to her senses.

Her cell phone vibrated in her hand. It couldn't be Steve. He'd hung up on her again. She glanced at the lit screen and touched the green button.

"Who's your favorite sister?"

"What do you want, Bonnie?"

"Who shit in your cornflakes?"

Tammy rubbed her temple. Worrying about Steve taking the twins had made her snap. "Sorry. I just got off the phone with Steve."

"It's been two years. He still giving you shit? He's got a new wife to make him miserable."

"Yeah, but he's still sticking his nose in my business."

"You know you're better off, don't you? The boys are, too."

Were they?

According to her mother, Tammy should have stayed married and ignored her husband's infidelity. She refused to live like that. Watching her father and mother had taught her a valuable lesson. Divorcing Steve had been the right thing to do.

How could she doubt it?

"I know that," she told her sister. "I also know they belong with me."

"What do you mean by that? Has he done something? You better tell me. Do I need to come down there and kick his ass?"

Bonnie had brown hair, but it should have been red like the rest of her sisters. She got fired up quicker than Tammy at the drop of a hat.

"Steve contacted the school. Asking for David and Christopher's records. He even hinted that he'd be moving them to another school."

"He can't do that. He can't do anything without your permission. Didn't he sign over custody?"

"Yes. But he's planning something." There was no doubt in her mind.

"I wish our father was still alive. He'd make Steve's asshole pucker up."

"Bonnie, you sure know how to make me feel better."

"He's a douche. Never mind him. I called to tell you what Ginger wants for graduation."

"It's months away."

"She believes in being prepared."

"I can't believe my niece is seventeen and a senior."

"Why? Make you feel old?"

Well, yes. But then, her sister was a lot older. "You mean like you? You are eleven years older than me."

"Don't remind me. I helped Mom change your diapers."

"So you keep telling me. Okay. What does Ginger want?"

"She's picked out an item for each of her favorite aunts."

"I thought I was her favorite," Tammy spouted jokingly.

"When she wants something, you are. Now, for you she's chosen perfume. *Amyris Femme Eau De Parfum.*"

Holy shit. "That's over two hundred dollars a bottle."

"You're getting off easy," Bonnie said unsympathetically. "She asked Vickie for diamond earrings and Nora for a tennis bracelet." Since Bonnie spoiled her daughter outrageously, Ginger had no idea that other people had to live on a budget.

"I love my niece but I have two boys to raise."

"You're her favorite." Bonnie snorted.

Smart alec.

"What does she want from you?"

"She expects us to get her a new car."

Of course. "At least you can afford it."

"Why don't you move back to New York? Al is divorced. He has money."

Al. Tammy had had such a crush on him. Until her father made it clear Al was off limits. At the time, she hadn't understood why her father did not approve of the son of his closest friend.

"He's also Italian," she said, "and it's a little shady where his money comes from."

"Don't be so picky," Bonnie shot back. "He's handsome and has lots of hair."

Tammy wanted to laugh. "Maybe at forty-two hair is import to you."

"One day it will be important to you, too."

She thought about the shaved heads that seemed to be the style these days. Then she thought about Shep. And the silver at his temples. Only one of his alluring assets.

"I'm not there yet."

***

Shep drove home with the window down, his elbow resting on the sill. The blowing wind cuffing the side of his head relaxed him. Fall. One of his favorite seasons. The breeze had a chill in the air, but he liked the cooler temperatures. If only it worked on his hot thoughts of Tammy.

The woman took up more of his time than he aimed to give. Although, to be honest, he liked thinking about the feisty redhead. Her smile lit up an entire room. Unusual eyes, though. The hint of different shades intrigued him.

A teacher. He pictured her reading a book to her kids. From the way she talked, the twins were full of energy. Of course, they were boys. He remembered him and his brothers at that age. The five of them got into all kinds of stuff. He marveled at how his mom had put up with their shenanigans. They'd raised plenty of hell, but when his mom spoke, they listened. Looking back, he'd rather take a lickin' from his dad than his mom.

Punching the Bluetooth on his steering wheel, Shep called Tammy's number. Even though he'd been thinking about her all day, this was the first chance he'd had to call.

"Hello." She sounded out of breath.

"Tammy? This is Shep."

"Uh. Hi."

"I hope I'm not interrupting you."

"No! I mean, of course not."

"I wanted to tell you about Eddie."

"Eddie?"

"My brother, the lawyer. Eddie said he could see you tomorrow."

"Tomorrow?" Then she screeched. "Really? That was fast. Tomorrow?"

"Yep." He didn't add that Eddie had rescheduled an appointment to fit her in. Brothers would do things for you. Eddie was a good guy.

"Thank you. Thank you. Thank you." Her excitement made Shep smile.

"All I did was talk to my brother. He's the one who's going to help."

"If not for you, I wouldn't be seeing him. You're a wonderful man to do this for me."

Out of habit, he started to decline her praise. Instead, he stopped himself, then enjoyed the sudden feeling swirling in his chest. Being humble was difficult when the woman you wanted to impress was the one issuing compliments.

"I told him you just wanted to talk. He said there would be no pressure. Ask questions. Tell your story. If he can help, he will. And there's no charge."

"What do you mean, no charge? Lawyers are expensive, I know that."

"He's my brother," Shep said while checking the rearview mirror. No way would he allow her to pay. As a favor, Eddie wouldn't charge her. If the office generated a bill, Shep would take care of it. He could sense her pride kicking in. "You're just going to talk."

"Just talk, huh."

"Just talk," he replied with his usual drawl, hoping to set her mind at ease.

"Will you go with me?"

She drilled him right down to the bone. The feeling in his chest amplified.

"If that's what you want. I'll go with you."

***

Today she would meet Shep's brother. Tammy paced her bedroom floor and looked in the mirror for the thousandth time. She tucked a curl behind her ear, then plucked it back out. She smoothed the jacket over her full hips, then counted to ten. Her nerves were jumping along her skin.

The navy-blue pants suit looked good on her and, she hoped, displayed an image of a professional woman. Was it too much? When the doorbell rang, she stumbled and cursed her new shoes. She shouldn't be wearing heels anyway. She kicked them off and stuck her feet into a pair of Sperry's.

The bell rang again. She took off at a run and remembered she wore her suit. *Shit*. She stuffed her feet back into her heels.

Before opening the door, she patted her hair one more time, then turned the handle and swallowed her tongue.

"Hi." Shep's slow drawl rolled over her.

"Hi," she managed to get out. She feasted her eyes and tried to calm her racing pulse. Damn, this man was hot.

"Can I come in?"

"Oh. Yes." She stepped back, trying not to stumble and reminded herself to breathe. Shep seemed to suck all the air out of the room.

"I, uh, guess the place looks familiar since you've been here before." What the hell was coming out of her mouth? She needed to jump-start her brain.

"Yeah. I didn't pay a lot of attention that night."

That night. Why had she brought it up?

"Thanks again for putting up with me and bringing me home." Would she ever get over the embarrassment?

"Bringing you home was no hardship."

Shep was so handsome. She drew in a slow breath to calm her racing pulse.

"You don't have to be nervous. Eddie won't bite."

How could she tell Shep his brother was not the one making her nervous? "I appreciate what you're doing for me. I mean, getting your brother to see me and all."

"Just trying to help out. There's no need to thank me. As for my brother, we're family." His eyes were warm and reassuring. His lips moved and she imagined leaning forward, tasting—

She jerked. My God, what was wrong with her? "Uh, no, I uh, I'm not worried about him. Well, I am, but ..." When her words failed, he just grinned. That sexy, come-kiss-me grin.

"Are you about ready to go?"

She blinked.

Good Lord, get a grip.

"Yes, all I need is my purse."

They said little as he drove through town and parked in "Lawyers Row". Taking her elbow, he escorted her into the building and didn't let go until they reached a very shiny elevator. Her nerves were on overdrive, but Shep calmed her in a way that eased her distress. She trembled. Not from fear of what this meeting represented, but from the tingling sensation she felt from his touch.

"Don't be nervous. Remember, Eddie won't bite."

The elevator doors opened to a bright room, a superb, cherry wood counter, and a pretty woman sitting behind it.

"Good afternoon. May I help you?" A beautiful smile and a pleasing voice, perfect for a receptionist. Jealously wavered right on top of her nerves.

"Yes, ma'am," Shep answered. His flawless manners were those of a gentleman. "We're here to see Eddie."

"I see the resemblance." The receptionist smiled. "You must be his brother."

Had Shep not been to Eddie's office before?

"Yes, I am. This is Tammy Michael. She has an appointment."

"He's expecting you. If you will have a seat over there, I'll ring his secretary." The woman nodded to their right.

Again, Shep took Tammy's elbow and guided her to several high back leather chairs. No expense was spared for this place.

"You all right?" he murmured close to her ear.

His spice cologne enveloped her, making her wonder what brand he wore. "I'm fine," she lied. She would be if she stopped fantasizing about him. God, he smelled good.

She and Shep had barely sat down when another beautiful woman approached them. Did this office only hire runway models? With so many gorgeous women available, why would Shep want her? She had to remember he was only with her because she'd asked him. True, he'd offered to help. He'd even gotten his brother to see her. That didn't mean he found her attractive.

"Hello. I'm Regina, Mr. Shepherd's secretary. Will you please follow me?"

Shepherd?

Puzzled, Tammy barely felt Shep's hand on her arm as they followed Regina down a luxurious hallway. She whispered out the side of her mouth.

"Is you name Shepherd?"

"Yep." That's all he said. Rather than have this discussion in the hallway, she sealed her lips, ready to pounce at the first opportunity.

A tall, impeccably dressed man stood beside a huge desk. He had that same speckled gray at his temples that made him look distinguished. "Welcome. Please come in."

"Eddie, this is Tammy Michael."

"It's a pleasure to meet you, Tammy." The deep smooth voice along with his silver-gray eyes, so much like Shep's, knocked her off balance even more than her anxious nerves already had. Eddie took her hand in both of his and held it while he talked. "I hope this guy hasn't been feeding you tales about our childhood. Only believe the good things he said about me. There are no bad things." He gave her a wink.

Right away, she felt at ease. "It's nice to meet you, too, uh, Mr. Shepherd."

"Please, call me Eddie. Mr. Shepherd sounds ridiculous in front of my brother."

"Okay. Well, uh, he hasn't said much. Only that you're a lawyer."

"One of the best, if I must say so myself. But I can't believe this guy has not been burning your ear with our escapades." He glanced to Shep as if daring him to ... what? Obviously, some kind of communication she didn't understand passed between them.

"I do have one question."

Both men turned to her and she realized Eddie still held her hand.

"Please, ask me anything." He patted her hand and then released it.

She stared directly at Shep. "Is your name Shep Shepherd?"

Both men laughed. It sounded like a perfectly reasonable question to her.

"Shep is short for Shepherd," he said in way of explanation. "In boot camp fire training, the men called each other by their last name. It stuck."

"What is your first name?"

"Jonathan."

"Why don't you have a seat?" Eddie gestured to an expensive, high-back chair.

Tammy eased into the soft leather and inhaled the rich fragrance. Plush. Eddie must be a successful lawyer. She hoped so anyway. She'd need all the influence she could get to fight Steve.

"Let's get to know each other. You can tell me about your ex-husband. Nothing is too much. Talk about anything you like."

It turned out she asked more questions than furnished information. She discovered that Eddie was a thirty-eight-year-old criminal lawyer who'd downsized to a civil trial attorney. He was taller than Shep, rather intimidating, but he brandished a smile that warmed a woman's insides.

As Shep and Eddie talked, she learned Eddie dwarfed his colleagues and evidently made a commendable presence in a courtroom. He kept himself in peak physical condition and used his appearance to his advantage. His track record was remarkable. Just listening to him speak, she could tell he was well-educated. For ten years, he'd never lost a case—until the last one. He didn't elaborate and she didn't ask why, but that's when he'd changed to strictly civil cases.

He asked her a ton of questions, yet made her so comfortable it was like having a conversation with a friend. Then he got down to the important stuff.

"Parents often wish to assert joint custody rights when going through the divorce process. Joint custody results in both parents sharing in the upbringing and responsibility for rearing children in some fashion. This arrangement differs from sole or full custody, where the decisions are made by one parent or party. Courts determine whether to award joint or sole custody depending on the best interests of the child, or in your case, children."

"The boys were so small, we didn't want to upset them. We have joint custody."

"Joint custody can mean different things and the terminology can be confusing. It can refer to 'joint legal custody' or 'joint physical custody.' Joint legal custody exists where the parents share decision-making authority for the child, but one parent retains primary physical custody. Joint physical custody exists where the child lives with each parent for roughly the same amount of time."

"Steve doesn't get them as often as he should. I've never denied him the right to see the boys. He ignores them on his own."

"I see." Eddie folded his hands, resting them in the middle of his desk. "That can be to your advantage."

"How?"

"We can argue his sudden about-face. Why does he want custody when he does not utilize his current visitation? There are a lot of things we can look at. But he hasn't served you with custody papers, yet."

"He's sneaky. He's up to something, I know it."

"Have you always lived in Virginia?"

"No. Steve and I were married in New York. His company transferred him and we moved here."

"To complicate matters, different states use different terminology when describing joint custody. For example, some states use the term 'shared custody' instead of 'joint custody'. Where did you get your divorce?"

"Here, in Virginia. We have joint custody, but the boys live with me. That is in our divorce papers."

"Did you bring them with you?"

"Yes." She dug in her purse. "I almost forgot them."

"Let me glance over your paperwork and I can tell you exactly what your rights are."

While she pulled out her divorce agreement, Eddie continued.

"Both parents retain important rights in a joint custody arrangement where each has input with respect to decisions on important matters such as the child's legal status, medical care, education, religious instruction, and extracurricular activities. However, the child will reside primarily with one parent. If a judge believes the parents will cooperate, he or she may award joint physical custody, setting a schedule assigning days to each parent."

"We cooperated just fine until now. Steve has visitation, but he pushes them off. He never has time for them. I don't understand why he's sneaking around now."

Tammy held her breath while Eddie scanned the document. He flipped the pages one after another, then carefully placed them on his desk.

"You have joint physical custody with no limitation. Which means your ex-husband can get the boys any time he wants."

"Wh— what do you mean?"

"It looks like your ex-husband has been biding his time. He has more power than he's led you to believe. According to this document, he can take them at any time."

Wind roared in her ears. Panic began to set in. The room grew hot. Her heart pounded and she started to sweat. She gripped the arms of her chair. Then she felt a warm hand on her arm.

"Tammy. I'm right here."

Shep.

She glanced up and immediately her anxiety calmed. He squeezed her hand, crushing her fear before it had a chance to swallow her.

"I didn't mean to scare you. *You* have the same right." Eddie's voice drew her attention to him. "I can't believe a judge gave you equal power unless he knew without a doubt the two of you were amenable."

"There was no judge. Only lawyers."

"Did you have your own lawyer?"

"Yes."

"I'm not sure he acted in your best interest. This agreement allows you both equal access with no prerequisites. The way this is written, the parents can physically fight over the children. No reputable lawyer would agree to this arrangement. You're fortunate your relationship with your ex-husband has been cordial this long."

"You're saying Steve can come take the boys away from me at any time?"

"He can pick up the boys anytime, anywhere without your permission, or without notifying you. Let me give you a scenario. Your ex-husband can physically pick up ... What are your sons' names?"

"David and Christopher. And please, just call him Steve."

"Steve can carry David to his car and put him in it. But you can yank your son back out. Same thing with Christopher. Can you imagine such a scene? Two parents in a physical altercation? It has happened. Imagine children having no idea what to do while their mother and father are fighting in a parking lot, yanking them back and forth. That's why an agreement like this doesn't work. The parents must agree on everything. If there is a disagreement, this document is worthless."

"All this time ..." Words failed her. One more instance where Steve had used his influence and she'd been dumb enough to think he was playing fair.

"If you think he's up to something, he may be getting ready to show his hand."

The idea terrified her. "What should I do?"

"You've already done it. You came to me." Eddie's grin took her alarm down several notches. If she wasn't so upset, she might think him attractive. Good looks ran in the Shepherd family. And compassion. Eddie was so easy to like.

"My cocky brother is good at his job," Shep said. "You can trust him."

When had he removed his hand? She wanted it back. As if he'd read her mind, he placed his palm over her knuckles and she quickly turned her hand over, lacing their fingers together.

It may have been forward. It may have been foolish. But she needed his strength. And he felt so damn good.

"Any skeletons in your—Steve's closet? Any domestic issues? Custody will not be awarded if one parent has been convicted of a domestic violence offense."

"Steve protects his image. He's squeaky clean."

Eddie's face turned serious and he leveled his gaze on her. "No one is squeaky clean."

"He doesn't break the law. Just the marriage vows."

"Raw emotions can often overtake good judgment. That's what I'm here for. Let me work with Steve's attorney."

"Steve hasn't done anything other than contact the school."

"That you know of."

"Well, yeah."

"Point made," Eddie said calmly and specifically.

Good Lord. What else had he done?

"Don't worry about anything until it happens. And then you come to me. I'll do the worrying for you."

Don't worry? How could she not? Come to him? Where else would she go? Now that she'd met Eddie, she'd most definitely take his advice.

CHAPTER 8

Since meeting Shep, Tammy had been on an emotional roller-coaster ride. He'd shown up like a knight right when she needed him. Steve knew how to push her buttons, using the twins to mess with her head. Shep calmed her, reassured her. He'd taken her mind off her troubles, then helped her face them.

"I really appreciate you going with me," she said as Shep pulled up to her house.

"You're welcome. Eddie's a good guy. And he gets results. He'll help you."

"I hope so. I can't lose my boys."

"You won't." He said it with such conviction, she wanted to believe him. Put her faith in him. A man. A man she could trust even after Steve had screwed her over.

"I'll help in any way I can," Shep's voice held strength and emotion, giving her the assurance she needed. When she reached for the door handle, he stopped her "Wait. I'll come around."

She knew he would. He'd been such a gentleman. He got out of the Land Rover, came to the passenger side, and opened her door. The vehicle wasn't too high, but high enough he took her hand. A little shiver raced up her arm.

"The boys are still in school. Did you take the whole day off?"

"Yes," she said as she slid out, her feet hitting the ground. "I didn't know how long the appointment would take. I figured I'd be stressed out. The boys don't need to see me like that."

"You didn't say much on the drive home."

She hesitated, giving him a sidelong glance. It amazed her how calm Shep made her. "I'm okay. Would you like to come in for coffee?" Any excuse to keep him close.

"Sure. I'd love a cup. Wait. It's almost lunchtime. Would you like to go get something to eat?"

"Why don't I make us lunch?" She dug in her purse for her keys.

"Sounds good to me."

The man was everything a woman dreamed about and hot as hell to boot. He sparked sensations in her she hoped someday to explore. For now, she needed to concentrate on opening the door.

Everything was tidy and in its place. Shep noticed that no toys littered the floor, which amazed him—with two six-year-old boys.

"Christopher and David share a bedroom, so I use the third one for a playroom. Otherwise, they would take over the house."

Could she read minds?

"Your house is nice."

"Thanks," she said, taking off her coat.

Since he lived in the country where it was cooler, he rarely wore one. She tossed hers on a chair. "Come on back to the kitchen."

He followed her through the open dining-room/kitchen combination. Kids' drawings were on the refrigerator. He smiled, pondering the cozy feel of the place. On one wall, a corkboard held a calendar, handwritten notes, and a few more pictures. From all the drawings, it was obvious Tammy loved her boys.

He watched her sexy backside as she moved about, getting ready to make coffee. When she pulled out a tray and lifted a white plastic thing, he drew his bows together.

"What's that?" He pointed to her hand.

"A pod for the Keurig."

"What's a Keurig?"

She smiled, and damned if he didn't forget what he'd asked her.

"A coffee pot." She lifted a handle on some sort of machine. "This is a Keurig."

"That's a coffee pot?"

"Yep. Makes a fresh cup every time."

"I like the sound of that." Still, he kept his eyes on the contraption. "What grade do you teach?" He scooted onto a high stool and stretched his long legs out.

"Third."

"And your boys are in kindergarten?"

"Yeah. Their birthdays are in November. The school cut-off date is September 30th, so they got a late start."

"The boys are six?"

"Six going on sixteen."

Shep chuckled, remembering his brothers at that age. Talk about full throttle. The only speed they knew was wide open. But his mom had known how to rein them in. He had a feeling Tammy could do the same. The spirit this woman exhibited showed she dominated her space.

Mere seconds passed and she placed a steaming mug in front of him.

"That was fast." He lifted the cup to take a sip.

"Milk or cream?"

"Black."

"Figures."

He hesitated. "How so?"

She popped a new pod into the machine and pushed a button. "You just seem ..."

"Go on." He took a sip and watched her over the rim.

"Strong men usually take their coffee black. Your profession dictates your time. I figure some days you don't have the chance to put anything in your coffee before you have to head out. Years of that routine," she shrugged, "I deduced you drank it black."

Strong men. Hmm.

She poured milk into her cup. "Would you excuse me just a minute? Make yourself at home."

Tammy disappeared and he wondered, since they were alone, if he made her nervous. Understandable—she'd been anxious going to Eddie's office. After meeting him, she'd calmed down. But a moment ago, she seemed jumpy.

Shep noticed some pictures on a mantle in the living space. He went in to check them out. Several photos were lined up in a row. A few of the twins in ball uniforms. Cute—they favored Tammy. And from what he could see, they were happy. He stared at the one of the boys with their mom. The sun glinted on her bright red hair, and her smile was as big as a proud mother's could get. The skin prickled on the back of his neck alerting him to her presence.

"Your boys?"

"Yeah. I signed them up for T-ball. You can tell by the photo they were full of themselves."

"Typical boys. They look happy." He turned and found Tammy had changed her suit for a pair of tight jeans. His gaze slid down her sexy legs before he could stop himself. Damn, she looked good enough—

Whoa. Bare Feet. Round toes with fire red polish. He felt a stirring behind his zipper.

"I couldn't stand those heels any longer. I hope you don't mind."

Mind? Hell.

Breathe.

At this moment, he needed something colder than coffee.

"Do you care if I kick off my shoes, too?" he asked in fun.

"Uh, sure. Be comfortable."

"I'm teasing." He gave her a smile, enjoying the way Tammy got all flustered. Made him want to push her further. Gave him an idea of what she might look like all hot and sweaty and ruffled with passion.

She stepped to the kitchen and he followed. He liked being behind her where he could devour her sexy backside. She pulled some containers from her refrigerator.

"Don't go to any trouble for me. A sandwich will be fine."

"I have leftover pasta from last night."

"Sounds delicious."

"Shrimp Alfredo. All I have to do is heat it up."

"A woman after my own heart."

Her face blushed red. Well. It slipped out. Thinking about it now, though, he meant it in more ways than just the saying.

She quickly took off the foil and added some plastic wrap, then put the dish into the microwave. "There. Just a few minutes."

"The guys at the station will be jealous."

"Why's that?"

"On my day off I get gourmet food and didn't have to cook it."

She laughed, a throaty sound that grabbed his gut. "You like to cook?"

"Don't have a lot of choice. We all cook at the station. But to answer your question, I do."

"What do you make?"

"Everything," he replied. "We get lots of practice. Since we have to eat each other's cooking, we make a variety of dishes. Chicken, steak, shrimp, veal. We have cookbooks, too."

"Well, if you do all that cooking, how about deserts?"

"I've been told that's your specialty."

"By Cassie and Mike, no doubt."

Shep gave a nod. "I hear tell that you like to bake cakes. You can bake me a cake anytime."

"I just might do that."

The microwave dinged, signaling the food was done. Tammy spooned some onto plates and gave him silverware.

"This smells delicious."

"Dig in," she said, taking the seat beside him. Her scent over-rode the food. Her sugary fragrance made him want to lick his lips. Lick her. Instead, he scooped noodles on his fork.

"Oh, man. This is good."

"Have some garlic bread."

"Homemade?" At her glare, he shrugged. "Sorry." He watched her eat and tried not to react at seeing her tongue dart out to lick a drop of sauce from the corner of her mouth. "You have other family around? Brothers, sisters ..."

"I grew up with three sisters. Bonnie and Vickie are twins." She propped her elbow on the counter, holding her fork in the air. "Poor Vickie. They're identical, but Bonnie's hair was straight and Vickie's hair was curly and stuck out everywhere.

Since she found product, it's better. In the middle is Nora, then me."

"Do they live close by?"

"New York."

"You're from New York?" He shook his head. "I never would have guessed."

"Yes, and why?"

"You're nice. Not at all like what I'd expect ..." He paused with the fork halfway to his mouth.

Fire snapped in her eyes. "And just what do you mean by that remark?"

"Now don't go getting your panti ... uh, feathers in a bunch. Most of the people I've met who are from the north are not friendly. They're snooty and bossy."

"Well, I'll let you off the hook. I am bossy."

"I didn't say you."

She waved his comment away with her hand. "Doesn't matter. I know I am."

"You're also friendly. And nice. And fun."

"Nice save."

He grunted. "Parents?"

"My mom is in New York. My dad is deceased."

"I'm sorry."

Tammy took a bite and he waited for her to finish. "I was close to my dad when I was little. He and Mom fought a lot, but being Catholic, my mom never got a divorce. I must have been about ten when he moved out. Mom got a job. Dad told her she didn't have to work, but she was determined. They fought about that, too. She said he couldn't tell her what to do and yada yada." Tammy twirled her fork in a circle.

He didn't know what to say to that, so he stayed quiet.

"I never saw either one of them with another person. Romantically, I mean. My dad had some shady dealings. I didn't find out until I went to college. I still don't know much. He died right after Steve and I got married. Not long after that, Steve's company transferred him to Virginia. Voilà."

He swallowed his food. "Voilà?"

"Here I am."

"How long have you been divorced?" he asked, then shoved another fork full of scrumptious pasta.

"Two years. The boys were four. It was a difficult decision and my mom almost disowned me, but it was for the best."

"Your mom gave you a hard time?"

"In my family, you don't get a divorce. Besides, we're Catholic."

"So, your mother would rather you spend your life married to someone who makes you miserable?" *Shit.* He shouldn't have said that. "Uh, I'm sorry. It's none of my business why you got divorced. I didn't mean to assume—"

"You're right. I was miserable. He cheated. I'm not putting up with that."

The shithead. What man in his right mind would cheat on this woman? Tammy was beautiful. Stacked, and when she smiled, her face lit up with a glow that reflected in her sparkling eyes. A man couldn't help but drown in them.

"You divorced him, but stayed in Virginia. Why didn't you go back home?"

"After the divorce, my sister tried to get me to go back to New York. Cassie told me not to make any decisions until I had time to think. Until I'd sorted everything out. By the time we moved from New York, I'd pretty much devoted my life to Steve. We were newlyweds. I wanted to make him happy. It wasn't until after we moved that I fell under a different spell. He told me what to do, when to do it, where to go. I'd lost touch with my friends, my family was in New York. But the worst, I lost my independence. I didn't realize it until it was almost too late."

Shep ate while Tammy talked, grateful she felt comfortable enough to tell him about things that were personal and had to be painful.

"Steve shattered my self-esteem, but when I found out he'd cheated on me, I found my backbone."

"Good for you. Although, I'm sure you would have reconnected with your friends in New York."

"Trying to get rid of me?" she teased with a sexy grin.

"Not a chance," he responded, facing her, and bumped her thigh with his knee. The teasing light in her eyes turned to smoldering wonder. The urge to kiss her speared him. He was a patient man. Tammy was worth some pampering. He calmed his racing pulse. "I'm glad you stayed in Virginia."

"Uh, yeah." She blinked. "Anyway, I made friends here, reinstated my independence. If I'd gone home with my tail between my legs, my mom and sisters would have taken over my life. I had to make it on my own. I put my degree to good use. I deserve the life I've made for the boys. For me. I love my teaching job. Cassie and I are BFFs."

"BFF?"

"Best buds."

"Mike likes her."

"No doubt. She and that man were drawn to each other like two magnets slamming together."

Shep would have to agree. He hoped for the same ilk of attraction between him and Tammy.

"How about you?" she asked. "Are you close to your brothers?"

"We keep in touch. We're spread out all over."

"My sisters and I fought and drove each other crazy growing up. We still do. Don't get me wrong. We love each other and would fight anyone who messed with our sisters, but … hey, we're human. Right?"

He could imagine her loving her family fiercely. And right away he wanted that kind of devotion directed at him.

His pager beeped.

"What's that?"

"My pager." He unclipped it from his belt.

"A fire?"

"Hooley, the fire inspector. I've been waiting on a report. Maybe he has something." Shep quickly put it back in place. "This was great. Thank you."

"You have to go?"

"Sorry to eat and run, but this might be important." He stood and lifted his plate.

"You don't need to do that." She hurried to stop him.

"My mama taught me—"

"I know, I know."

"Your boys will be home soon."

"Wow," she said, glancing at her watch. "I didn't realize it was that time." She bit her bottom lip. "Shep."

Her serious tone cleared the fog he'd fallen into while watching her worry her lip. Her solemn eyes made him want to yank her close and fill them with yearning.

"Thank you."

He definitely needed to kiss her. It was probably way too soon. So, he did the only thing he could.

"You're welcome."

CHAPTER 9

Procedures were tedious but needed to be presented in a way men would understand and remember. Updates were infrequent, but often Shep would look for anything that might help make a firefighter's job safer.

When Shep answered Hooley's page, he'd agreed to meet in thirty minutes. Those had to be the longest thirty minutes on record. The incident at the training site was an ongoing investigation that needed answers now. True, Shep hadn't been in charge, but five teams were on site that day. Station Eight was one. Every firefighter, trained or not, had been yanked into action by the unexplained explosion. He hoped the fire inspector's call meant he'd found out what had been the cause.

Two raps on the door drew his attention from the manual he'd been studying. He welcomed the intrusion.

"Enter."

When the door opened, Hooley filled the space. "Glad you called me back," Hooley said as he entered.

"I hope you've got some news."

"Got something to show you."

Shep noticed the large case in Hooley's hand. "What's that?"

He closed the door then placed the case on Shep's desk.

"My computer, among other things." Hooley pulled out a laptop and turned it on.

"You going to make me wait or tell me what I want to know?" Shep spat, irritably.

Damn his impatience. Usually, Shep was more controlled. He was the one who calmed others. Even when he chewed a guy out, he did so with a cool head.

"And here I thought patience was one of your strong points," Hooley snorted.

"Normally, I'd agree. Men were hurt on that site. Have you found anything?"

Hooley took a seat before he answered. "I found out a lot of things. One, the incident at the training site was not an accident. Fact. Someone set the explosion."

Shep ran a hand over the back of his neck, then dropped into his chair.

"Arson," Hooley continued. "I've got evidence."

"Evidence?" Shep rebounded. "How was that possible? Wilson was in charge. He's not careless. If anything, he's a fanatic when it comes to procedures."

"Before I tell you the rest, I'd like your team to take a look at some film."

"You got the film?" Of course, he did. What else would Hooley be referring to but the video taken on site for training purposes? "I'm normally not so slow. Evidently, you found something on there, too."

"I want your guys to watch this video before I tell you what I found."

Shep gave a nod and strode to the door. The team's shift was over, but he'd seen Jared outside. Maybe he was still here.

Shep stepped to the rail and took in the scene below.

"Johnson! Is Jared still here?"

"He's outside with Edgar and his new Harley. Want me to get him for ya?"

"Yeah," Shep shouted back.

Johnson gave a shrill whistle, then motioned with his arm and pointed up to Shep. Two seconds later, Jared sauntered inside the bay.

"What's up?"

"Call in the team."

"All of them?"

"Everyone." Without another word, Shep turned on his heel and marched back to his office.

Twenty minutes later, the entire crew filled Shep's small space. Hooley hit a button on his computer and the screen came to life. Shep watched right along with Mike, Jared, Laredo, and Cooper as the horrific explosion blew up on the display. His muscles grew taut at the gruesome scene. When the footage ended, every man sat stunned for a few moments, most likely remembering their movements on that day.

"I didn't see anything out of sync," Cooper said with noticeable disappointment.

"It was a clusterfuck." Jared fisted his hands.

Things might not have happened as planned, but Shep was proud of the way firefighters had responded. "Every man went into action. Looks to me like they did exactly what they were supposed to do."

"Take another look." Hooley played the recording again and slowed down the feed. "Look for anything suspicious or out of the ordinary. Anything. Anything at all."

When the clip stopped, Hooley hit the feed again. By the fourth time Mike spoke up, pointing out one of the guys from Station Nine.

"Captain Wilson says this isn't one of his men," Hooley said.

Between the film and Hooley's statement, Shep's head was spinning. It was bad enough suspecting a firefighter. But if this guy didn't belong to Station Nine, who the hell was he?

"Got too much gear on to see who he is," Mike said. "The number on his helmet is definitely Station Nine."

"Every Captain at each of the five stations on sight that day has seen this film. Every firefighter has been identified but one. Him." Hooley pointed to the same man Mike had indicated. "I've been calling in every member of each firehouse to see if we can figure out who this guy is. No one has recognized him."

"At least we know where he got his uniform." Cooper stepped around Mike. "Some guy just waltzed into Station Nine and took their gear?"

"It's only five miles from Station Eight," Mike added. "Someone could just as easily have filched a suit from any of the firehouses. Who the hell would do that?"

"And why?" Laredo uttered.

"This guy could be anyone," Hooley explained. "We have no idea of motive. He could have chosen a firehouse randomly or he could have a beef with a certain individual."

He could be anyone. That didn't tell them a goddamned thing. Firefighters were hurt. Some nut-job was running around out there setting off explosives. Stealing equipment from firehouses.

"This guy is good," Hooley warned. "He left no trace or clue of his identity. This is our only lead and you guys can see for yourself, it's not much."

"Until we know more," Shep began, catching the eyes of each member of the team, "Maybe we better keep an eye out, since we leave our doors open most of the time."

The men nodded in agreement.

"All right." Shep used a tone signaling the meeting had come to an end. "Keep your eyes and ears open. That's it for now. Thanks for coming in."

"Thanks for calling us, Cap," Mike said as he stood.

"We appreciate it," Jared added.

"Yeah, thanks," Cooper and Laredo chimed in, then they all headed out. As soon as the door closed, Shep exploded.

"Son-of-a-bitch! Gas tanks. Placed and opened at just the right time. Some sick bastard knew what he was doing. Knew firefighters would be there. Knew men would be hurt. Or killed." He wanted to punch something. Better yet someone. The fucker who planted those tanks.

"I know what you're feeling," Hooley said, standing to his full height. "Every firefighter feels the same way. We all would like to get our hands on the bastard's neck."

Shep seethed as he fisted his hands. Every nerve in his body danced with indignation. "What kind of monster targets firefighters? Because that's exactly what this maniac did."

"He's a pro, that's evident. A professional at explosives. Maybe special forces. My hunch, he's had military experience."

"I know that guy had on Station Nine's gear, and I know he probably stole it. I just don't want to believe a firefighter was responsible."

"I doubt he's a trained firefighter."

"It's a miracle Ryan lived."

"I'd heard a piece of metal ripped his leg from his knee to his groin. Glad he got to keep his leg."

By the grace of God.

"He's a die hard. I just hope his injury isn't bad enough to keep him from his squad." Shep would want to keep fighting fires no matter how bad he might be hurt. He knew Ryan felt the same way.

"The man has a good sense of humor. If he can't come back, he'll be okay."

Shep braced his hands on the edge of his desk. "It's hard to believe someone deliberately set out to kill one or more of us."

"I don't want to believe it either." Hooley gathered his computer and put it back into the case.

Shep straightened and held out his hand. "Thanks for coming by. Will you let me know as soon as you hear anything else?"

"You know I will. Just be alert."

"You can count on that."

***

All the guys took a turn in the kitchen, but for some reason, Shep found himself doing most of the cooking. He had to admit, the compliments boosted his ego. Maybe he couldn't do anything about the incident at the training site, but cooking calmed his racing thoughts and kept the frustration at bay. He tore off the packaging and had just dropped chicken pieces into a bowl at the sink when the sound of a woman's heels echoed down the hall. The hair stood on the back of his neck.

"Yoo hoo. Captain." Damn that singsong voice drove him right up a wall.

Shit. Alice Daniels. So much for calm. The woman had set her eye on him and he needed a thicker hide to escape her talons. Too late to escape.

"There you are."

He turned slowly, wishing her appearance was his imagination. No such luck. The woman wore shorter skirts than some teenagers. Even if she did have a great figure, she exposed entirely too much of it. The shade of her hair came out of some bottle, which didn't really matter since most women colored their hair. What he didn't like—absolutely hated—was her sudden appearances without warning. And her visits were getting more frequent. He supposed he should be glad Alice wasn't stalking him.

"Hello, Ms. Daniels."

"Now, now. You know my name. Why don't you try that again?"

Damned if he would. With a clenched jaw, he said, "What brings you by, Alice?"

Her smile reminded him of the cliché about the cat. He sure as hell was not the canary.

"I know you men cook every day. I made some homemade bread last evening. I brought you some." A dish towel covered the pan in her hand.

"You didn't have to do that. But the guys love homemade bread."

"What about you, Shep?"

He cringed hearing his name roll over her tongue. She breathed the word as if it was a caress.

"I like bread as well as the next man."

She moved around the counter and stepped in close, so he held out his hands to take the dish from her, keeping some distance between them. She leaned against the granite and posed, cocking a foot, resting on her toe. That brought her skirt a bit tighter. He wasn't interested.

Now would be a good time for dispatch to call. He should be ashamed wishing for a 911 emergency. He wondered if he could sneak off a page to one of the crew. The woman had eyes like a hawk. They narrowed and she looked at him through the slits. He felt like a piece of meat.

"Smells good, Alice. You bake this last night?"

"Um, yes. If you want, you can warm it in the oven for a few minutes just before you eat."

"When the men find out you brought bread, they won't wait."

"When is your next day off?"

Heat crawled up his neck.

"I rarely take one. I'm always on standby."

"Do you take any time off?"

"Don't make it a habit." He avoided right out lying to the woman. He wasn't about to let her get any ideas, though.

"But you can't stay here all of the time."

"I always have work to do." And he did. A house and land the size of his required constant upkeep.

Her eyes grew wide and she no longer seemed relaxed. "You have another job?"

"No. The fire department is my life." Let her make of that what she wanted. It was the truth.

"Your life?" Her lips turned down in a pout, and she swayed from one hip to the other. "Sounds rather lonely."

At times. But he hoped to change that.

"Don't you know all work and no play makes a dull boy?" The woman purred, reminding him of a damned cat.

"I have responsibilities, and I'm no boy." Not some kid she could push around.

"I can see that," she said, eyeing him up and down like he was some damn lollipop.

Hell. He walked right into that one.

"Sorry, I don't have time to talk right now, Alice." He placed her dish on the counter and propped his hands on his hips. "I've got to start dinner and I'm waiting on an important call." At this point, a call from anyone would be welcome.

"Oh, well, uh ..."

"You know we stay pretty busy at the firehouse."

"Okay," she reluctantly agreed. "Enjoy your bread. I'll see you around then."

He stepped to the sink and turned on the water. Fearing she might slip up behind him, he quickly turned it off and grabbed a towel, then put more distance between them by walking to the fridge.

"Bye, Alice. Have a good day."

She made a sound like a huff, then grabbed her purse and back down the hall she went. Thank God.

With the chicken in the oven, Shep had just started chopping vegetables when Mike and Cooper strolled in. Where the hell had they been ten minutes ago?

"Hey Cap. What are we having tonight?" Cooper leaned over his shoulder and snatched a slice of tomato. Shep smacked his fingers with the blade of his knife.

"Dude!"

"Keep your fingers out of the food. We're having chicken fettuccini and salad."

"You're the best, Cap." Before Cooper cleared the doorway, Shep stopped him.

"Finished with the tanks?"

"Yep. Full and ready for the next run. Spares are gaged and loaded on the shelves."

"Restock the MIDI?"

Cooper glanced to Mike.

"Yes. The kid helped."

"Helped? I did most of the work while you got all moon-eyed with your girlfriend on the phone."

Mike had never been serious about a woman before. Cassie sure had changed his mind. "Then you can stay and heat up the saucepan," Shep said to Cooper.

"Come on, Cap. No one can make the sauce like you."

"It's time you learned."

"What's this?" Mike pointed to the dish Alice brought.

"Ms. Daniels brought home-made rolls."

"She tried sneaking by me while I was loading the tanks." Cooper flashed a shitty grin. "She's got the hots for the Captain."

"Alice is attractive, but too intimidating for my taste," Shep grumbled. "The woman refuses to understand I'm not going out with her."

"You know she doesn't bake that stuff." Cooper snatched a slice of cheese and dodged out of the way before Shep could catch him.

"Who bake what stuff?" Jared strode into the kitchen and right into the conversation.

"Al-lice," Cooper purred in a singsong tone.

Christ. He sounded just like her.

"The real estate agent? She been by here again?"

"Of course. She's after Cap." Cooper's grin was infectious.

"She bring more food?"

"She picks the stuff up over at Mason's Bakery."

Shep stopped chopping and stared.

Cooper grabbed a bottle of water from the fridge. He tossed it to Mike, then pulled out two more for Jared and himself. "Old man Mason told me. The stuff she brings in here is from his place." Cooper made a sign of crossing his heart. "I swear."

The conniving female. Whether she cooked or not, he would not give her any reason to continue to pester him.

"You know what, Cap?" Jared asked.

"I'm afraid to ask." Shep kept his eyes on his task.

"If we can get rolls and stuff at the bakery, we don't need her."

Shep hiked a brow. "We don't need her *period.*"

"But she brings us food." Cooper piped up. "Free food."

A niggling suspicion pricked Shep's mind. Cooper could spout out jibes as well as the rest of them, but more than once he'd mentioned money. Was he strapped for funds?

Cooper had arrived on the scene two years ago. Hadn't given much information and never talked about his past. On his application, he'd written *San Francisco* as his last address. Being on the opposite coast, Virginia was about as far as one could get if the kid wanted to disappear.

Everyone had a past. Shep was no different. Cooper worked hard, showed the men respect, and was damn good at his job.

Maybe he'd speak with Mike, feel him out. See what he knew.

CHAPTER 10

The drive home had been long and taxing. The sun shining on this cold autumn day would normally have Tammy enjoying the fall season. Today, she stressed over Steve. Knowing her husband, she fretted over what he might do. It was killing her.

Her doctor wanted to give her a prescription for stress, but she hated taking pills. Her blood pressure was through the roof. As upset and mad as she'd been, it was a wonder the pressure cup hadn't exploded.

She tossed her purse on the counter and trudged down the hall, her feet feeling as though she had steal weights wrapped around her ankles. She'd lost ten pounds. Her doctor had liked that but not the way she'd lost it.

Worry never did anyone any good, he'd told her. He also said she should surround herself with friends to help her during this *trying time*. Humph. What she'd really like to do was castrate Steve.

Just as she kicked off her shoes, her cell rang. She dashed to the counter, dug in her purse and glanced at the blinking screen.

Steve.

She remembered the last time she'd called him and the way he'd answered.

"What do you want, Steve?"

"I'd ask who pissed on you, but I don't have time for your snotty attitude."

There went her blood pressure.

"I just got out of a meeting. I'm—"

She interrupted. "You're at the office?" How like Steve to make his kids wait while he took a meeting.

"You need to get the boys." And just like Steve to push them back off on her.

"Where are they?"

"At school, smart ass."

"You haven't picked them up yet?" She checked her watch. School let out forty minutes ago. "I had a doctor's appointment. You promised—"

"If I go now, I won't be there for another forty-five minutes."

She bit back a stream of swear words. "They knew you were supposed to get them, Steve. You just left them there?"

"You're wasting time. I can't make it."

Her phone beeped, letting her know another call was coming in. Probably the school. She checked the screen and recognized the number. Sure enough.

"I've got to go." She hung up on Steve and immediately answered the incoming call.

"Hello?"

"Tammy?"

"Oh God, Madelyn, I'm so sorry. Are the boys okay?"

"They're fine. Susie took them to her room to see the animals."

"Thank you. I'll be right there."

"Wasn't their dad supposed to pick them up?"

Tammy bit her tongue to keep from calling him an SOB. "Yes. I just found out he didn't. I'm on my way."

"Take a breath. Everything is okay. I'm here until 4:30 anyway."

Tammy had taken the afternoon off, so she'd lost track of time. The boys had been waiting almost an hour. Her head pounded. She rubbed her temple as if that would ease the throbbing.

"I'm on my way."

"Take your time. They aren't going anywhere. And they're no trouble. Susie enjoys having them."

"Just don't let Christopher touch that snake. He's already asked if he can have one."

Madeline laughed. "Typical six-year-old boy."

"Thank you. See you in fifteen minutes." Tammy had gone from worry to exhaustion to a frantic frenzy, and ready to commit murder in a matter of minutes. She just wanted to sit down and cry.

Her ass of a husband had not only forgotten he had a wife, he'd forgotten his children. Dumping on her like always and then expecting her to fix everything. If the bastard thought he was getting custody, she'd see him in hell first.

***

Shep tossed down a pen, tipped back in his spring-loaded chair and locked his fingers together behind his head. He wished Hooley would get some clue on that guy in the film.

He shoved out of the chair and strode to the shelf of manuals. Grabbing the one he needed, he took it back to his desk.

Ten minutes later, a rap sounded on his office door.

"Come in."

"Anything I can do to help?" Mike asked, stepping inside.

"I've been going over the updated manual. Nothing new. It outlines the procedures in detail."

"But?" Mike asked as he settled in one of the two chairs in front of Shep's desk.

"I keep going over procedure and that man on the film. How was he missed?"

"We did everything by the book," Mike declared.

"So you said. I know Wilson. That's why it puzzles me how some perpetrator managed to expose gas without him knowing. And then managed to get out of the way before it exploded?"

"The bastard was watching us, waiting for his opening."

"To time it precisely ..." Shep couldn't grasp how an outsider could have gone unnoticed. Too many firefighters were on the scene, too many eyes observing. After all, this had been a learning exercise. "Someone should have seen something, smelled the gas—"

"Hell, Cap. I was there, too."

"I just wish Hooley would find out who that guy was. We can't let this happen again."

"Again? We don't know how it happened this time. What can we do? Put guards at our training sites."

"That's not a bad idea." Shep raked his brain in irritation. "How did the son-of-a-bitch find out about the training site? The location, the time? How the hell did he get his information?"

"For this to happen the way it did, this character had to be planning this strike for a while."

Shep stared through the window, into the open area of the bay. Even though the idea pricked at his brain, he refused to acknowledge that a firefighter might have had something to do with this. Who would sink low enough to hurt men who put their lives on the line every day? It had to be a criminal. Or some bastard with a warped mind.

"I agree. He had to be watching," he said out loud. "Observing firefighters for quite a while. He wore a firefighter suit, blended in. Close enough to set it up, but at a distance where he wouldn't be in the fallout."

Mike fisted his hands. "What pisses me off, the cocksucker intended for men to get hurt."

Shep released a sigh, knowing frustration would get them nowhere. "Hooley's on it. He's a good investigator and he won't stop until he gets his man."

"Does he have any leads?"

"You know Hooley. Closed mouth. He won't give up anything until he has all of his facts."

"What about the film?"

"After you guys had your say, he made the rounds, visiting each fire station again. The perp covered himself pretty well."

"*No one* recognized that guy?"

Shep shook his head. Another reason he wouldn't believe the guy was a firefighter. Not from around here, anyway. Still, he couldn't ignore the fact that this man had moved among the crew as if he knew what he was doing. Comfortable in fall-out gear. Either he was familiar with the process or the guy had a big set of balls.

"Look, Shep. I know we were supposed to stay away from the site, but things like this just don't happen. Besides, it's been weeks. Jared, Laredo and Coop, we just wanted to scout around. See if we could come up with some sort of explanation."

Mike knew how important it was not to mess with a suspicious fire scene. Shep didn't need to read him the riot act.

"I just hope that guy on the film was the only one," Mike muttered

Only one?

Shep couldn't have been more stunned if Mike had punched him in the gut. "I can't believe I didn't consider another conspirator. After Hooley's visit, I presumed it was the one guy."

"He knows too much," Mike said shaking his head. "Which brings up the question again. Did a firefighter have a hand in this?"

"I'm not ready to believe that, or the idea of an inside source. This guy could be working alone."

"Our arsonist has balls. If he walked right in and helped himself to Station Nine's equipment, what's to keep this guy from entering any of the stations?"

The same concern disturbed Shep.

***

"I hate you. You're just so friggin' happy all the time."

"Orgasms could have a lot to do with that."

"Shut up," Tammy said, holding up her hand. "I do not need to hear about your multiple orgasms when I am having none."

"You can change that," Cassie smirked.

"Tell it to Shep. No! Don't. And don't tell Mike. He'd tell Shep. I don't need the embarrassment."

"Then don't complain."

"You have the man of your dreams. You're with him all the time. I'm entitled to complain. Steve is driving me crazy ..."

"And ..."

Shep's image popped into Tammy's head as clear as if he stood right in front of her. She closed her eyes and groaned. "I want him so bad my stomach hurts."

Cassie snickered, knowing exactly who Tammy meant. She kept up with Tammy's subject changes as if she could read her mind. The mocking sound fueled Tammy's annoyance.

"If Mike didn't love you so much, I'd say something snarky. But any dig at you is wasted. The world can see Mike's devotion. He's like a puppy with his tongue hanging out. It's disgusting."

"I can't believe you would compare Mike to a puppy."

"All right. A Great Dane."

"That's more like it." Cassie lifted her cup. "I feel the same way."

Tammy sighed and propped her chin against the palm of her hand. "I wish I could experience a love like that. Or at least a man who would give me an orgasm."

Cassie spat out her coffee. "Give a girl some warning."

"Okay, okay," Tammy said in the middle of her laughing. "Only part of that spill was joking."

"Only part? Don't settle for less than what you want."

"Cassie, I have two boys. I come with baggage."

Cassie smacked her mug on the counter, causing Tammy to jump. "Do you hear yourself? If anyone else said that, you'd rip them a new one." Then Cassie slid a hand across the surface and placed her palm over Tammy's fist. "You can have it all. Exactly what you want. I think Shep is the man to give you your dreams."

"Ha," Tammy spouted, wanting to believe it so badly. Her daddy didn't raise no fool. Common sense had saved her on many occasions. "He is a dream, that's for sure. But I'm not a teenager. I see the real world and have no illusions. What would a man like him want with me?"

"A man like him? How well do you know him? Shep likes you. Didn't you two hit it off at the *Pitt Stop*?"

"Oh yeah. He had to take my drunk ass home."

"You had fun. He did too. And he called you afterwards. Right?"

He called. Worried she'd think he'd taken advantage and wanted to set things straight. She could still hear his deep voice. So sexy, he had nearly melted her bones. She was hopeless.

"Yeah, he called. To tell me nothing happened so I'd let him off the hook. After all, Shep is pretty hot. It's entirely possible he has no real desire for me." Wasn't that a disappointing thought?

"You're wrong. You're nice as well as pretty. You've got a chest most women can only dream about. You're a barrel of laughs. Shep likes you."

"He's helping me. There's a difference. Steve is being cagey. Shep's brother is a lawyer. Shep is all involved in my mess, offering to help with my situation. There's nothing personal about it. No intimacy. How can I have a relationship with a man who thinks he has to save me?"

"Give him a chance. Push all that other stuff to the side. Take some time for yourself. Get to know him."

Get to know him. She wished she could have quiet moments with Shep. He wasn't Mr. Muscles and thank God, a far cry from Mr. Sunglasses. Shep sported confidence, dignity, a composure that made her sit up and take notice. What would he think if he knew she wanted to rip that shirt off and see what he had underneath?

Get to know him. How?

"Remember when I asked you about bringing Mike and the other firefighters to school for a show and tell?" she asked Cassie. "I could do that."

"That's a great idea. Only instead of Mike, you should ask Shep. A perfect excuse to see him. No pressure."

"Not with forty kids around," Tammy said cynically as she held her cup to her lips ready to sip.

"You need time together, where your ex has nothing to do with the two of you seeing each other."

She tucked a curl behind her ear. "I don't know if he'd go for, well, you know, just me and him. Like a date."

"Why not?"

"A date means, you know, a date. Like the guy is interested."

"Where's that outrageous flirt from the *Pitt Stop*?"

"Don't remind me." Tammy hung her head.

"Why not? You didn't do anything wrong. Okay, never mind. Start with the school. The kindergarten class would love it if the firefighters came to school."

"And brought their big red truck."

Cassie grinned. "Then see what develops."

How bad could it be? The man was a dream. As Tammy's dad would say, nothing ventured, nothing gained. *Don't wait around. Go out and get what you want.*

Damn, she wanted Shep.

CHAPTER 11

An audience of worshipful men watched her every move, looking like high school boys at a strip club. Tammy had thought it would be a good idea to bring sweets to the firefighters at Station Eight. Now, she was reconsidering whether or not it had been a wise decision. All she had to do was walk across the parking lot to the firehouse. The one in which Shep worked. The hunky firefighter. Who made her weak in the knees.

Nerves assailed her. Where was her courage when she needed it?

Tammy thrust her chin up and gripped the handle on her container. Managing children was her specialty. If she could handle a rowdy bunch of third-graders and her twin six-year-old boys, she could deal with these guys.

Men liked to eat, that was a no-brainer. Men ogled women. That too wasn't news. But the way they looked at her? She would expect the appreciative stares if Cassie was the one strutting across the parking lot. Or maybe some skinny model, runway type. But *her?*

Tammy had strawberry blond-red hair which irritated the hell out of her. Why couldn't it be a deep auburn that men seemed to think was sexy? Even with her five foot six frame, she carried more weight than she wanted. Some men liked curves. Speaking of which, she did not lack in the boob department. Her girls were bold and proud. She suffered the backaches to prove it. She supposed these guys could be looking at *them*. After all, boys would be boys.

She recognized Jared right away, leading the pack. She held the container of baked goodies up as if she needed to show her reason for coming. Before she could say a word, Jared called out.

"Hey, sexy. You bring that for me?" He'd gone right into flirt mode. What else would she expect with all the flirting going on between them at the restaurant the night they'd met?

"Hello, handsome. How do you know what's in here? It might be something you don't want."

"Let me see." He reached forward as if to take her Tupperware, and another firefighter shoved him out of the way.

"Where are your manners, *Baboso*." A man with olive skin, all teeth and devilishly good looks, took a step toward her. By his mocking comment and his accent, Tammy figured this guy was Hispanic. "Allow me to apologize for my"—he glanced to Jared—"*friend*. I'm Laredo. May I help you with that?"

Oh, he was a fine devil.

"Why thank you, Laredo." She couldn't help but take a peek at Jared, who immediately maneuvered his way back in front of his *friend*.

"Out of the way, buddy. Tammy and I already know each other."

"Then I'm not surprised she did not bring this for you." Laredo turned back to her. "Forgive him, *querida*. He was raised by animals."

She laughed out loud but heard a snort. Glancing to the sound, she found the owner. Another firefighter, just as tall as Laredo and Jared.

"I'm Tammy," she said to the new guy.

"I remember. I'm Cooper." He gave her a blinding grin.

Good Lord. Was *drop dead gorgeous* a requirement on the sign-me-up-to-be-a-firefighter application? "You remember?"

"I saw you at the Mexican restaurant. Ignore those two and I'll show you where to put that." He gave her a sexy wink. Fine-looking and full of himself. All this testosterone was making her feel young again.

"Down, pup." Ahh, a voice she recognized. The young flirt jerked his head.

"I told you not to call me that."

Mike, the size of a tank and probably as strong, strode toward them. "You guys about done?"

Three bodies shifted to attention. Intriguing, the way these guys froze and all conversation stopped. Except for Cooper.

"Hey, Hoss. Tammy brought us some goodies and these two yahoos are fighting over our food."

"She say that was for you?" Mike asked with a nod in her direction.

"A woman bringing a container to a firehouse full of hungry men? What else could it be?"

"Don't worry. Alice will bring you something."

Cooper's face immediately turned sour. Tammy wondered if Alice was his girlfriend.

"We worked up an appetite. As a matter—"

"Can it, pup." Mike smiled at her. "Hi Tammy. These jokers giving you a hard time?"

"Nothing I can't handle." She gave a flirty smile to both Jared and Laredo. But Shep was the one she wanted to see. "I know you guys cook a lot and probably eat better than most people do at home. I didn't know if you baked. I'm always baking, so I thought you guys might like a homemade cake."

"We love cake." At a glare from Mike, Cooper snapped his mouth closed. It was easy to see who was in charge of this bunch. Or maybe it was because of Mike's size. He was a bear of a man. All brawn and muscles, but with a sexy smile that would take a woman's breath.

"That's mighty nice of you. Why don't we take this cake up to the main room? We have to walk right by the captain's office. I'll bet he'll want a piece of cake."

Tammy wondered if that was Mike's way of saving her from asking about Shep. She'd more than likely turn red if she had to publicly announce Shep was the man she wanted to see.

It was pretty obvious the guys ragged on each other. That meant they got along. Including her in their fun made her feel welcome.

"Jared, it's good to see you again. Laredo, it was nice of you to come to my aid. Cooper, it was nice to meet you."

"Oh, I'm coming with you. I want a piece of that cake before Hoss gets to it."

"Hoss?"

"He means the big guy." Laredo gave a nod toward Mike.

Cooper patted his stomach. "Yeah. If I get to the table last, there'll be nothing left."

Before Mike could retaliate, she shoved the container toward Cooper. "Would you mind carrying this for me?"

He looked like a cat that had lapped up all the cream. "Sure thing. Right this way." He gave an exaggerated bow, then turned and strode across the cement floor to a stairway.

"You're not leaving us behind." The voice had an accent. That was Laredo.

The guys bantered back and forth as they trailed behind her. Self-conscious of her backside looming on the steps above them, she tried not to blush. Although, her face did feel hot. That was more than likely because she knew Shep was in his office.

Mike stopped and rapped on a closed door. The other three continued down the hall.

"Enter." Shep's voice vibrated from the other side. She concentrated on her breathing as Mike turned the door handle.

"Hey, Cap. We have a visitor."

Shep's eyes grew wide when he spotted her. Nerves danced in her stomach, and his welcoming grin made her knees weak.

"Tammy. Come in," he said as he stood.

"I hope I'm not interrupting. You look busy."

"Of course, not."

"Tammy brought cake," Mike explained. "Cooper took it to the main room."

"Tell him he'd better save me a piece."

"Will do, Cap. Tammy. Thanks again." Mike closed the door and the room suddenly seemed much smaller.

"That was mighty nice of you. Those guys are a hungry bunch."

"I guess you better hurry or you might not get any."

"They know better." Shep came around his desk to her and her mouth suddenly went dry. God, he looked good. Anxious bumps danced along her skin. She had the urge to walk right into his arms and wasn't sure what held her back.

"So, this is your office."

"This is it. You caught me on a slow afternoon, as far as response calls. I'm buried in paperwork." His slow hum set off a tiny shiver down her spine.

"You sure I'm not intruding?"

"Never. It's nice to see you anytime."

Darn it. A blush heated her cheeks. This man made her lose all concentration to the point where she felt several emotions at once. Before she'd met Shep, she'd have sworn she didn't have a shy bone in her body. "When I was talking to Jared and the others, I kept waiting for the alarm to go off."

As if her words had provoked the thing, a loud siren wailed, reminding her of air raid signals she'd heard in war movies. She damn near jumped out of her skin.

"Easy there." Shep crooned, stepping closer. "It's twelve noon. The siren goes off every day at this time."

"Oh." Her hand pressed over her racing heart. The thing pounded like a jackhammer. "Twelve o'clock and all is well?"

"Something like that. Won't you sit down?"

"Sure. I have a few minutes." She moved to the sofa and Shep sat beside her, his closeness stirring her blood. He seemed pleased to see her.

"Thank you for bringing cake."

She swallowed before speaking. "Cassie said Mike was working today. I had to make cupcakes for the Cub Scouts, so I figured I'd whip up a cake at the same time. Christopher and Michael are at a campout. Just for the day. When they're older, they get to go *overnight*." She used her fingers to make the air quotes to signify it was special to the boys.

"Sounds like a big deal."

"It is to them. They're having a picnic and my contribution was cupcakes. I dropped them off and decided to drive over."

"I'm glad you did. You must have gotten up pretty early if you've done all that baking."

"I made the cakes last night. All I had to do this morning was add the icing."

"Sounds delicious. Can't wait to try it."

"Then go. Now."

"I didn't mean—"

"From what Cooper said, you need to get in there before Mike."

"Mike has a good relationship with Cooper. He more or less took the kid under his wing. Cooper likes to pick on him."

Didn't look like much of a kid to her. That boy was a grown ass man. "I'd like to see your station if that's okay. Why don't you get a piece of cake and you can take me on a tour?"

Shep gave her a grin that melted her insides. Full sexy lips. She wanted him to kiss her. *But not here.* She leaped from the couch before she did something stupid, like lean into him.

Tammy looked good enough to eat. The way she hopped up made Shep wonder if his expression had given away his thoughts. He grinned. She was jittery. Couldn't be because they were in his office alone.

Shep slowly rose to his feet, his eyes locked on Tammy. Something about this woman stirred him up quicker than an alarm.

"I'd love to sample your cake and give you a tour." He opened the door. "Ladies first."

When she gave him that coy smile, his belly did a little leap. Mmmm. Felt good.

"The big room, it's more like a lounge, is down this way." He'd love to watch her walk, but he figured it'd be safer if he led the way. The guys' voices streamed down the hallway. When he and Tammy stepped into the room, the buzz stopped.

Damn, she looked cute when her face flushed like that.

"Tammy, this cake is good," Jared called out.

"Yeah. This has got to be the best cake I've ever tasted."

"Don't talk with food in your mouth," Mike snapped at Cooper.

"Gee, Hoss. Can't help myself. This is great."

"Leave some icing for the rest of us," Laredo chimed in.

Shep noticed half the cake was gone. "You pigs leave any for us?"

"Snooze, ya lose." Cooper shot back. Then he froze and looked ready to choke. "Gee. I'm sorry, Tammy. Here, let me get you a plate."

Throwing Tammy's name out there guaranteed a spot at the table. The men jumped to action.

"Here, *querida*. Sit next to me."

Shep was ready to say no, but he glanced to Tammy for her reaction. She beamed.

"Thank you, Laredo." She damn near bounced over to take the chair next to him.

A little green envy clouded Shep's vision. He took a seat between Mike and Cooper.

"Here you go." Cooper handed Tammy silverware and a napkin. The kid had manners. Shep had to give him that.

Jared dragged his chair closer to Tammy. "I want another slice. Tammy, you can bring us cake anytime."

"Just what you guys need. A sugar fix to give you energy for cleaning up the station."

"Now, Cap. I did my chores today."

"You can inspect the trucks, Cap." Laredo kept the rigs shining. If paint could be washed off, their trucks would be bare.

Mike snorted. "Might need to get some new rags, Cap. Laredo done wore out the ones we have."

A shit-eating grin covered Laredo's face as if Mike had just given him a compliment. Then he leaned toward Tammy. "Would you like to see the ladderback?"

"Yes, I would."

"You will see your reflection, I promise. If you'd like to climb into my truck, I'll help you."

Before Tammy could reply, Shep spoke up. "I'll be giving Tammy a tour of the station."

Not just Laredo, but all eyes turned on him. *Hell*. Had he tipped his hand? The guys were used to him sounding bossy, but jealous? They wouldn't let him hear the end of this.

Mike stood. "You guys got your treat. Let's hit it."

Jared gave Mike a smirk, then shoved the last bite into his mouth. After a few mumbles, the crew threw away their trash and followed Mike.

"They're fun," Tammy said with a grin.

"Good thing we came in when we did or you might not have gotten a piece of your own cake."

"I wasn't expecting any. I brought it for you." At his raised brow, she quickly added. "For everyone. All of them. The guys."

She was just adorable.

"Thank you. Coffee's hot. There's always a pot. Want some?"

"Sure. I'm a coffee drinker."

Shep grabbed two mugs and poured coffee, handing one to her. "Milk?"

"Just a bit. Thanks."

He sat next to her and reached for his piece of cake. When she took a sip of her coffee, he stared at her lips, wondering if she tasted as good as her cake. Her tongue flicked out to catch a drop of icing. The sight lanced his gut. Older, wiser, and a hell of a lot more patient, he relished the warm sensation rolling through him and then concentrated on eating his slice.

"Good coffee. I was expecting mud." Even her voice did things to him. Soft, sweet, and frank, without intending any insolence.

"It doesn't last long enough to turn into glue," he said. "Most times, the team drinks water. Although, coffee is perfect with cake. I'm sure Mike had you in mind when he made it."

"Me?"

"Sure. I imagine he put on a fresh pot for our guest."

"Oh. That wasn't necessary."

"We might be a bunch of men, but we have manners. And rules, when it comes to the job and keeping our house clean."

"Our house. I like the way you refer to the fire station."

"We spend more time here than at home." Shep shoved a piece of cake in his mouth. "Mmm, this is really good."

"You guys are going overboard. It's just a cake."

"You kidding? I've tasted lots of cakes. This is delicious. The team wasn't kidding or just being polite."

"Well, I do take pride in my baking."

He finished in three bites and gulped some coffee, comfortable to just be near her.

"I'm ready," she said as she finished.

He took her paper plate to the garbage. "All right then. Let's go.

He showed her the bunk room, knowing the guys would not have left clothes or junk lying around. Sure enough, it was in top shape. He took her downstairs, directed her to the rigs and explained the purpose of each one. Tammy asked a lot of questions. Her interest pleased him more than he would have thought.

Laredo had to show off the quint; Jared got a little cocky with driving stories and Mike showed her the maps.

"What are those for?" Tammy pointed at a pair of droopy pants in a puddle around a pair of boots.

"Those belong to Elf. He's more old school."

"Elf?"

"Elf is taller than me," Mike explained. "He's on the next shift."

"I can't imagine someone bigger than you."

"I didn't say bigger. He's *taller*." Mike held a hand above his head. "Six-five."

"Wow. That is tall."

Only a couple inches taller, but Elf's slender form made him look small next to Mike. Hours in the weight room shared some responsibility for Mike's size. Many mornings, Shep had seen him hitting the iron.

"So why does he leave his boots there, like that?"

"We use GPS now. Before that, we used maps. These maps are various charts of the city and county. Every street, every house, building, and structure is on the maps. Elf likes to take a glance at them before the trucks head out. He keeps his boots and turnout pants here, ready to jump in his gear and save time."

"Two birds with one stone, so to speak."

Mike gave a nod. "You got it."

"Jared showed me the GPS in the firetruck."

"Each rig has one."

"There's so much equipment in the cab. I never realized there'd be so much to see in a firetruck or at a station."

"We're not through," Shep added. "One more stop." He took her to where Cooper attended the air tanks.

"My turn." Cooper grinned when he saw her.

"We saved the best for last." Tammy teased, unaware she'd just made Cooper's day.

"You know, Tammy. I'm not that young. I bet you're only, what, two years older than me?"

She laughed out loud. "You are a *Don Juan*. I'm a lot older."

"I like older women." If Cooper wasn't such an outrageous joker, Shep would kick his ass right now. But he knew the kid was harmless.

"I have two boys. You like women that come with a package deal?"

"The more the merrier."

Cooper was so full of shit. As for Shep, he liked Tammy's package very much. As for her *package deal,* he loved kids. One day he might have a dozen.

Cooper showed Tammy the tanks and the two continued to flirt. Shep stood back and admired the woman who attracted him more and more.

"Wow. That would be great."

Uh oh. What?

"Shep. Could you come to our school? The kids would love it."

"We can schedule a date." Upon occasion, schools hosted a fire safety exhibition. He'd like visiting Tammy at her school. He glanced at Cooper. "You just volunteered your day off."

"Day off?" Tammy asked, surprised.

"I don't mind, Cap. If it's for Tammy." The shit gave her a wink. If he kept it up, Shep might whack him yet.

"Sounds like a good idea." Mike joined them. "I'll go. Which school?"

"Verona Elementary. Our kindergarteners would love it."

"Count me in." Shep turned to see Jared and Laredo coming up behind him.

"*Me así como.*"

Looked like they all wanted to go. "We can't very well send the whole crew to the school on their shift. If a call came in, the station will need the rigs," Shep explained. "Off shift, we can take the quint and one more. Leave the necessary rigs at the station. If the quint is needed, Laredo will have to leave."

"All of you want to come? That's just super. Maybe there won't be any fires that day. We can hope for the best."

"An idealist. Perfect." There Jared went, flashing that sensual grin.

What had this station come to, all these guys acting like a bunch of Casanovas?

CHAPTER 12

A page from the office alerted Tammy that Shep had arrived. Her student teacher would take care of her third-grade students while she escorted the firefighters to the kindergarten group waiting in the cafeteria. As she approached the office, she saw several men hauling equipment into the foyer, but her eyes sought only Shep.

His back to her, he stood beside Mike. Trying to control her excited jitters, she slowed her steps and slipped to his side.

"Hello."

He spun with surprise. "Hello yourself."

"Hi, Tammy."

"Hi, Mike."

"You remember Cooper" Shep indicated a man carrying a fire suit and a tank.

"Hello, Tammy. Good to see you again."

"Thank you for doing this. I know it's your day off."

"Wouldn't miss it." He gave her a sexy grin. *Oooo, he's going to be a heartbreaker.*

"Cooper and Mike will do the demonstration," Shep explained. "Laredo is outside with the quint."

"The quint?"

"The ladder truck. The kids always get a kick out of that."

"Oh, yeah."

"Where do you want us?" Mike asked.

"Follow me." Her heels clicked on the hallway tile and Shep fell into step beside her. "The kindergarten classes are in the cafeteria. The tables have been folded up and a space made for your demonstration." She glanced to Shep. "I thought you'd be wearing your fire uniform."

"Best way to scare the daylights out of a group of preschoolers is to have a firefighter enter a room in full gear with SCBA on air. We start in street clothes and work all the way up to fully bunkered out. The intent is to show that inside that *scary* outfit is still a human being. Not to be afraid."

"That makes sense."

"This isn't my first rodeo. We visit a lot of schools. You've never seen a presentation on fire safety?"

Tammy shook her head.

"What about your boys?"

"Today. They know you're coming and they've been rowdy since the announcement."

The moment the men stepped into the lunchroom, a riot of energized shrieks and excited screams resounded of the cement block walls. Shep took control of the situation as though he'd commanded groups of children on a regular basis. Impressed and awed, she watched the men do their thing.

Shep gave a speech, then Mike described each item as Cooper dressed the way a firefighter got ready for an actual fire. Shep came over to stand beside her. The man was too distracting. And his scent made her want to lean in and rub her nose along his neck.

"Cooper is great for this. Not only does he love the play-acting, he likes kids."

Tammy floated back to earth and saw that, by now, Cooper had on some sort of hood.

"What's this for?" Mike asked the children.

"You look like a baby," said one child. The others laughed.

"He might look like a baby, but this protects his face and neck. We don't want to get burned."

"Am I ready?" Cooper asked.

"No," all the students replied.

"You need your coat." A child pointed to the coat in Mike's hand.

Cooper put on the coat and fastened it up. She never realized how much these guys wore when they headed out to a fire. Every time. That was a lot to carry.

He put on a mask, pulled the hood over it and again spoke with the kids. The interaction was unbelievable. Every eye was trained on Cooper and Mike.

"Is it heavy?" one little boy asked.

Cooper had put on an air tank. He nodded to the child and answered, "About fifty pounds." His voice was muffled by the mask, Mike took over.

"Everyone take a deep breath. The air you just brought into your lungs? There's air in this tank. About forty-five minutes. When you're working hard, you're breathing harder and sucking more air. In that case, you might only have thirty minutes."

Now Tammy understood why they didn't wear their gear into the school. Cooper looked like a monster from a scary movie—to anyone who didn't know he was a firefighter.

"Everything is protected. Is he ready to go fight a fire?"

"Yes," the students yelled.

"Noooo." Mike shook his head. Cooper held up his bare hands.

"Gloves. He needs gloves." Mike looked at Cooper. "Where are your gloves?"

"In his pocket," a few kids answered. One being her own Christopher. How did he know? Maybe because Cooper was patting his leg. He dug into the fire pants and pulled out his gloves.

The demonstration had been a big hit. She'd even learned a few things.

"How about now? Am I ready?"

"You sound funny." Another boy spoke up.

Cooper disconnected his breathing tube.

"If you see a firefighter that looks like me, what do you do?"

"Jump out the window!" Good Lord, was that her David?

"I know he looks scary," Mike said. "No, you don't jump out of a window. You go toward him."

"Don't be afraid of me. I'm here to help. I'm the same man as before I put on all this gear."

Then Mike addressed the children. "If you're in a building that's on fire, do you want to hide?"

"No," the children called back.

"All of these things protect us so we can go into burning buildings. If you see him, someone who looks like this, you go to him." Mike motioned with his hands as he talked. "We're here to help you. If you see a guy like this, don't be afraid."

"Give me a fist bump, guys. I'm still the same person, no need to be scared." The children lined up to give Cooper a fist bump. "See. It's just me."

In a matter of minutes, the kids surrounded Mike and Cooper. Some tapped on the helmet, a few were knocking on the toes of his fire boots.

"He's amazing," Tammy said.

"He's a ham," Shep responded.

"I had no idea. This was a great presentation. All kids and adults need to see this."

"You spread the word. We'll show up."

Tammy allowed the vibration of Shep's voice to rumble through her belly.

Remember you're in school.

"Which ones are yours?"

It took Tammy a moment to realize Shep was asking about her boys. "That's Christopher and that's David."

"How in the world do you tell them apart?"

"It's easy. I'm their mother." She smiled with pride. He gave back one of his own.

His sexy grin launched a torrid of emotions sizzling through her blood.

"Who wants to see a firetruck?"

Screams and hoots and jumping feet erupted.

Once again, Shep took control, then Mike and Cooper herded the children outside.

***

The next morning brought a brisk wind. Shep headed out early on errands and finished them in no time. All morning, he kept replaying the visit to the school over and over in his mind. So much so, he was making a big deal out of an hour of instruction and conversation. Even during the quiet moments while he'd stood beside Tammy, he basked in her presence. He just couldn't get the spirited redhead out of his mind.

One thing he knew, the more he saw her, the more he wanted to be with her.

He turned at the light, drove a few miles and found himself on the same street as Tammy's house. Would she mind an unscheduled visit?

Why not?

He pulled into her driveway and threw the shifter in park.

He rapped on her door and hooked his hands in his back pockets. The front door opened and Tammy's eyes flew wide. The fragrance of vanilla drifted from inside.

"Shep!"

"Yep. It's me."

"What on earth are you doing here?"

Not the welcome he'd hoped for. Or expected.

"Looks to me I arrived just in time." He took a sniff.

"In time?"

"Yeah. There's a pretty awesome smell coming from inside. Has my mouth watering."

"Oh, yeah, I've been baking."

He could feel the energy bouncing off her. She tossed her hair from her eyes, then her hands fluttered about like she was swatting a fly.

"Can I come in?"

"Oh. Yes. Where are my manners? Come in. Come in." Damn, she looked cute all flustered.

She closed the door and motioned for him to follow her. "Smells great in here. What are you making?"

"I've got two birthday cakes and another one for a teacher's baby shower next week."

"Darn. I was hoping to sample something."

Tammy laughed. "You're in luck. I trim my sheet cakes. Then I put the chunks in a dessert bowl and add pudding. The boys love it."

"Sounds great."

"I happen to have some," she said as she pulled a bowl from the refrigerator.

Tammy closed the refrigerator door and found her face level with SAFR branded over a carved, navy-blue pec. She had thought Mike was ripped. He might be big, but Shep packed some pretty impressive pecs.

Her tongue tripped over itself. Her hands wouldn't be still. *Oh my God. Oh my God.*

Since she had the day to herself, she'd decided to catch up on her baked goods. She had three orders for next week. With one cake in the oven and two tiers on the cooling rack, she had just wiped flour from the counter, ready to mix up her icing when the sound of the doorbell had startled her. She'd grabbed a dish towel to clean off her hands, padded barefoot to the front of her house and found *him*.

She blew a stray curl from her eyes.

Shep looked incredible. And here she stood, wearing an apron with butter and flour splattered all over it. She hoped she didn't have the darn stuff smeared on her face. After the divorce, she'd forgotten how to be sexy.

Until now.

"The boys wanted to see the Derby at the Scout hut and Steve is picking them up afterwards. I ..." She needed to stop babbling. She must look a sight, and from her heated cheeks, she'd just turned red. With her hair and fair complexion, her face gave away every emotion.

"I guess I should have called," Shep said sounding uncertain.

"Oh, heavens no," she hurried to say. Although, if he had, she'd be cleaned up and maybe even wearing something sexy. Not covered in flour.

"Glad I didn't or I would have missed out on this."

Some of the tension eased from her shoulders. Then his sensual grin made her taut again. She placed the bowl on the counter while he pulled out a barstool. "How about some whipped cream?"

His dark brow, sprinkled with silver, arched. "Is that a trick question?

She took a container of Cool Whip and scooped a dollop into his bowl. He hiked his brow again. She laughed and scooped two more.

How did the man stay in such excellent shape?

"Would you like coffee to go with that?" When it looked like he was about to hike his brow again, she shook her head. "Never mind. Stupid question."

"Not stupid. Just not necessary. I'll never turn down a cup of coffee."

Tammy popped a pod into the Keurig.

"Forgot you had that contraption."

"It's still coffee."

"Are you going to sit down and have some with me?"

One of her weaknesses was sampling sweets as she baked. She'd already eaten more than she should. *What the hell?* She'd run an extra mile on the treadmill. She prepared a bowl for herself. Shep stood and pulled out a chair as she came around the counter. Chivalry was not dead.

"My mama taught all us boys manners."

"I like your mama. Thank you."

"My pleasure." He sat back in the chair next to her. "Where's your whipped cream?"

"Calories," she said just before shoving a spoonful of heaven into her mouth. She would enjoy every bite.

"Why that's just un-American." He rose and removed the Cool Whip container she'd just put in the fridge. "Only one for you," he said as he scooped a hefty portion into her bowl.

"One of your scoops equals two of mine."

He chuckled. A most amazing sound that did wonderful things to her girly parts.

"Now, dig in."

Tammy watched Shep as she raised her spoon to her mouth. The man was even appealing while he ate. She focused on his lips, then the knot at his throat as it bobbed up and down. She imagined putting her lips there—

"This is really good."

She blinked, popping out of her sensual daydream.

"Don't think I've ever had cake and pudding together."

Her face flushed again, so she grabbed her coffee and took a swallow, hoping he wouldn't notice. The coffee only made her hotter.

"I'm glad you like it," she stammered. "The boys gobble this stuff down."

"I would too, but my mama—"

"I know," she said, waving her spoon. "Are you so polite all of the time?"

"Nope. Catch me when I'm hungry after a full day of fighting fires and I'll gobble food just like the rest of the men."

As an image of the firefighters stuffing their faces appeared in her mind, the oven dinged. She turned the dial to off, then removed her cake and set it on the cooling rack. Perfect.

"I guess I'm in the way."

"No! I mean, you're not." Her words came out more urgent than she'd meant them to.

"I'm taking you away from your work. Can I help?"

Shep's presence alone distracted her. Thinking of his masculine body in her small space made her mind whirl like a spinning tornado. If he helped, and they brushed up against each other ... *Damn it.* Her face heated again.

"You haven't told me why you're here."

"Do I make you nervous?" He spoke in that low drawl, shooting sparks through her chest.

Of course, he made her nervous. Because she wanted him to kiss her, and she hadn't been around a man in a long time. Especially one who triggered such thoughts. She hadn't felt sexy in years. With her divorce, and raising rambunctious twins, she couldn't remember the last time she'd cared enough to worry about her sensual impression. Shep stirred her blood. Made her think of things like kissing, and more. She wanted more.

First, she had to get over these damned nerves.

CHAPTER 13

"Do I make you nervous?" Shep spoke in a low drawl, trying to keep the humor from his voice. She pleased the hell out of him.

"No," she said, tucking a curl of her fiery hair behind one ear. "Why would you think I'm nervous?"

"You're fidgety. Your hands are all over the place. You won't look me in the eye. You're not at all like you were at the *Pitt Stop*."

For some reason, that irritated her. Her body stiffened and her eyes flared with fire.

"No, I'm not inebriated. And I don't plan to behave that way again. So, if you're looking for a girl just for a good time—"

"Whoa, now," he said, holding out his hands. "You've got the wrong idea. I meant comfortable, relaxed ... open."

"I'm sorry."

"Don't apologize," he told her. "Ever." He held her gaze and watched a flush creep up her neck and over her cheeks.

He stepped closer. Her nose scrunched up, drawing his attention to the freckles sprinkled there.

"Feel better?"

"How do you do that?" she asked.

"Do what?"

"Make me feel composed when only a moment ago I wanted to fight."

His ego shot up a few points. He'd like to make her feel a whole lot better. "I don't want to fight." He had the hots for Tammy. There were no two ways about it. Did he dare kiss her? He'd been looking forward to the moment when he could see if she tasted as sweet as her cake with pudding.

"I had a blast flirting with you at the *Pitt Stop*. Thought maybe you did too."

"I did," she croaked. Her breath came out in short gasps. "I was aware of most of the evening. You're a good dancer."

All right. Keep it simple. "You do a mean two-step."

Her pretty smile was back. "I had a great partner."

"Thanks." *Partner.* He liked the sound of that.

"I know. Your mother taught you. You said you were glad because you got women that way."

He frowned. "I don't remember saying it exactly like that."

She shrugged.

"At the Mexican restaurant, you seemed to hit it off with Jared.

"I wasn't with Jared. Of course, you know that." She twisted her hair around a finger. "It's obvious he's a player. We were just having a bit of fun."

"Fun is okay." He waited, studying her, aware of her chest rising and falling with each breath. She rolled her bottom lip in as her top teeth grazed the skin. Fascinated, he couldn't move. He should. He should step away. Or step closer. Kiss her, while she remained immobile. Did she want him to kiss her? All the signs said she did.

Too soon. She had kids. She was sweet and nice and kind. Damn, he wanted sweet and fire. He'd bet with her red hair, she'd be fire. Give him fire. He damn near strangled at the thought.

He cleared his throat. "I probably should be going. You're busy."

"You don't have to go." Her quick breath and hoarse voice told him she wanted him to stay. He'd better get the hell out of here before he acted on his crazy desire.

Maybe not so crazy, but fast. Hard and hot. And way too soon. Too soon for a woman like her. A woman he would want to keep.

"I have a dog at home. He'll be looking for me."

"What kind of dog?"

Talking about Hutch would help. "An Alaskan Malamute."

"They are so pretty. The boys want a dog."

"But you don't?"

"It's not that. Who will take care of him? Feed him? Then do we tie him up all day? The boys could give a dog plenty of exercise, I suppose. But we go out so much. Stay on the road. And when they go to their dad's, who is going to house break him?"

"Boys that age can handle those duties. A dog would be good for any kid. Hutch is more the size of a bear. You wouldn't want one like him. He'd be too big for your house and two rowdy boys."

"I'd rather have a big dog. One that could stay outside."

"Boys will want to sleep with him."

"Good Lord, I didn't think of that. Besides, one dog, two boys. Do the math."

He chuckled. "Guess they could take turns."

"Are you kidding? All three would be in the same bed."

"Until you make up your mind, they can play with Hutch."

"You have a big yard?"

He thought of his eighty-three acres. "I live in the country. If I was home more, I'd get some pups. I like having dogs around."

"With your profession, I guess you never know when you have to leave or how long you'll be gone. I suppose Hutch is big enough to take care of himself."

"Mostly." No time like the present. Shep might as well get her view on his *profession*.

"A firefighter's life isn't much different from another individual."

She braced her hands on the counter and gaped at him. "I can not believe you said that."

"Why?"

"Why in the world would you say such a thing?"

He shrugged. "It's a job. I go to work, put in my hours, go home. Get a paycheck."

A full blob of pudding wavered on the spoon she pointed at him. "You fight fires."

"Yeah. That's what firefighter means."

"Don't be obtuse," she said with a huff.

"Big words. Your teaching profession is showing."

"You fight fires," she said distinctively. "You go into burning buildings while everyone else is running out."

As if he didn't know. "That's what I'm supposed to do."

"Don't make light of this," she said smacking her spoon on the counter. "Your job is dangerous."

"A lot of jobs are dangerous." He wasn't arguing, just stating a fact. But he needed to keep this conversation going to figure out how she felt about him being a firefighter. See if she would be willing to accept his profession.

She held up her hand. "Stop. At least admit your profession is hero worthy."

"I don't like—"

She held her hand up higher, cutting him off. "Please. I know men like this macho stuff, and some brag and some take it in stride. You evidently are one of the humble types. I like big, strong, silent type men."

His pulse shot up. Curious, he awaited her next words.

"But give credit where credit is due. You're a hero."

Damn it. He took a breath.

"Ah, ah. Don't speak." Tammy wiggled a finger at him. "You. Are. A. hero. Do not deny it. I'm not saying you should be glorified in the papers, although I think all firefighters and policemen deserve just that. I'm not saying you should receive a medal or free stuff or a parade down Main Street."

He brooded in silence, waiting for her to finish. He didn't mind Tammy singing his praises, but he'd rather she noticed him as a man first and his profession second.

"What I am saying, is that you are a courageous man. A strong man with a good heart. If not, you wouldn't do what you do. There are people out there who appreciate you. Who appreciate what you do. Every person who has had any experience with fire appreciates a uniform at a glance. I'm sure it takes a special man, a strong individual to do what you do. You risk your life to save people, their homes, whatever. Look at the night Mike and Jared saved that woman who wrecked. They weren't even on duty."

God, he loved seeing her all fired up. The woman was radiant on her soapbox.

"Women love strong men. Good looking men. Built men. Hot men. Give me a man with a conscience, compassion, and morals any day. That's what makes a man."

"We have women firefighters too."

"You know what I mean. And you're right. Women are strong. If a woman can do the job, she deserves a shot at any profession, same as a man."

He stood and held out his hand.

"What?" Tammy asked in confusion.

"I don't want you to break an ankle when you climb down from your pedestal. Fire and brimstone, woman. That's a pretty tall soapbox you climbed up on."

She blushed.

Simply delicious.

"Well. I may have gotten a little carried away. But you are a hero. Don't devalue your worth."

"You think I'm worth something?"

She gave him a glare that could have melted ice at the North Pole.

"I'm a simple man with simple tastes," he said sliding back onto his stool. "Don't make me out to be something I'm not."

"Don't act like you're less than what you are. You're good. Courageous."

"Now it's your turn to stop. I do my job. Not for hero worship."

"You don't need to tell me that," she said, squeezing his hand. "I may not have known you long, or very well. But I do know the kind of man you are."

He grinned, enjoying the feel of her hand on his. So, Tammy thought she knew him? If she paid attention, that meant she was interested. "I like my job. I love what I do. Always have. I've never wanted to do anything else."

"Do you ever get scared?"

He rubbed his thumb across her knuckles. "I wouldn't say scared. Maybe cautious. I'm responsible for my men. Firefighters are trained for most any circumstances. For me, I get pumped up knowing I have to act fast. There's no room for worry or doubt. I rely on my training and confidence, focusing on the goal. To put the fire out, save lives. When I was younger, it was great to get an adrenaline rush. Even then, I applied myself to the job. The emphasis has always been on what needed to be done."

"I have every confidence in you. I know you're a good captain."

"You do, do you?" He liked hearing her say she believed in him. Maybe his profession wouldn't scare her off.

"I can see where charging into a burning building might be a thrill seeker for some. But I know you're a conscientious and caring man. You'd never put anyone in danger. I've always been a pretty good judge of character." Her face crinkled up into a scowl. "Except for my husband."

Just like that, a cloud shadowed Tammy's mood. And he'd thought they were making progress. He wanted to chase her shadows away. Slay her demons. Her husband. Ex.

"Is he giving you a hard time? We can go talk to Eddie again."

"Not yet. But I'm afraid it's just a matter of time. He's demanding more time with David and Christopher. Don't get me wrong. I think the boys need their father. I just wish he'd shown them more attention when he was here."

"Too busy?"

"With his cheating, yes."

Shep didn't like Tammy being sad. Actually, she looked pissed more than anything.

"I have an idea," he said, hoping to put a smile back on her beautiful face. "Why don't you bring the boys to the station? Mike saw a young boy when he was at the hospital and promised him a visit. He's supposed to come next week. Why don't you bring David and Christopher and the boys can meet each other?"

"You sure you want three rowdy boys at your station? That's like a playground with all those big, flashy trucks. My two can be a hand full by themselves."

"Todd is around ten, I think. It would be good for them."

"If you're sure."

"I'm sure. I'll give you a call and get the exact time and date. I guess I better go and let you get back to your baking. Thanks for the cake and pudding. What do you call that, anyway?"

"I call it cake and pudding." She laughed.

"Jumped into that one, didn't I."

"With both feet. I'm glad you stopped by."

"Me too."

***

"How are things with Shep?"

Of course, Cassie would ask just as Tammy shoved a chip into her mouth. Salsa and a margarita were just what she needed after a day of drowning in confection.

"I'm completely smitten." It was the first night they'd had a chance to visit their usual haunt in quite a while. With Cassie practically living with Mike, she and Tammy's get-togethers at El Puerto's had dropped considerably.

"Smitten? I see you're still reading historical romance novels."

"If you weren't so wrapped up in Mike, you'd be reading too."

"Why should I read about hot guys when I have one of my own?" Cassie asked. "Maybe soon you'll get to live your own fantasies."

"I do remember saying that. Right here in this booth."

Tammy thought back to the particular Friday evening when they'd first set eyes on a group of firefighters entering this restaurant. The night Tammy flirted with Jared and Cassie met Mike. It hadn't taken long for Tammy to recognize Jared as a playboy. Still, she'd had fun. But Mike and Cassie only had eyes for each other.

"God, this margarita tastes good," Tammy said puckering up her lips. "Goes great with hot sauce."

"I'd rather my mouth did not feel like it's on fire. And, I'll stick to my beer."

"Have you noticed how many puns we use since meeting our firefighters?"

"Yeah." Cassie gave a soft laugh. "And I've noticed how wild you are these days since you're seeing Shep."

"Seriously?" Tammy snorted. "How wild do you think I can get with two six-year-olds hanging around?"

"There is such a thing as a babysitter."

Tammy nailed Cassie with her eyes. "Are you offering? That would cut into your time with Mike."

"You don't have them all the time."

"Don't remind me. Suddenly Steve wants them more. He's up to something." Tammy's ex put a bitter taste in her mouth. She took a sip of her drink to get rid of it.

"You think he's going for custody?"

"I'd bet on it. Cassie, I'm scared."

"Don't be. You've got a lawyer. And you've got Shep to lean on. Do it."

She stared at the straw she twirled in her glass. "I've relied on myself for so long."

"I know you're independent. You've really changed these last two years."

"I had to." Anger spiked as she recalled how Steve had turned her into a meek stooge. "I'll never let a man rule me again."

"Sometimes you need a man to be strong for you."

She stopped stirring and smacked her hand flat on their table. "Cassie, you saw what Steve did to me. Yes, I let him. But, still. He turned me into a pathetic creature I despised."

"You were not pathetic. You trusted him. He was your husband for goodness sake. He was dominating. You see that now. You won't let that happen again."

"You're damn right I won't."

"All I'm saying is, it's okay to lean on a man. Shep isn't like Steve."

"Good Lord, you don't need to tell *me* that. Those two are as different as black and white."

Cassie took a sip of her beer then set the bottle down. "I think Shep would be good for you."

"He's great, period. Fabulous." Tammy wiped at the salt coating the rim of her goblet. "Kind, giving, big-hearted, supportive, solid, sexy ... My God, he is sexy."

"It's wonderful, isn't it? Having an attractive man want to be with you?"

"Cassie." She stared at her friend. "You and Mike are in the same category. You're both gorgeous, charismatic."

"You can have with Shep what I have with Mike."

Tammy chewed her lip. "You two are so perfect together. Anyone can see you're in love."

"It started with trust. Mike is everything to me, and I do mean everything. You can have trust with Shep. That man looks at you the way Mike looked at me when I wasn't sure if he was interested."

"Really?" She so wanted to believe that Shep liked her more than mere attraction. Cassie seemed to think so. "I like Shep a lot."

"Lean on him, Tammy. I think he'd be there for you in anything."

Was it wishful thinking? Or was Cassie right? Tammy just needed to be sure her infatuation was not clouding her judgment.

How she would love to lean on Shep, among other things.

CHAPTER 14

On rare occasion, Station Eight got a slow day. The crew would rather be fighting fires than logging gear, testing hoses, filling air tanks, taking inventory—the tasks were endless. But those things had to be done. A rig and the squad had to be equipped and ready to go at a moment's notice.

Shep inhaled and smiled. Oven fried chicken. Cooper was taking his turn in the kitchen. He was young, but Shep saw something in him. Something the kid didn't see in himself.

Laredo had the music cranked up again. Shep didn't mind. The guy was a hard worker, had a friendly personality, and took everything that was thrown at him. Jared and Mike were restocking the MIDI, last Shep checked. Now would be a good time to call Hooley. Shep wanted answers. He had little patience when it came to waiting.

Before he could prop his feet on his desk, a sharp rap hit his office door. He knew it would be Mike.

"Enter." Shep couldn't read Mike's face. "Got something on your mind?"

"Nothing. The guys are keeping themselves busy. Glad to have some free time without a crisis."

Shep knew better. Mike would rather be saving lives than twiddling his thumbs. He had something on his mind, all right. If Shep had to guess, he'd say Cassie.

"Cassie said you took Tammy to see your brother."

Shep leaned back in his chair, making the seat creak. "Yep."

"Getting something out of you is like pulling teeth with a pair of pliers," Mike said with aggravation. Shep wanted to grin.

"What do you want to know? I took her. Eddie talked to her. Figure she already told Cassie all about it."

"Would you care to tell me?"

"Tell you what? Eddie is going to help her."

"I'm not concerned about Eddie. What about you and Tammy? Did she forgive you or is she okay with you taking her home after the girls got bombed?" Mike was a friend as well as a crew member. The two had gotten close enough to share some things from their past. Since Mike's girlfriend happened to be Tammy's best friend, Shep guessed he and Mike were supposed to share.

"She's all right with it."

"That's it?" Mike shook his head. "At least tell me what happened after you took her to see Eddie?"

"I took her home, too." At Mike's glare, Shep figured he could throw a bone. "She invited me in for coffee."

"Now we're getting somewhere."

"You want to have a sleepover and talk like a couple of girlfriends? Share secrets?"

"Why don't you just admit you like her?"

Sure. He could admit that. "I like her. Took me by surprise when she asked me to go with her."

"And then she asked you in for coffee."

"Yep." Shep stretched his arms behind his head and propped his feet up on his desk. "How are things going with you and Cassie?"

"Fine."

If Mike realized the switch in topic, he didn't say anything. After a few more seconds of silence, Mike's face clouded like thunder.

"Well?"

"Well, what?" Shep asked innocently.

"You want to know, so why don't you ask?"

Wasn't his way. If a man wanted to say something, he should spit it out. Shep had never made a habit of asking another man his personal business. If it had something to do with Station Eight, he'd be crawling up someone's asshole. "Figure if there's anything you want to tell me, you will."

"She's getting too close," Mike blurted.

Shep's suspicions were correct. He'd seen Mike change. Letting a woman inside your head could be dangerous, or just what the doctor ordered.

"*She* is? Or *you* are?"

"I can't have a relationship." Mike's expression ranked somewhere between anger and terror.

"Seems you already are."

"I can't … I can't afford an attachment, you know that."

"I don't know any such thing. You've babbled such nonsense before. I don't see any reason you and Cassie can't have a future."

"Future? You forget my mom walked out on my dad because of his profession?"

A hang-up Mike couldn't seem to get over—his fear of a woman rejecting him because of his job. Yes, some women could handle their man being in danger and others could not deal with the stress—like Mike's mother.

"Don't mean Cassie will."

"It takes a certain kind of woman to accept her husband being a firefighter."

Husband? Were things that serious with Cassie? Or did Mike mean his father? Mike had been just a boy when his mother bailed. Cassie was nothing like Mike's mom. From what Shep had seen, Cassie was a remarkable woman. She was perfect for Mike.

Shep wondered if Tammy would be open to a relationship with a firefighter. But they were talking about Cassie.

"You think Cassie wants some pencil pusher?"

"My job is too dangerous."

Shep lifted his feet from his desk, slowly lowered them to the floor and scooted his chair forward. He braced his arms on the edge and locked eyes with Mike. "If a woman loves you, she'll accept your job."

Mike gave a harsh laugh. "You're one to talk."

Sure, Shep was single. Because he made a mistake as a teenager which he had no intention of repeating. He wanted the right woman. The next time he said *I do* and promised to love a woman till death do us part, he had every intention of doing it. But that was a tidbit he kept to himself.

"I hope to marry someday. To the right woman. You and Cassie make a fine couple. From what I see, that woman loves you. Don't throw that away."

"I want her in my life. I want her for keeps. But I can't let go of the fear that she'll leave."

So, it was serious. "Look, Mike. You'd be—"

Three loud tones came across the intercom. Shep shoved from his chair without finishing his sentence and rushed out the door. He snatched a paper from the printer, scanned the address and sprinted down the stairs.

Within minutes they were at the scene of a crash. He pulled behind a police car, assessing the scene. Laredo drove the quint to the front of the wreckage with Jared and Mike maneuvering the MIDI right behind. One officer directed traffic away from the blocked intersection. Another one came to meet Shep.

"Captain Shepherd," Shep introduced himself, not recognizing the cop. Most of the men in blue knew him. Just as the officer opened his mouth, a loud crack echoed between the buildings. The officer flinched and pushed Shep behind a police car.

"Get down! That's a gun."

A gun?

Fuck.

Two more blasts sounded and Shep thought the hammering of his heart clanged as loud as the gunfire. He pressed his mic.

"Shots fired. Shots fired. Stay back. Don't get out of the trucks. If you're already out, stay the hell on the ground. We're in the middle of gunfire."

His heart raced. "What the hell is going on here?" he roared at the police officer.

"I have no idea."

"Why weren't we notified of the danger?" Shep was furious. His men had charged into a critical setting totally unaware. They'd bungled into an unsecured scene.

"There was no situation," the cop spat out, clearly frustrated. "A traffic accident. Protocol."

"Then who the hell is shooting at us?"

"I don't know." While the officer radioed the incident to his superiors, Shep took roll call, making sure no one had been hit.

"Check in," he barked over the radio.

Each member of the crew replied back.

"Stay put," the cop said. "Chief is sending backup."

Did the idiot think he was going anywhere?

"Cap. Better get those cops away from that car. It's going to blow if we don't get those flames out."

He faced the officer. "Get your men away from those vehicles. My guys can't put the flames out with a sniper firing rounds." No more shots had been fired, but the shooter could still be there.

Sirens sounded as more officers arrived on the scene.

"Those flames aren't getting any smaller, Cap. Do you think the gunman is gone?" Mike's voice buzzed through the radio.

"Hold." He turned to the officer. "My men are not making a move until it's clear."

"We have uniforms going into the building where the shots came from. When the scene is secure, I'll let you know."

Shep radioed Mike. "The officers want to secure the scene before we move."

"They better fucking hurry or we'll be directly in line of the explosion."

"Uniforms entered the building where the shots came from," he shouted back. "Hold your horses."

"What about the drivers of those cars? Anyone still in them?" Jared's voice cracked through the speaker.

"You mean you don't know?" Shep tried to see from where he crouched. Were there people in the line of gunfire and at risk from burning flames?

"We never made it from the truck," the radio barked.

"Son-of-a-bitch." He faced the cop. "I need an answer. There might be people out there?"

Static and shouting came over the policeman's radio. "The shooter is gone. The scene is secure."

Shep wasted no time. "All clear. Get to it!" He squared off with the officer. "What the hell happened here?"

"No idea. Guess you got the call on the scanner, just like me. My captain is here, now."

Shep saw Chandler, the police captain, and marched in his direction. "Any idea of what the hell we drove into?"

"Thought maybe you could tell me," Chandler replied. "Officers responded to a traffic accident, then we got a call saying shots were fired at firefighters."

"That's exactly what happened. What I want to know is how we ended up in the middle of a shooting."

"I'm sorry. I have no idea. There was no indication of a gun or a hint of any kind that a shit show could happen."

Adrenaline pumped through Shep's veins, right along with his fury. "My men were shot at. No warning whatsoever."

"I'm as much in the dark as you. No explanation, but we'll find out. The shooter got away. There's no evidence of more than one. No sign of him, other than shots were fired."

Shep's temple throbbed. His pulse had slowed somewhat, but anger still had him in its thrall. He needed to check on the team. "Let me know when you learn something."

Glancing to the quint, he saw Laredo give him a salute. No worries there. He retraced his steps, then went straight for the MIDI. Jared pushed a gurney toward an officer lying on the sidewalk, where Mike was crouched. When he stood, Shep let out a sigh. Everyone accounted for. Mike caught Shep's eye and approached, carrying his helmet.

"You hurt?"

"Naw, Cap. We stayed behind the MIDI while the shooting was going on."

"There a reason you're not wearing your helmet?"

"I took it off while I was checking out the officer's wound," Mike answered.

"Whose blood on your face?"

"One of the officers got shot."

Shep glanced over to the man being put on the stretcher. "Damn, what a clusterfuck. I'd rather fight fires than bullets any day."

"You and me, both."

"Let's wrap this up and head back to the station."

"You got it, Cap."

Shep drove back to the station, thinking of the bullets they'd dodged and how the team managed to enter a dangerous scenario. At least the men had come back in one piece. He stowed his gear so it could be cleaned and checked for the next run, and had just collapsed in his chair when the door to his office flew open. He turned with a reprimand ready on his tongue for barging in, but one glance at Laredo's face told Shep something was wrong.

"Cap. You gotta see this."

"What is it?"

"We think Mike took a bullet. His helmet, anyway."

Shep bounded out of his chair. "You've got two seconds to make sense."

"Mike's helmet has a hole. A bullet hole."

Shep charged out the door and down the steps, Laredo on his heels. Unless some maniac had charged the station, the bullet hole had to be from the shooter at the accident site. Several shots were fired. Both Mike and Jared had been pinned down behind the squad. He'd seen blood on Mike's face, but—

He marched forward, heading straight for Mike's large frame.

"What's this I hear about a bullet hole?"

Jared handed him a helmet. Mike's helmet. Shep frowned as he studied the hole. He ground his teeth together, feeling a muscle tighten from his cheek to his temple. Fury pierced his chest. Fear clenched his stomach.

"Looks like the bullet went through here."

"I remember hearing a hiss," Mike said, clearly confused. "As for the shield, I figured it got scraped."

A fraction over …

"Laredo. Take him to the hospital," Shep ordered.

"Now wait a minute. I'm fine."

Fuming, Shep scowled at Mike, clearly displaying his doubt and his ire.

"He's got blood on his head," Cooper said. Shep remembered seeing Mike without his helmet. Blood on his temple.

"A scratch," Mike shot back.

"Yours?" Shep asked. His intent evident, for Mike had said earlier it was the policeman's. "*Not* the officer?"

Mike shrugged, which just pissed Shep off.

"Get your ass to the hospital and don't say another damn word." If Mike opened his mouth, Shep was mad enough—and scared enough—to deck him.

He could have been killed.

"The rest of you, get this gear stowed."

He glared at Laredo, who was already moving in Mike's direction.

"Come on, Mike. We'll take my truck."

Fortunately for everyone, Mike didn't say another word. Shep rarely spoke in the tone he'd just used. When he did, every man, or beast, knew to get out of his way. He would never admit to the team that fear was at the root of his anger.

These guys were his family. Close as any brothers could be. They lived together, ate together, slept under the same roof and spent more hours with each other than their wives or partners. He'd bonded with each of them. The knot in his gut twisted his insides. His exasperation—strung tighter than an overextended rubber band—ready to snap.

Voices echoed in the bay door. He glanced at his watch. Some of the crew for the next shift were arriving.

"You"—he pointed to Jared—"alert the next shift—"

Before he could finish what he was going to say, tires squealed in the front lot. A van rolled up, TV3 News painted on the side.

"Shit. I was hoping to be gone before they found out."

"Didn't take them long," Jared said.

No, it hadn't. And now, with the added business of Mike ...

"You gonna tell them about Mike?" Cooper asked.

Shit. He had to. He just wished he'd had time to plan a statement. "Can't hide something like that."

"I wouldn't be surprised if they didn't have a reporter follow Mike and Laredo to the hospital," Jared added.

People came running inside the bay, microphones held in their hands.

"Might as well get this over with."

CHAPTER 15

Giving Mike's name to the press was a mere formality. Shep was sure they already knew the name of every guy at the station. Hoping the shooting wouldn't hit the news before he had a chance to inform the Chief, he'd hurried to his office. Delivering the details of the incident had gone about the way he'd expected. Now, there was one more person Shep needed to call.

Over the past few weeks, he'd seen a light in Mike's eyes and a bounce in his step. With a level head on his shoulders, Mike was one strong individual. But he'd never let himself fall in love or make a commitment to a woman.

Cassie had changed his mind. If Mike was even thinking about marriage, he had to be hooked. Shep couldn't think of a better woman for Mike. A teacher. Sparks had flown the minute they met. Those two belonged together. Cassie was sure to be upset when she found out.

Tammy was her best friend. He decided to call Tammy.

"Hello."

The sound of Tammy's cheery voice made him feel better. The woman was like a ball of energy, just bursting to get out.

"Tammy. This is Shep."

"I know. I have you programmed in my phone. I even gave you a special ringtone."

A special ringtone?

She sputtered as if she hadn't meant to tell him that.

"I mean, uh, you know. In case you needed to get in touch with me. For Eddie. Uh, he might need to contact me. So, I wanted to make sure I answered quick. Uh ..."

Any other time he would tease her and egg on her nervous chatter. But he'd called for a reason. One that if he dawdled, she wouldn't take too kindly when she found out.

"Tammy. Where are you?"

"I'm at home. Would you like to come over?"

"I have something to tell you."

Silence. What was she thinking? Good Lord, he'd scared the shit out of her. And it was about to get worse.

"Hey."

"I'm here." Her soft voice came back over the line, filled with worry. He hated making her worry. "You sound serious."

"I need to ask a favor and it won't be pleasant."

"You have my attention. First, tell me, are you all right?"

"I'm good. It's not about me."

"What happened?"

"We had a 911 call today, a traffic accident downtown." He hesitated when he heard her gasp. He hated to alarm her, but she had to know. *Cassie* had to know. "Some guy showed up with a gun and took pot shots at us. Everyone is okay."

Again, silence.

"Tammy. Did you hear me? Everyone is okay."

"Please tell me the truth. Don't spare anything." The catch in her voice tugged at his heart.

"I am. The thing is—"

"I knew it," she shrieked.

"Now, hang on. Listen, okay?"

He heard her inhale and blow out. "Okay."

"The thing is, one of the bullets struck Mike's helmet. He's okay, but I made him go to the hospital to get checked out."

"His helmet?"

"I know it sounds bad. Actually, it's a miracle he doesn't have a hole in his head."

"But he is all right?"

"I sent him to the hospital to make sure. He was standing up when he left, but a bullet to his helmet scared all of us." He didn't like admitting to weakness, but who the hell wouldn't be scared if they were on the receiving end of a gun? The hole in Mike's helmet had given every man on the team a reality check.

Shep still couldn't believe they'd stumbled into a situation that bizarre. A sniper. *Christ.* What next?

"I'm waiting to hear. I'll let you know when I do."

"Oh, my God. Cassie."

"That's why I called. I thought maybe you should be the one to tell her. She might take it better coming from you."

"You're sure he's all right?"

"No. Like I said, he was standing when he left. Breathing, walking, talking. But he's in shock. We all are. It's difficult to believe he took a shot to his helmet and he's still walking around."

"His helmet. So, it didn't actually hit *him*."

Shit.

"Well ..."

"Jonathan Shepherd! You tell me this minute. What are you not telling me?"

There was nothing wrong with his hearing. At least there hadn't been until now. Tammy shouting in his ear just might have damaged his eardrum.

"Calm down. The bullet creased his temple. He had blood—"

"His temple! Oh my God. It could have killed him. He ... oh my God. Shep—"

"Hey. I told you. He's okay. A little blood. No—"

"Blood! Just spit it out instead of leaving a trail of bread crumbs. Tell me all of it."

"That is all of it. He had some blood on his temple. You're not any more scared than I was when I found out."

"When you found out? Weren't you there? Did you see him?"

"I meant when I saw his helmet and realized the blood on his face was his."

"There is definitely more to this story and you're going to tell me the whole thing. Later. I've got to find Cassie."

"There's one more thing."

"Dammit. Will you quit dolling out tidbits? Speak!"

This woman had a temper to match her fiery red hair. "Reports and news cameras were here at the station. It's bound to be on television."

"Are you serious? Is there anything else?"

"That's it."

"I'm ... Shep?" She'd gone from exasperation to worry in a ripping second.

"Yeah."

"Are you okay?"

Damn. Her concern for him rocked him back on his heels. He wished he could reach through the phone and yank her to him. Hold her in his arms. He needed her sweetness to soothe him. Tammy had the perfect balance of fire and serenity, but his head spun the way she leaped from one emotion to the other.

"I'm good." He wanted to add *babe*, but caught himself.

"I'm glad you called me. Thank you," she purred into his ear. Then she quickly shot out, "Now, I've got to go."

The call ended and he realized Tammy had hung up on him. *What a woman.*

***

Shep rolled his shoulders as he headed to the waiting area. Mike was being unreasonable. Most people got out of Mike's way when he got in a snit, but Shep, being his captain, probably got more leeway than most. Mike might be big, but Shep never backed down from an argument—especially when he was right. The doctors wanted Mike to stay in the hospital. The blockhead was determined to go home. This was one argument Shep might lose.

Every member of the team stood when they saw him enter the waiting area.

"He's fine," Shep told the group before they could ask. "He's being an ass."

Aware of Tammy's gaze on him, Shep focused on Cassie.

"The doctor wants to keep Mike overnight for observation, but he's determined to leave. Maybe you can make him listen to the doctor."

Cassie's eyes were wide as she hung on every word. She didn't move a muscle. Didn't utter a sound.

Jared placed an arm around her shoulders. "Cassie? Did you understand Shep? You can see him."

She gave a little nod. Tammy walked with her to the set of double doors, so Shep dropped into an empty chair.

"How is he, Cap?" Laredo asked, sitting next to him.

"He's fine. Mad as a damned hornet. I figure Cassie will calm him down."

"She sure will. She'll set his ass straight," Cooper added.

"Looks like Mike's in it for real." Jared joined the group.

Yep, it did. It also looked like Cassie was in love with Mike. Just the medicine he needed.

Shep smelled Tammy's perfume before she sat beside him.

"Hi," she said.

"Hi, yourself."

"Thanks for calling me."

"Thank you for telling Cassie."

"She wasn't home, wasn't answering her phone. I nearly went out of my mind trying to find her."

"Where was she?"

"Grocery store. Of all days for her to go grocery shopping."

He chuckled. "Some people like to eat."

She looked at him like he was dirt. With a glare so adorable, he wanted to kiss the irritation from her lips. *Feisty.*

"At least you found her," he said.

"I called everywhere. By the time she answered, it was on the six o'clock news. She ran out of her house before I could get to her."

"She saw the news?" Shep cursed under his breath.

"Hey, Cap." Jared stood before Shep. "Since the big guy is okay, we might as well head out."

"Cassie's been back there long enough to talk him into staying. We gotta tell Hoss goodbye." Cooper might follow Jared around, but he was attached to Mike. Shep imagined the guys wanted to see for themselves that Mike was fine.

The guys ambled down the hall to find Mike and Shep was glad to have a few minutes with Tammy.

"Are you going to wait for Cassie?"

"If I know her, she'll be spending the night with her man."

Her man.

Had a nice ring to it. Shep wondered if Tammy would refer to him as her man. He wouldn't mind belonging to her.

Tammy's cheeks were flushed and the top of her breasts pinked above the neckline of the shirt that hugged her curvy body. Just right for a man's hands.

She took his breath. Her smile, her bubbly personality, and her fine physique.

"You know, I rushed here for Cassie. But I wanted to see with my own eyes that … that all of you were okay."

All of you. He'd noticed Tammy's hesitation.

"This isn't something that usually happens. Firefighters never enter an area where there are guns. Today was a fluke. No one knew a shooter was anywhere in the vicinity." He hoped to ease her fears and let her know this incident was unusual.

"Are you trying to tell me you aren't normally in this kind of danger?"

He shifted to face her. "That's exactly what I'm trying to explain."

"Just how is this more dangerous than running into a burning building?"

"No one's shooting at us."

"Shep—" she sputtered. He'd swear she was counting to ten. Then she punched his arm.

He flinched. "What's that for?"

"Men. Humph." She crossed her arms and rolled out her lip in a tempting pout.

"All men or just me?"

"You make me mad. Battling fire is every bit as dangerous as dodging bullets. But you are the one whose nuts. You run into the fire. Most people run away from a gun."

She had him there.

"My line of work is risky—"

"Risky! It's treacherous. Daring. Unsafe."

"I have to stop you there. We are trained. We're as safe as we can be. Firefighters don't charge into a building without a plan. Those men are skilled. Qualified to do their jobs."

Tammy grasped his arm. "I never meant to insinuate otherwise. I know you're competent. You save lives. I admire you."

"Don't admire me, Tammy. I'm just an ordinary man."

"Oh, I could so debate that statement with many contentions. You, Shep, are no ordinary anything. Man or otherwise." She inhaled a deep breath and let it out in a dramatic sigh.

Damn, this woman was good for his ego.

***

The man in the hospital bed was not the brother. Did the cocksucker have a horseshoe up his ass?

Seth strode back to his vehicle, his muscles tight with tension. Leaning against the back bumper of his SUV, he lit up a cigarette, tilted his head to the sky, then released smoke into the air.

Goddammit.

His blood boiled with vengeance. His brother had lived in hell, survived hell, for two years before those bastards finally killed him.

A brother for a brother.

He'd promised.

A brother in the Staunton Fire Department. A fireman. Another fucking hero. How convenient that bit of knowledge fit perfectly into his plans.

How hard could it be? Accidents happened every day. Seems natural—due to his profession—a hotshot could fall in the line of duty.

A brother for a brother.

But the bastard was still alive. A headshot. His aim had been dead on. Now what?

Calm the fuck down.

He inhaled deeply, sucking smoke into his lungs. Resting his head against the cab, he closed his eyes and exhaled.

Patience.

Using the same technique he'd used on various missions, Seth forced his pulse to slow to a steady beat. A calm mind accomplished more than reckless strength.

No one in this town knew him. His target would find out soon enough. For now, he preferred to stay under the radar.

Still, he had a plan. First, he had to find out if this one would survive. He crept back inside and found the fireman had been moved to another floor.

Slick as a whistle, he made his way upstairs. *Give a flirty grin to a pretty nurse and you had her eating out of your hands.* Casually, he took a stroll to the room number that the cute ponytail had given him. A blonde woman crawled onto the bed with the big guy lying in it.

Son-of-a-bitch.

Seth pulled his cell from his pocket and hit the keypad, calling the one man he trusted without question.

"What?" a groggy voice came over the line.

"Carl. It's me."

"Seth? Been a while, man."

"Yeah. Got anything goin' on?"

"Naw. I need a job. You got something?"

"Sure do. Taking a man out."

"No shit. You got a plan?"

He had a plan all right. Make the bastard suffer the way *his* brother had suffered. Grab him by the nuts and show him how it felt to lose a brother.

"Yeah, I got a plan," he answered, "but the guy is a fireman. Got the eye of the public, you know what I mean?"

"That will bring some heavy heat." Carl's gruff voice echoed over the line. Carl didn't complain. Not once in the hot desert of Afghanistan. He'd been one of the most competent men in Seth's unit. Loyal to a fault.

"Yeah," he agreed. It would bring heat. They'd just have to deal with shit as it came. "I'll give you the details of why later. You in?"

"Sure, man. I owe ya."

Seth had given his all to the military. Dedicated to serving his country. But when he received the news of his brother's death, he'd signed up for a new mission. Revenge. He arranged the place and time to meet Carl, then ended the call. Seth shoved his phone in his pocket, turned around, and—

Froze.

A nurse stood, glaring at him. He'd never had difficulty with women. Charmed quite a few, in fact. There would be no charming this one. After an intense stare-down, she stuck her nose in the air and strutted on down the hall.

Goddamned bitch had seen him. Heard him.

How much had she heard?

He thought back over his conversation, trying to remember the exact words he'd said. Was there anything to incriminate him?

Fuck.

Just what he needed. A nosy nurse. A loose mouth.

Someone to finger him.

CHAPTER 16

Christopher dragged into the kitchen as though he had cement on his feet, with a mulish look—one Tammy had seen too often lately. Normally, he and David charged though the house at a dead run.

Steve had demanded more visits with the boys and she'd agreed to keep the peace. She had never denied him access or time with the twins. He'd simply chosen not to see them. Now, he acted like a candidate for father of the year. At first, the boys had loved going to their dad's. But more and more she'd seen their temperament changing.

"What's up, tiger?"

"Do we have to go to Dad's today?"

Uh oh. She didn't like the sound of that.

"Do you want to go see your dad?" she asked carefully. She would not discourage the visits, but she damn well wouldn't make the kids go if they didn't want to.

"Naw. It's no fun over there."

"Is that the only reason you don't want to go?"

His little eyes bugged out like he'd said something wrong.

"Of course, you don't have to go if you don't want to. I thought you might like spending time with your dad." If Steve was actually taking the time to be with his children. He hadn't before. Why would she think he was now? Was Steve pushing them off on his wife?

"Really?" Christopher's whole attitude changed.

"Yes, really." She smiled hoping to put her son at ease.

"Whoopee," came from the hallway. Then David burst into the room.

She crossed her arms and arched her brow the way she did when they were in trouble. "Were you hiding around the corner?"

Two pairs of guilty eyes gaped at her, then quickly glanced at each other.

"He made me do it." Christopher pointed to David.

"He didn't want to go either," David shot back.

Before the boys got into an arguing match, she stopped them. "Wait. I had something else planned today, anyway."

"You did?"

"How about a field trip?"

"You mean we gotta go to school?"

"No. But we are going to visit a place that is kind of like going on a field trip."

"Are we going to the Safari Park?" Christopher hopped up and down like a jumping bean. Seeing his brother, David jumped right along with him.

"Yay. We're going to the zoo."

Excited squeals and yelps pealed through the kitchen. She gave them three minutes before trying to calm them.

"Nope. That's not it."

"What is it?" Christopher stopped bouncing before David.

"Are we going to like it?"

"Let me see." She put her finger to her temple and pretended to think. "Yep. I think you might like it. But I'm not sure. Maybe I better ask you and see."

"Aw, Mom. What is it?"

"Tell us, Mommy." David jerked on her shirt.

"All right. I guess I should. How would you like to go see fire trucks?"

"For real?"

"At school?"

Did David think everything was at school? She needed to fix that.

"We're going to the firehouse. Station Eight."

The squeals and screams started again. She covered her ears and watched the two boys dance around each other.

"A real firetruck."

"We're going to the firehouse."

"We're going to see firemen."

Suddenly, David stopped. "Will it be the same firemen that came to our school?"

"Yep. The same men. How about that?"

"You're the best, Mom." Christopher slammed against her, throwing his little arms around her as far as he could reach. Not to be outdone, David wiggled in beside his brother.

"Yeah, Mom. You're the best."

***

Shep heard the twins before he saw them. Then he heard Tammy reeling them in. Remarkable how the sound of her voice spiked his pulse. Excitement swirled in his body as he eagerly awaited, seeking her form in the open bay door.

Mike had promised Todd, the boy he'd met at ER, a tour of Station Eight and Shep had invited Tammy's sons. Even though Todd was a few years older, Shep figured the three would get on great together. Todd and his father were standing next to Mike and turned in unison at the clamor of the rambunctious twins.

"Hello boys," Shep called as David and Christopher came into sight.

"Hi, Shep."

"We're here." David hopped from one foot to the other. "Wow. Look at that."

"Remember what I said." Tammy might as well give up. They were too excited, and they were boys.

"Christopher, David, there's someone I want you to meet." Shep gestured to Todd and the boys followed. "This is Todd."

"Hi, Todd," the twins said at the same time.

"I'm Christopher. Are you here to see the fire trucks with us?"

Tammy always used his full name when speaking about Christopher, but Shep was surprised to hear the boy repeat it the same way. Figured the boy would go by Chris or something.

"Hi. Yes. Mike invited me."

"Mike?"

"Wow. You're big," David said to Mike.

"Yep. I'm Mike. You guys want to come with me?"

"Woohoo!" Howls echoed through the bay as they skipped off to the rigs.

"Boys—"

"Don't waste your breath. They'll be fine," Shep said, grinning. "Tammy, this is Daniel Williams, Todd's father. This is Tammy, David and Christopher's mom."

"Hello, may I call you Tammy? I'm pleased to meet you."

"Of course. I'm pleased to meet you, too." She glanced at the boys climbing on one of the firetrucks. "Are you sure they won't hurt anything?"

"Mike has it under control."

"Your son seems so well mannered," Tammy said to Daniel. "I guess my children look like hooligans."

"No. They look like typical boys. I'm afraid I'm to blame for Todd's quiet nature. He's very mature for his age. You see, I'm gone a lot. Todd thinks he needs to be the man of the house and take care of his mother."

"That's impressive. You should use the term *proud* instead of *blame*."

Daniel's eyes widened. He might have been surprised at Tammy's words, but they only confirmed what Shep already knew. Tammy was an exceptional woman. Anyone who spent time with her had to see her inner beauty.

"I am proud of him. As for today, it's hard to say who is more delighted about this visit." Daniel glanced over at his son. "Todd is eager and excited. Being gone so much, I rarely see him this way. I'm very pleased he met Mike at the hospital."

"At the hospital?"

A look of guilt crossed Daniel's face. "Again, my fault. I'd built a tree house for Todd a few years back. He thought it needed to be bigger. I've shown him how to use my tools, and he took it upon himself to use them in my absence. He fell onto a saw."

"Daniel." Shep wanted to ease the man's mind. "You carry a burden where there should be none. Todd is a healthy, thriving young man. You and your wife have done an excellent job raising him. Mike is a bit the quiet, reserved type. Look at him." Shep gave a nod in Mike's direction. "He seem happy to you? Look at your son. I'd say he's perfect."

Todd climbed onto the rig right along with Christopher and David. Even with the twins exhibiting their boisterous energy, Mike had them firmly in control.

"Daniel. Take it from me," Tammy said. "Boys will be boys, and you can't keep them from getting hurt. I've got double trouble."

Daniel smiled, and Shep admired his spirited redhead even more.

"Like Shep said, Todd is fine. All parents share an accountability of guilt, but it's better to enjoy children and not blame ourselves when things happen."

"True," Daniel said, his tender gaze aimed at Tammy. "However, something tells me you, too, are a worrier. I doubt you follow your own advice."

"Touché."

Seeing the two smiling at each other created a rush of envy. If Daniel wasn't married, Shep might be worried. He shrugged it off.

"I think I'll join my son. Those firetrucks look particularly interesting. How about you?"

"I've had the tour. You go right ahead and enjoy yourself."

"I will." Daniel gave a big grin to Tammy, then a nod to Shep.

"He seems like a nice man," Tammy said.

"That was seemly, what you said."

"About blame? All parents feel that way. It's hard not to."

"Some more than others," Shep said. "I think you balance it quite well."

"With two six-year-olds, it's not easy."

"You're remarkable," he said out loud.

She blushed.

And adorable. And I want to kiss you right now.

"Stop. I'm just me.

Over an hour later, the boys were still going strong but Todd's father decided it was time to leave. Tammy promised the boys would visit each other. She was glad Christopher and David had made a new friend.

Shep had the afternoon off, so when he offered the boys ice-cream, all she could think about was her children on a sugar high. She'd been glad they burned off their energy climbing on trucks and running around the firehouse. Now she'd have to deal with sugar in their blood.

She liked seeing Shep with her boys. Liked the twinkle in his eyes as he watched them, talked with them, *listened* to them. Steve had always been too busy. Then Shep asked her if he could invite them back to his place to see his dog.

Asked her. First.

Of course, David and Christopher were ecstatic. So here they were, driving on a country road headed to Shep's house. Tammy had to admit, she was anxious to see his home.

The top of an A-frame came into view as Shep drove over the rise. Her mouth fell open. The house looked big enough to hold a family of ten. The road ended, so this had to be his. The rustic exterior and location fit Shep perfect. A large meadow was situated to the side, and an outline of the forest beyond could be seen over the roof of the beautiful structure of wood and stone and glass. She stared at the large window centered directly above two stone pillars in the middle of a house that had some of the biggest logs she'd ever seen.

"Are we here?"

"Is this your house?"

The click of seatbelts releasing jerked her out of her daze.

"Yep. This is it." Shep shoved the shifter into park and cut the engine. He was out of the Land Rover before she could think.

"Where's your dog?"

"Yeah. What's his name?"

"Hutch."

"I like Hutch."

"Where is he?"

"Can we see him?"

"Come on. We'll go around back." Shep shot her a grin. "You coming?"

"Come on, Mom."

"Hurry up, Mom."

She quickly climbed from the car and hurried to catch the twins. A walkway of stone curved around the side. A lot of work had gone into this place. The back was stunning, but she barely had time to notice. Shep went to a porch, opened a door, and a huge monster loped out.

Delighted squeals rent the air. And here she thought her boys were all squealed out.

"Wow."

"Hi Hutch."

"He's big." Christopher tried his best to get his arms to reach around the dog's neck.

"He licked me," David shrieked.

Good grief, with all the commotion, she couldn't tell which kid screamed the loudest.

"Hutch." Shep crouched and scrubbed the dog behind his ears. "This is David and Christopher. They've come to play."

"Look Mom. He likes us. Can we take him in the yard?" Christopher, the more daring one, had to ask.

"Sure. Make sure you stay where we can see you. Don't go into the trees."

Before Tammy could object, they took off.

"Don't worry. Hutch won't let them stray off too far."

Tammy finally found her tongue. "What breed of dog is he?"

"Alaskan Malamute."

"I thought that was what you told me. I've not seen one that big."

"You're thinking of males that weigh eighty pounds. Hutch is a breed that weighs one-hundred-thirty-five."

"Good Lord. They could ride him like a horse."

Shep laughed. "Yeah, they probably could. Want something to drink?"

"No. I'm full of ice-cream."

"We can sit on the porch and keep an eye on them."

She looked to the meadow where her children chased the big dog. "I'd like that."

"Sure thing."

The boys ran around the yard in circles, cheering and laughing as the dog bounced and licked their hands. Sitting on the back porch with Shep felt natural. Not awkward at all. They watched the boys romp and play with his dog and for the moment, everything seemed right in the world.

"You have a beautiful place."

"It's home. I love the wide-open space."

"I can see why. You can see all the colors of the rainbow from right here on your back porch. Various shades of green in the field and beyond to the trees. The way purple and pink outline the mountains, it looks like a painting. Gold and white swirls in a blue sky. The sun's rays streaking out behind a cloud. It's breathtaking."

"You see what I see."

"I can imagine how you feel, too. It's overwhelming. Peace, beauty, life ..."

She felt his intense gaze and turned. His gray eyes blazed with a heat that seared her soul. They could be two lovers or two friends. Or parents watching their children—

My God, Tammy. Fantasize much?

"Hey, Shep. Look at this." David had climbed onto the dog's back.

"Oh, my God."

Shep laughed. "They figured it out."

"Ride 'em cowboy," David yelled. Christopher ran beside them, whooping.

"Will they hurt him?"

"Are you kidding? Hutch loves romping with them. Been a while since he's been around little kids."

"How long have you had him?"

"About five years. A family with two boys had a house fire. The dad was in the military and gone a lot. After the fire, the mother and kids moved into an apartment. They had no idea Hutch would get so big and was thinking of getting rid of him. He was still a puppy but weighed about eighty pounds. He took to me right away and I brought him home.

The boys came charging to the porch, saving her from herself.

"Mom, I'm thirsty." David breathed hard from his running.

"Me, too." Christopher trailed behind the dog.

"I've got water, tea, and soda."

"Soda!" both boys squealed.

She gave up. Today was special. She was enjoying being with Shep and her boys were having the time of their lives. What was a little more sugar on an already natural high?

Shep had not been prepared for the way his heart lifted as he watched the two radiant boys playing with his dog. The joy on their little faces grabbed a piece of his heart.

"Here ya go, Champ." Shep placed a Dr. Pepper in front of ... *David?*

"Thank you."

"And Sprite for you." *Christopher?* Since Shep wasn't sure, he didn't use their names.

"Thanks, Shep."

"Just what they need—more sugar. May I use the ladies—uh, your bathroom?"

"At the bottom of the stairway, on the right."

Tammy went inside and he sat with the boys on the porch while Hutch thumped his tail.

"Mommy doesn't let us have soda and ice-cream the same day."

Shep studied the kid's face. A few more freckles. *That's David.*

"My daddy has a step mommy," Christopher said. Shep was pretty sure that was Christopher. The kid needed a nickname. "Daddy wants us to call her Mom. She's not my mom."

Uh, oh. What did he say to that? Nothing.

"I'm not gonna call her Mom." David lifted his can and took a gulp.

"Did you kiss my mom?" Christopher asked.

Oh, hell. Where'd the kid come up with that? "Uh, no."

"My dad kisses *Marleeene*."

"I called her Marly," David piped up, "and she didn't like it."

"Her name's *Marleeene*." Christopher dragged out the name, clearly showing his dislike. "She wants us to call her Mom."

"I don't know." David shrugged. "She gave Daddy a funny look when he said that."

"I guess it's okay if my mom kisses you," Christopher continued.

Shep wasn't sure how this conversation was about to go. "I like your mom. I like you boys, too."

"Are you getting married?"

Whoa. Two pairs of eyes were fastened on him. Tammy was still inside, so Shep had to handle this carefully.

"Kissing someone doesn't mean they're getting married."

"My dad kisses *Marleeene.* They got married." *Freckles. David.*

"Okay. Uh. Sometimes a man and woman can kiss if they like each other."

"You mean like a girlfriend? Is my mom your girlfriend?" David asked.

"I got a girlfriend." Christopher puffed out his chest.

"You mean Jane?" David swiveled to his brother. "Did you kiss her?"

"Naw. Yuk. Kissing is for grownups."

Shep could only imagine Tammy's reaction if she heard her boys.

Christopher pointed at him. "Like you. You're growed up. Mom's growed up. My dad's growed."

"Mom said *Marleeene* was a baby. She ain't no baby."

Little ears were always listening and Shep figured they weren't supposed to hear that. He could only imagine what Tammy thought of the woman. The wife of Tammy's ex must be younger.

"She's growed up 'cause she kisses Daddy."

The back door opened and Tammy stepped out.

Thank goodness.

CHAPTER 17

Being a member of a fire department, accidents were a given. Firefighters were trained to expect the unexpected. But how the hell were they supposed to deal with sabotage?

Shep tapped his fingers on the printed report. Proof. The explosion at the Wimer property had been no accident. He still couldn't wrap his mind around why. If someone would deliberately set an explosion at one of the training sites ... Who knew what could happen next?

Every man on the team had been anxiously waiting for news. He had nothing to give them. Patience might be a virtue, but he had none with this scumbag. Unable to sit in his office any longer, he opened the door and stepped back in surprise. Mike stood there with his arm raised.

"You got something for me, Mike?"

He pointed a thumb over his shoulder. "Chuck's here to see you."

Shep glanced to the side and saw Chuck. "Come on in."

"You can come in too, Mike," Chuck said. "This concerns the entire department."

"You here officially?" Shep asked.

"Investigator Hooley is on the Wimer property case. He shared some information with me."

Shep wondered if Chuck had read Hooley's report.

"There's a detective in our department working closely with the fire inspector and Hooley asked for me to help with his investigation."

Shep sat down and leaned back in his chair, while Chuck continued.

"I've never known Hooley to ask for help before, and you can bet I was surprised when he asked for me."

"I'm not," Mike said. "You're one of the best guys on the police force. You're scrupulous but fair. You've been on the force for how long?"

"Nine years. Seems more like twenty."

"Does that mean you're working on the case now? Did you get promoted?" Shep asked.

"Congratulations, man," Mike told Chuck.

"No. Unofficially, I did not. I'm staying in uniform and working—I guess you could say—undercover."

"Undercover?" Mike blurted. "Holy shit!"

"I'm working the street, keeping an eye on traffic, looking for anything unusual. Keeping an eye out for strangers. Hooley showed me the film."

"You saw the film?" Mike shot a glance to Shep then turned in his seat toward Chuck.

"Hooley wanted another assessment from a police officer's view. We size people up and look for details a normal citizen might overlook."

"That sounds reasonable," Shep said with a nod. "So, tell me, Chuck. I'm sure Wilson pointed out the firefighter who didn't belong there. You have any idea who that guy is?"

"Wilson pointed out the man. Most of his face was hidden by his mask. He knew where the camera was and kept his head turned."

"That fucker was right there in plain sight of everyone." Mike vaulted out of his chair to pace the room. Shep had a few choice names for the bastard, too.

"That tells us something," Chuck said, his eyes locked on Shep.

"Tells you what?"

"We think this guy is a pro."

"You think he's a firefighter?" Mike asked as he dropped back into his chair.

"Not necessarily," Chuck answered, meeting Mike's gaze. "He's cool. Composed. Unruffled. Like you said, he was right in the middle of the action. Walking around like he belonged there. Wearing Station Nine's gear."

"Bold mother—"

Chuck kept talking. "The guy has balls. At some point, he walked right into Station Nine and stole their gear. A smooth operator. And if he can do that, there's no limit to what this guy might do."

Shep had gotten that impression reading Hooley's report. "So that you will know, I've talked to the men and instructed them to be alert. Mike has the idea, if this character got away with sneaking around one fire station, what's to keep him from hitting the others."

"That man has a brass set." Mike flexed his arms. "But if he comes in Station Eight, he's going to get his ass kicked."

"Like I said," Chuck stated, "This guy could be capable of anything. I think you need to be prepared for that."

An eerie weight settled over the room.

Chuck faced Mike. "Did you see anything, anything at all? The way he walked. Did he talk with anyone?"

"No. Nothing."

"I've talked to the other stations. No one remembers anything suspicious. He doesn't have to be a firefighter or an EMT. But he could be in the prison system."

"Prison?"

Chuck gave a nod. "Like I said. He could be a professional. A criminal."

Shep took all this in. An explosion. An arsonist. The possibility of a firefighter committing this crime had rankled. But a criminal? A professional? Prison? Those ideas chilled his blood.

"Why are you here, Chuck?"

"For whatever reason, this guy has targeted the fire department. He's already proven he's dangerous. There were five teams on sight that day. He could be pursuing any of them."

"You think we have a target on our backs?"

"It's possible. That's why Hooley brought me in. I cover every scenario, every possibility. The Wimer house exploded. Firefighters were hurt. It was no coincidence. Hooley found evidence of gas, propane, and explosives. Those items do serious damage. This guy isn't playing games. He's out for blood."

"Is?"

"The Wimer property is isolated. Our perp did his research and more than likely made several visits to the site. From what I understand, the timing was precise. He had to enter the property and set things in motion for the explosion to go off at the exact moment. That takes detailed planning. And accuracy."

Mike's eyes locked onto Shep's. Without any outward sign, dread came through loud and clear in his troubled gaze. After a lengthy silent communication, Shep turned back to Chuck.

"What aren't you telling us?"

Chuck scraped a hand over his jaw. "I don't like this, but I feel you need to be prepared. Especially after the incident downtown. The bullet to Mike's helmet may not have been an accident. I hope to God I'm wrong, but this perp could be a killer. One of you could be his next victim."

***

Shep stood at the top of the stairway, watching Chuck exit the bay. He'd stopped to chat with the team as they performed their tasks. As usual, Laredo had the stereo blaring, but it started raining so he'd brought the quint inside. He held a cloth, ready to shine the already gleaming red paint. Cooper stood next to him.

"Might as well round them up," Shep told Mike.

"They're probably chomping at the bit to find out what Chuck had to say." He exchanged a glance with Shep, then lumbered down the steps.

Shep strode to the game room to see if anyone else was there.

"Hey, Nate. You off today?"

"Yeah. Two days on, three days off. You'll see me around here for the next two days. Contractors painting at my house."

"Hold down the fort for me, will you? The squad will be in my office."

"Will do."

Nate had joined Station Eight as a volunteer eleven years ago, and Shep was damn glad to have him. Like today, when Nate had time off, he'd come into the firehouse and hang out. If a call came in from dispatch, he'd climb on the truck with the rest of them. Even though it was raining, calls came in. In these conditions, there were more traffic accidents than fires.

As he stepped into his office, he heard the clomping boots of his squad coming up the stairs. Mike entered first with Cooper right behind him, then Jared and Laredo.

"What's up, Cap?" Obviously, Laredo couldn't wait any longer.

"Gee, man. You anxious to get your ass handed to you?"

"If my *culo* is in the slinger, I want to know," Laredo growled back at Cooper.

Shep picked up Hooley's report, then dropped it back on his desk. "The official word came back from the training site."

"Hooley told us he found explosives," Cooper reminded everyone.

"Now it's in writing," Shep said. "A hunt is out for the man who did it. Officer Preston is working on the case with Hooley."

"Chuck?" Jared burst out.

"Keep it under wraps. He's working as a detective, but keeping a low profile. He's staying in uniform to observe traffic. So, no one will question if he pulls over vehicles in case our guy might be in one of them."

"Holy shit. Chuck's undercover?"

Ignoring Cooper, Shep continued. "Hooley showed him the film from the training site. Even though the guy was wearing fire gear, Hooley thought Chuck might recognize something the rest of us wouldn't. Like the way the perp walks or something."

"I still can't believe an outsider walked right in and helped himself to Station Nine's equipment. How's Captain Wilson handling that?"

"As you can imagine, Laredo, he's livid."

"That fucker was right there in plain sight of everyone."

Shep stayed on target. "Chuck thinks this guy is a con. Whether or not he's in the prison system, our arsonist has balls. He's already proven he's dangerous. Mike was with me when

Chuck gave his opinion. I'm passing that information on to you."

"So, Chuck's meeting was official. I thought he was pawning his sister off on Shep."

Shep didn't even want to think about what Jared meant. He didn't need another female on his hands. He still had to put a stop to Alice and her surprise visits. "Chuck said this firebug could be capable of anything. He warned us to be prepared."

"For what?"

Cooper was young and had a long career ahead of him. Hell, none of the men had signed up for this.

"He seems to think we might have a target on our backs. This guy isn't playing games. He's out for blood." Shep swallowed the dread clogging his throat at what he had to say next. "The bullet to Mike's helmet may not have been an accident."

"Of course, it wasn't an accident!" Jared shouted. "Some fucker was shooting at us." Shep locked eyes with Jared, remembering he'd been in the MIDI with Mike.

"That just goes to show this guy is desperate. He's already proven he's violent."

"Wait a minute. You think the shooter is the same guy as our arsonist?"

"Chuck thinks it's possible. I want you guys to be alert." No reason to tell them to be careful. That word was not allowed in firefighter training. Skill, diligence, aptitude, competence—those were the ones that made a firefighter safe.

"Just what we need. Some joker gunning for us when we're trying to save lives."

"If this bastard has targeted the fire department, he could be watching every move we make." Mike's expression alone should scare off any aggressor. But Shep knew the man benched four hundred pounds. If he caught the thug, there wouldn't be much left of his ass.

"You mean, like a stalker? Fuck."

"Sheds a whole new light on first response, huh, pup."

"I'd rather tackle a burning building without a sniper on my back."

Stunned and bewildered, the team went back to work. Shep's mind spun as he thought about the mysterious events surrounding Station Eight, with no resolution in sight. He could barely fathom some criminal was out to get them.

Firefighters.

The men he was responsible for.

***

"This was a good idea." Tammy liked her coffee, but she usually only drank it in the morning. When Cassie suggested iced Frappuccino's from Starbucks, the idea sounded too good to pass up.

"You looked like you were dragging."

"I was. Jeremy Chittum was wild today. There's no way he'd been given his medication. I think his mother overdoses him on the weekend and then on Monday, she sends the kid to school wired."

"That's sad. I have a little girl in my class who needs to be on meds, but her parents refuse to give it to her. I can understand they'd be scared to medicate, but they don't understand the child is unable to calm down enough to learn. Her attention span is non-existent. And the poor thing keeps getting into trouble. It's not her fault."

"Parents." Tammy sucked ice through her straw and soon developed a brain freeze. "Oh my God. Take this before I drink it all."

"Mmm mmm. I love white chocolate." Cassie ignored her.

"Can you give me a perm?"

"You don't need a perm. You have lots of curl."

"Too much. A perm can straighten some of my unruly curls."

"Who told you that?" Cassie asked while stirring the ice with her straw.

"Holly. You just pour on the lotion and comb it straight."

"Sounds like something she would say. She should spend more time teaching than surfing the internet. Do not do that."

"What about color then? Will you color it for me?"

"Your hair is a beautiful shade of red. Why would you mess with it?"

"I've had this shade all my life."

"I do like your new cut. Where is this sudden urge to change your hair coming from?"

Tammy swiveled sideways, facing Cassie. "I want to spruce things up a bit."

"Steve is an asshole. You're fine the way you are. He insulted you and tried to blame you to excuse *his* behavior. You can't believe anything he said. You're pretty, Tammy. I'll give you the same pep talk you gave me. Look in the mirror."

"I'm not that bad. My sisters never stomped me into the ground. As for Steve, I gave him the power to hurt me. It's just that ... well, Shep is so hot."

Cassie swung her whole body to face Tammy. "Listen to me. Steve is a hound dog. His cheating had nothing to do with you. Shep is attracted to you. Go with it."

Tammy considered that. Did Shep find her tempting enough to kiss? "You don't know how much I want to. I'm not expecting much. Maybe a little kissing, a little tongue." Who was she kidding? She wanted him to grab her caveman-style and ravish her. Just like the hero in her romance novels.

If he did, she might embarrass herself. She had no clue what she would do. Sure, she might want him to be infatuated with her, but it had been so long since she'd even dated a guy. Yeah, she'd flirted and had a blast, but there had been no threat. No chance of him actually making a move on her.

"Gee, Cassie. I have two boys to take care of. I've never seriously considered being intimate with someone. Certainly not someone as sexy as Shep."

"Why not?"

"Have you seen the guy?" Tammy snarked.

"Yeah. Right next to Mike."

"They both are hot. Shep makes my eyes blur and my mind go all gooey. A girl can dream, but when it comes to reality, he'd never be interested in me."

"Tammy, it's okay to dream. To make those dreams come true, you have to act. How much preaching did I have to listen to from you?"

Tammy waved a hand. "That was different. Anyone could see the guy was bonkers over you."

"This time it's me looking at you two. I think you should go for it."

She wanted to. Oh, how she wanted. To actually have a chance with Shep. The reasonable voice of her conscience told her no way. What would he want with a mother of two six-year-olds? At this point, she'd settle for a hot interlude. A quick roll in the hay. Romance would just be icing on the cake.

Would he consider it? Did she even tempt him? She was so frustrated. The caffeine did not help one bit.

"Shep is kind and considerate. A good Samaritan," she said on a sigh.

"You'll never know if you don't try."

"I really like him. What if I fall for Shep?"

"Wouldn't that be a good thing? You wanted your own boy toy—this is your chance to live your own fantasies."

"I'd love some hot sex," Tammy whispered. "Shep's just the guy to give it to me. But he's the type of guy I can see myself falling hard for. What if it's just a fling for him? I have my boys to consider."

"According to Mike, Shep doesn't date. You're the first woman he's shown an interest in. So maybe ..." Cassie shrugged while placing her lips over her straw.

"That's because he's helping me, or rather his brother is. Shep is getting caught in the middle."

"Shep likes you. If you want to sex things up, buy a matching bra and panty set."

Tammy frowned. "We're not at that point yet."

Cassie wiggled her eyebrows. "But you want to."

"Yeah. You're right. I'd like to entice him at least to the point where he might see my bra and panties. For now, he isn't even at the hand holding stage. Besides, they don't make matching lacy sets for a woman my size. These girls"—Tammy slightly mashed her boobs together with her arms—"need special handling."

"I'm glad to know someone with bigger boobs than me."

"The thing is, I pack the other curves to go with them."

"Why don't you take one step at a time? Go out with Shep. Then see what happens."

For all her talk about sex, Tammy couldn't be with a guy just for a sexual interlude. She might have been a tad wilder in college, but those days were long gone. Nowadays, she yearned to feel like a desirable woman. If Shep made a move, she would probably melt. She'd just have to hope her heart survived.

"You ready? I need to get going."

Cassie slung her purse over her shoulder and scampered in front of Tammy. "You can still buy sexy lingerie. How about red?"

"That would look just dandy with my red hair," Tammy said deadpan.

"You like pink. Get hot pink."

"Or maybe purple," she shot back just before she spun on her heel and walked right into a hard chest. Good thing she had a lid on her Frappuccino. "Oh, I'm sor—"

"Are you Tammy Michael?"

A large guy in a suit towered over her. She narrowed her eyes wondering how this man knew her name. She'd never seen him before, and he was standing way too close.

"Yes, I am."

"This is for you."

When he held out an envelope she automatically took it. A bad habit.

"You've just been served."

CHAPTER 18

The son-of-a-bitch did it.

Tammy stared at the papers in her hand, wanting to scream. Fury burned in her blood. She'd known Steve was up to no good. Even though she'd suspected he might try taking the boys, she never thought he'd actually do it. He'd filed for custody. That was enough to scare the living daylights out of her.

Her father had been the driving force behind her confidence. He'd shown all of his daughters how to be strong. She'd just forgotten it for a while. The last two years she'd done fine. Now her stability was being threatened again.

She should have expected this from Steve. Still, it rankled. And the first person she wanted to run to—Shep. Not Cassie.

Cassie was as close to Tammy as her sisters. The best friend any girl could have. At least Cassie had been there when that suit had handed Tammy—no, served her—the custody subpoena. Cassie had been supportive, but she wasn't the one Tammy needed right now. She wanted Shep and no one else.

She jumped in her car and drove, longing for his comfort, and safety. *Shep.* He'd been there for her. Whether she wanted to talk, cry, pull her hair out, his low voice and his smooth drawl eased her tension and calmed her fears to a reasonable level that she could think.

At the end of the long drive stood a huge log house with rock pillars on the porch, and a large window centered directly above in the A-frame top. She could appreciate its beauty more so now. The last time she'd been here, the boys had been with her, she'd barely had a chance to take it all in.

Shep. Her inner compass brought her to his door. He was strong, confident, everything she was not at this moment. The man who made her customary boldness vanish waited in that house. At least she hoped so. His SUV was parked out front, so he had to be here somewhere.

Being near him made her feel safe, and she desperately needed him to be in charge. Like the night of her intoxication. He'd taken her home and put her to bed. He watched over her. Tended to her. He'd been considerate, compassionate. She could use some of that right now.

He made her think of things long denied her. Like passion. She hadn't had sex since ... since way before her marriage dissolved. It wasn't likely she'd have sex anytime soon. Not with the dreamy fireman anyway.

Her cheeks heated. Why in the world was she thinking of sex now? Her courage was failing fast.

Get a grip.

Good Lord, she should have called. But she'd been so shocked, so overwhelmed, she'd had no idea if she was coming or going.

Since she had acted without thinking and her car was sitting in front of his house, she couldn't very well drive off. She jerked the car door open and climbed out. Just then, Hutch came loping from the side of the house.

"Hey, boy. How are you doing?" If she hadn't already met Shep's dog, she'd be scared by his size alone. There was no doubt in her mind he could tear up an intruder. But she and the Malamute had made friends. He nuzzled her hand like a big old teddy bear.

"Where's your master? He around back?"

Tammy followed Hutch back down the same path he'd come from. As she rounded the corner of the house, her jaw dropped. Her body temperature skyrocketed and it had nothing to do with the sun or the weather.

Shep stood there, swinging an ax. He looked just like a hero on the cover of one of her romance novels. Rough, rugged, and bare from the waist up. Unable to move, she stared. And stared. From his sweaty shoulders down a damn fine, chiseled chest. The ax came down and she noticed the tattoo on his arm. A lion's head. And underneath some kind of bird or feathers. She'd never pictured Shep as a tattoo kind of guy.

Could the man get any sexier?

Her mouth hung open, so she quickly snapped it shut. Even her dreams had not measured up, or created a likeness as tantalizing as the mortal before her. No vision in her mind came near to the provocative picture she presently saw. Her stomach fluttered as if a whole cocoon of butterflies lived there.

"I wondered who was out front. Since Hutch didn't bark, I figured it had to be someone he knew."

"Me," she managed to croak.

"Good day for chopping wood."

She swallowed, her throat dryer than the Sahara Desert.

He continued, "With the temperatures dropping, I'll be needing it."

He swiped a towel around his neck and chest. Tammy told herself to breathe as her gaze followed the movement. Oh, how she envied that towel. She'd like to be draped over him, around him, rubbing up against that glistening, rock-hard body.

"Come on in," he said, stepping to the porch. His sexy tread reminded her of the graceful gait of a big cat. Her eyes devoured; she'd already swallowed her tongue. His muscles rippled as he lifted a shirt from a hook on a post and covered those mouth-watering abs. The pain in her lungs reminded her once again, she needed to breathe.

Good Lord, she probably looked like an idiot, standing there all agog. But damn, she never got to see anything this delicious. She forced herself not to stumble and make a complete fool of herself, knowing there wasn't a chance in hell he hadn't noticed her reaction.

She stiffened her resolve. What did it matter? The guy was hot. A woman couldn't help but get turned on.

She stepped past him as he held the door. Even all sweaty, he smelled like wood and all man.

"What were you doing with your shirt off? It's October?" She'd gotten some of her control back and then she had to go and mention his naked, sweaty, chiseled six-pack.

"The temperature might be cool, but as you can see, I worked up a sweat."

Oh, yeah. She'd seen.

Shep gently wrapped his fingers around her wrist and tugged her to the side. Before she could react, he closed the door and pressed her back against it. His powerful hands, one on each side of her head, blocked her in. Even though a few inches separated his body from hers, she felt the heat. His beautiful gray eyes held her immobile, hypnotized, mesmerized. He leaned closer. She licked her lips.

His eyes turn hot, molten. She braced her hands against the wood at her back, needing something solid to hold on to. Her chest rose and fell in anticipation. He didn't ask to kiss her. He just leaned in and put his mouth over hers, his lips soft, yet firm. She released a little sigh.

God, she'd dreamed of this. His kiss. Then there was no more thought, as Shep took possession of her mouth, kissing her slowly and thoroughly.

All too soon, he pulled back.

"Why are you here?" his low voice rumbled.

"Uh ... I forgot."

He chuckled, shooting a wave of pulsations through her chest.

"Why did you do that?" she dared to ask him.

"You looked like you needed it."

Then, just as unexpectedly, he backed away.

"Why don't you make yourself comfortable while I go put on a dry shirt?"

She sagged against the door, unable to do anything but watch him swagger up a wooden stairway. She wasn't sure her legs could hold her. If she wasn't so overwhelmed, she'd think she imagined it. She touched her fingers to her lips. *No.* Shep's touch had burned to her core.

Wow. Just wow.

For the first time, she noticed a fire in the big stone fireplace. She moved toward the flames, still feeling the impact of his kiss. A cozy setting. Even if it had not been intentional, the scene in his home was romantic. The crackling fire in the hearth, the smell of burning wood gave a cozy ambiance. He kept a neat house. Blankets adorned the masculine leather and wood furniture. Large pieces, lots of wood, and she was sure some were antiques.

Tastefully done in blue and brown and cream, his home had the décor of the outdoors, more so than any appearance of a man cave. His taste in furniture felt comfy, relaxed. Just like the man. Shiny, thick wood beams crisscrossed the ceiling and framed the huge upper window. Long windows at the bottom of the stairs framed a panoramic view of the Blue Ridge Mountains that most people only dreamed about.

She strode to the door and tugged at the laces of her boots.

"You don't need to take off your boots," Shep said as he descended the stairs. "Believe me, these floors have taken some harsh traffic. And with Hutch, I don't worry about my floors."

Normal. She needed to act normal. As if the kiss had not completely shaken her to her bones. She needed to appear unaffected. Not let him see how much she hoped he would kiss her again.

"Your place looks very tidy."

"I give it a good scrub every once in a while. I like clean," he said, rolling his sleeves up a turn. "Habit. No sense in riding the guys to keep the station spotless if I don't practice what I preach."

This man impressed her more every day. Nerves made her ramble. "Your home is lovely, but you know that. I may have already told you. Oh, well. It's worth repeating. It's fabulous."

"I don't know about that."

"Are you kidding? It's huge. I mean, look at this kitchen."

"Tammy. Take a breath. It's just a house."

She needed to fill her lungs with air, probably needed an oxygen tank after his surprise kiss. Had his lips really been on hers?

"When I'm nervous, I prattle."

"Are you nervous?"

How'd you guess? Anxious. Panicky. Desperately wanting him to kiss her again.

"Uh, a little," she fudged.

He stepped closer. "You have no reason to be nervous."

Her head was spinning. Between his deep voice and his sexy drawl, goosebumps pebbled on her skin. She thought he was going to kiss her again. She hoped he would kiss her again. A good soul-searing whopper.

He blinked. "A nice glass of ice tea is just what I need. But as you said, it's cold."

"Not in here," She muttered. After that kiss, she might never be cold again.

Hearing her, he grinned, and his eyes sparkled in understanding. "How about something to drink. Hot or cold?"

"Hot please. Coffee is fine."

"I've got hot chocolate."

"That would be awesome. Chocolate is my weakness."

"Mine, too." Shep laughed that soft, gut-rolling sound. Her belly did a little flip. His growled.

"I worked through lunch. Will you join me?"

Now this was right up her ally. Being in any kitchen came as natural as breathing to her. And this gave her the very thing she needed to behave naturally. "Only if I can make you lunch."

"You're my guest. But I won't turn down your help."

She followed him around the island. He stopped and met her eyes.

"Can I get the milk or do you have instant?" she asked, ready to jump right in. "Want me to boil some water?"

"Nope. I'll do it." He grasped her hips and easily lifted her onto the center island. Stunned, she grabbed his shoulders. The breath shot out of her lungs. "You just sit there and look pretty."

Sit—she could do. Pretty—if he thought so. But breathing—impossible.

She didn't know whether to grab him or close her mouth, which most likely hung open in shock. His wink started her mind working again. *Damn.* He'd had his hands on her and she sat there like a deer that had been caught in a car's headlights. Twice he'd touched her. Flabbergasted her. Then went about his business as if it was an everyday occurrence.

If her heart could stand these little shocks, she could get used to this.

He moved about as a man obviously used to culinary skills. She enjoyed watching him in his space. He looked as comfortable as she did in her own home. You had to love a man that took charge in a kitchen. And in other things.

Being around someone with so much strength … A man who knew his own mind, what he wanted and acted on it. She could still feel the pressure of his hands on her hips. Shep had lifted her as if she weighed nothing.

He drew water and placed a glass measuring cup in the microwave. When he reached for a box of chocolate mix, his muscles bunched, pulling the back of his shirt taut. Her mouth watered.

"Afraid it's instant," he said. "I cook. But being a bachelor, I have some quick, easy stuff, too."

Quick. Easy. Right. The hot chocolate.

A bell dinged and Shep poured hot water into two mugs. Then he turned to her. Her breath caught in her throat. Was he going to touch her again?

"Now. What would you like?"

You.

"Uh …"

"Do you have time to stay for dinner or do you have to get the boys?"

No. She was certain Steve had purposefully made sure he had the twins when she was served custody papers. He must have expected her to go off the deep end.

"Steve has the boys for the night."

"Want to tell me what put that look on your face, or you want to eat first?"

So, Shep had sensed her mood, although she shouldn't be surprised. He connected with her, showed an interest in her thoughts. Something Steve had never done.

"What I'm thinking should kill my appetite."

"Hmmm. Maybe I can entice you with steak and baked potatoes? I picked up a few and haven't had a chance to freeze them yet. I like them better fresh. Your timing is perfect."

"Steak sounds wonderful."

"Great." He opened a cabinet. "How about some cheese and crackers to tide us over?"

"With hot chocolate? I'd rather have marshmallows."

"Marshmallows it is." He took a bag from another cabinet, then poured the white fluffs into a bowl. "We can drink our cocoa by the fire."

Before he had a chance to lift her—whether he intended to or not—she hopped down from the counter. His brow arched, and she suspected he had been planning exactly that. A tingle shot up her back.

She grasped her mug and padded to his living-room space. She liked the open floor plan of the entire lower level. The stone fireplace, couch and chairs, wood furniture she wondered if he'd made by hand. She took a closer look at the kitchen table, island, and the long counter with cabinets.

"Did you build your house?"

"Yes, I did. Every stone, every log."

"I like your open floor design."

"Less construction. And I like wide open spaces."

She took a seat on the sofa and inwardly smiled when he sat beside her. He handed her the bowl, then filched three marshmallows and plopped one into his mouth. Even his chewing was sexy.

"Are you going to tell me why you're here?" Shep got right to the point. No beating around the bush.

"Can I just drop in for a visit?"

"Anytime," he said in that long, smooth drawl. "But something tells me there's a reason. Whatever the motive, I'm glad you came to my home."

Tammy chewed on her bottom lip and his gut twisted. He wanted to reach over, jerk her onto his lap and nibble those lips again. He'd known Tammy would taste sweet. And tantalizing. Still, he'd couldn't help giving in to his temptation. The only way he'd managed to maintain control of himself was by planting his hands on the door. Touching her with just his mouth was more than enough to fire his lust. If he'd wrapped his arms around her, he might not have come up for air. Might not have let Tammy go.

The woman was irresistible.

His instincts told him this was not a social call. He never ignored his gut. Tammy wrapped her arms around herself, unconsciously lifting her breasts that already rose with her fitful breathing.

"Are you cold? It gets chilly out here in the country."

"No. I'm okay."

Obviously, she was not.

"You can talk to me about anything. I hope you know that."

Her gaze flashed to his. "I do. You're kind and sweet."

He lifted his mug. "It's the chocolate." He liked seeing her smile.

"You make me feel at ease. Just like that. 'It's the chocolate.'," she mimicked. "You always know what to say to make me feel better."

"So, there is a reason for this visit?"

She worried her lip with her teeth. "I received a court summons for custody today."

Damn it. He'd known Tammy long enough to know her kids were her world. Her ex was an asshole and had just proved it.

"You were expecting it, but it was still a shock?"

"Yeah. Something like that. I knew. I mean I suspected. But I kept hoping he wouldn't do it."

"I'll help you through this," he said, taking her hand. He would. He meant every damn word. If he got a chance, he'd help her ex right into his fist. But that wouldn't solve anything.

"I guess that's why I came here. I knew you would. You do. You actually do more than help. You give me strength."

That made him feel good. "Did you call Eddie?"

She shook her head. "No. Cassie was with me. A man in a suit walked right up to me in Starbucks. He had to know who I was. Asked me if I was Tammy Michael then said, 'you've been served'."

"Starbucks? Your ex must have provided a photo." He'd had her watched. Stalked. Shep's veins filled with disgust.

"I hate to think of Steve spreading my picture around." Tammy's dismal voice grabbed Shep in his gut.

He didn't like it either. The idea of her ex flashing Tammy's photo about in public as if she was a criminal. Who else had the bastard showed it to?

Tammy popped a marshmallow into her mouth, then tried to hide behind her hand while she chewed. *Adorable.*

"Man, these are good. I love the chewy texture."

He grabbed two more for himself, pleased that her spirit had returned. She didn't need to dwell on her asshat of a husband. "I can get some hangers if you want to toast them."

"Really? In the house?"

"What's a fireplace for if you can't do the things over a fire that you can do outside?" He gathered kabob skewers instead. "Here. This should do the trick."

Together, they added the marshmallows to the rods and roasted them over the fire. Tammy was such a good woman. She needed to have a little fun in her life and not the constant worry of losing her children. Something as simple as toasting marshmallows put that little girl glow on her face. And he was damn happy to share this with her.

"My brothers and I used to toast marshmallows over a fire," he told her. "We ate more charred black than white goo."

"You held them in the flames too long."

"Yeah." He chuckled. "But it was fun. My brothers, Roger and Billy, would burn theirs up for the hell of it. Then get mad when we ran out."

"I bet your mom had her hands full."

"She did with me and my brothers."

Tammy glanced up, meeting his gaze. "You sound like you had a happy childhood."

"Five boys? We were wild. But Mom could rein us in pretty easily. How about you? Fun childhood or sibling horror stories?"

"My mom and dad separated when I was little. They did terrible things to one another in the name of love and family. They pulled and pushed, ripping us all up in the process, each claiming that what they did was for us kids. They did not set a good example." She took a marshmallow and seemed to study it. "If my mom hated my dad so much, why did they ever get married? All they ever did was fight. He gave her what she wanted. After he moved out, he never came back to the house. Mom wouldn't allow it. She's Catholic, so they never divorced.

I don't know why. If I'd listened to my mom, I would never have had a relationship with my dad."

"But you did," he said softly.

"Yeah. As for thinking love can last forever, well, look at me. My mother lectured me about how my father pledged his love for her and he left. My ex promised me forever, and he left. Then she berated me when I divorced Steve."

"Because she doesn't believe in divorce?"

"She'd rather live alone. Not me. I wasn't about to spend the rest of my life shackled to a man who didn't want me. Ending things with Steve had been difficult, but for the best. My father would have beat the shit out of him."

Shep shared the same sentiment as her father.

"My dad was very protective of all his daughters. Too bad he didn't live long enough."

"Tell me about your sisters?"

"Bonnie and Vickie are twins, the oldest. Then Nora came a few years later."

"So, twins run in your family."

"Yeah, and they don't skip generations. Bonnie took care of me a lot and let me follow her around. Vickie was the wild one of the bunch. How about you and your brothers? Who's the oldest?"

"Eddie. Only by two years, but there are times he talks to me like I'm a baby."

"Older siblings do that. I bet you were a cute baby."

"You don't think I'm cute now?" He couldn't resist teasing her.

"I didn't say that. Since you're fishing—"

"Fishing? Woman, when I fish I use a line and some bait."

"I've never heard you use a line," she mocked. "As for bait ..."

"Yes. Go on." When she hesitated, he coaxed her to continue. Playful Tammy he liked. Shy Tammy made him want to push her. Draw her out where she hid no secrets from him.

"I have a few other words I'd use instead of cute."

His breathing slowed. "Such as."

"Fishing."

"That's not fishing."

"If you say so."

Damn, this woman kept him on his toes. He liked sparring with her. "I think your red hair generates your spunk."

"My hair? Spunk, huh. You ain't seen nothing yet."

That's what he wanted to see. Feisty Tammy. Not sad or troubled Tammy.

"You're distracting me from the topic."

He liked distracting her. "I've already forgotten the topic."

"Cute. You're not a baby anymore."

He grunted. "Not by a long shot."

She glanced up at the top of his head. "A few threads of silver."

"Everyone in my family grayed early."

"You think it makes you look old. Far from it. It's distinguished looking."

He raised his mug. "I'll take it."

Her fingers flittered through a few strands at his temple. He felt the tingle all the way to his gut. The woman didn't have a clue what she did to him.

"It's only a few sprinkled here and there. Besides, I think it's sexy." Her hand smacked over her mouth and her eyes grew wide.

He grinned. "Sexy, huh?"

"Well, that horse charged right out of the barn. Yes, Shep. I think you're sexy. Now are you happy?"

Very.

He sipped cocoa and kept his gaze on her.

"What you said about my red hair is true. It's gotten me into more scrapes. I have a bad habit of blurting out what I'm thinking. No filter."

He gave in to the grin tugging at his lips. "I like a woman that says what she thinks. Better than being all shifty and flighty and expecting a man to read her mind."

"You're not unobservant. I think you can read a woman quite well."

"Is that so?" He narrowed his lids, searching under her layers. Although he'd suspected her attraction all along, he hadn't detected anything more than interest.

Until that kiss.

Pure magnetism.

Tonight, Tammy needed his friendship. She'd had a shock. It made him feel good that she'd come to him. Whether she knew it or not, she was vulnerable. No matter how much he wanted her, he would not take advantage.

CHAPTER 19

Thirty, smirty. At the moment, Tammy felt like a teenager. Having a man's attention made her feel young again, and she was far from an old woman. Most considered thirty to be the prime of their life. Even forty. So, she figured she was just getting started. Shep made her giddy beyond belief. He'd shocked her, pinning her to the door and kissing her. A flash of desire had barely begun, a hint of need that was quickly ripped away. Only a few seconds, but enough to whet her appetite for a whole lot more.

They'd talked for hours. Had a divine dinner, then said goodnight. He'd walked her to her car, stared at her as if he could devour her, then tucked her inside and sent her home. Which was probably for the best. She'd been on an emotional roller coaster since she'd received the custody subpoena. Not a time to hop into the sack with a hot firefighter, no matter how much she'd wanted to. When she and Shep got to that point—and she hoped they would, knew they would—she could do so with a clear head. She respected him all the more for recognizing that.

Tonight would be her first date since her divorce. She wanted to forget the things she wanted to forget. With so much trouble from her ex, she needed a break for one night.

Cassie was the sweetest person in the world, and her sibling was nothing like her. Her sister believed money grew on trees. Or men, anyway. But Jennifer did like children, and she'd offered to take the twins for the evening. The boys liked Cassie's sister and she had promised them movie night. They loved dressing up like the characters in the movie, and then watch the film.

After dropping the boys off, Tammy hurried home and got ready for her dinner date with Shep. He would arrive in thirty minutes and she still hadn't decided what to wear.

It had been so long since she'd dressed to impress a man. Between being a third-grade teacher and raising two six-year-olds, casual had been the way to go. She didn't own anything sexy.

She dug in the back of her closet and found a few dresses she'd forgotten about. *Crap. Twenty minutes.* She prayed they would fit. She jerked the green one from the hanger and tugged it over her head. As she smoothed it over her hips, she glanced in the mirror. It fit her perfectly and the color matched her eyes. She must have lost a few pounds. Even though it was shorter than she remembered, she couldn't help but feel good.

Another glance at the clock showed she had no time to spare. She added a touch of makeup—she hardly ever wore any—and finger combed her hair. The shorter cut was much easier to care for.

Just as she grabbed her purse, she heard the purr of an engine outside. She peeked through the curtain of her front window and saw Shep's Land Rover. Then damn near swallowed her tongue as he climbed out of the driver's side.

The man was definitely one of a kind. She hurried to open the front door.

Standing on her doorstep, Shep looked good enough to eat. She put her tongue back in her mouth and told herself to breathe.

"Hi."

"Hi," he said in that sexy drawl.

"Come in." She stepped back and inhaled his woodsy scent as he walked by.

"Smells good in here. You've been baking."

"I made a birthday cake for one of the teachers. It's cooling on the racks and when I get home tonight, I'll add the icing."

"Tonight?"

That's what she normally did. By his expression, maybe he'd imagined something else. Maybe he wasn't planning on bringing her home. Maybe he wanted her to stay with him. Or maybe his intention was to make wild, passionate love to her when he brought her home. In that case, hell with the cake.

Right. Her imagination was on overdrive.

"I keep late hours," she said as if she needed to explain. "I do a lot of my decorating after the boys go to bed. If I worked on my cakes with them around, there'd be more eating than baking, and I'd lose a lot of business.

"You have a cake business?"

"Not really. I love baking, and a lot of people like my cakes. Someone is always asking for a birthday cake or one for a special occasion like a party or celebration. I've even done wedding cakes."

He shook his head. "I don't know how you have time. Teaching all day and taking care of two boys. That has to take up most of your day. Unless you don't sleep."

"I sleep. Like the dead. I'm exhausted by the time I get in bed." Talking about the bedroom gave her other ideas. A dangerous topic with a sexy man. "I enjoy baking. Although I do spend a lot of hours on the road taking David and Christopher to the scout hut or T-Ball."

"And yet you made time for me."

The way he said it sent chills racing over her skin.

"Thank you," he said in his low sexy drawl.

She blinked, her body melting into a puddle of goo. She was quickly falling under his spell. She prayed with all her heart this was real.

"You look beautiful."

Her breath caught. "I haven't heard that in years."

"You should hear it every day."

Damn her pale complexion. Her face must be beet red, now. "Thanks, but you don't need to compliment me."

"Not compliment a beautiful woman? It would be a crime not to. Ready to go?"

He opened the passenger door for her, just like a real gentleman. She couldn't remember Steve ever doing that for her. Even when the twins were born, he let her fend for herself.

The smell of leather and wood hovered. Confined in the smaller space, she could enjoy the cologne he'd used sparingly. She buckled her seatbelt and glanced over, briefly catching him in profile. Damn, the man was drop-dead gorgeous. Why hadn't he been scarfed up by some woman? Her gaze drifted lower to his molded chest. She wondered if it was as hard as it looked. When he'd trapped her to the door, he'd only touched her with his lips.

He turned the key and the engine roared to life. Then he gripped the steering wheel, drawing her attention to his long fingers. Strong fingers. Nice hands. Her heart did a crazy little leap.

In minutes, he pulled into a lot she recognized. The Mexican restaurant where she'd first laid eyes on him and a whole bunch of firefighters.

"I know you like Mexican."

"It's my favorite spot."

"Wait for me."

She frowned. *Huh?* "Where are you going?"

He grinned. "I'm coming around to get you."

Oh.

He opened the passenger door and took her hand, helping her out. Funny how something so simple as holding hands could delight her so.

A hostess seated them and gave them menus, another one brought chips and salsa. She'd been here a dozen times with Cassie, but tonight everything seemed different. Aware of the man sitting across from her, she supposed, made her more conscious of her surroundings.

"Did you notice me, that night?" she asked, meaning the night the entire fire department had shown up.

"How could I not?"

She just wanted to sigh. "Yeah. I guess you saw Jared and me … uh…"

"Flirting?" he supplied with a teasing grin. "Couldn't help that either."

"I feel really embarrassed."

"Why?" He laid down his menu. "The two of you were having fun. You and I had fun at the *Pitt Stop*."

"That was different."

A sexy brow hiked up. "How was that different?"

Was he kidding? He and Jared were as different as night and day. Of course, she'd flirted with Jared. In fun. Being with Shep went to a whole dissimilar level. "Well, with Jared I was just goofing around."

"And with me?"

"With you ..." How could she tell Shep flirting with him was so much more than just playing around? She couldn't. "I was having fun." Well, that sounded lame.

His expression gave nothing away, but his eyes held a hint of mischief. She was beginning to think he liked flirting more than he let on.

"Having fun?" he coaxed.

She met his gaze. "You're a lot of fun. And I like you."

"You didn't like him?"

"Of course. He was too darn cute." Then she leaned forward as if she was about to reveal a secret. "I can spot a player a mile away. Jared was entertaining and nothing more."

His sexy lips curved into a huge grin. Evidently, she'd said the right thing.

"You know you're dangerous when you do that," she told him.

"Do what?"

"Give me that killer smile."

"Killer, huh?" Then he gave her the very grin she'd been talking about.

Lordy yes. A panty melting grin. It had been entirely too long since she'd gone out with a man. But Shep—why was he with her? "Can I ask you something?"

"Go ahead."

"What are you doing with me?" This time, both eyebrows hiked up to his hair line. "I mean, you're a handsome man. You could have any woman you want."

He laid down his menu and folded his hands over the top of it. "Maybe I don't want."

His eyes bore into hers, holding her captive. The intensity robbing her breath. She wanted to ask him to explain but feared his answer. *Don't rock the boat.*

"You are definitely the hottest man I've ever been with," she breathed. "Oh my God. I just said that out loud."

He leaned forward, and all she could do was stare at his lips. She couldn't form a coherent thought.

He gave her a wink.

A wink!

"You're a lovely woman. I enjoy your company. I like talking with you." He sat back, his eyes still locked with hers. And to use your own words, you're fun. I like you, too." He picked up a menu. "Let's order dinner, and later I'll see if I can answer your question more thoroughly."

***

Dinner was great, but the ride to Shep's place had been torture. Tammy spent the entire drive wondering about his comment. How would he answer her more thoroughly? Would he kiss her again? Would he do more than kiss her? Was she ready for this?

When he asked her to come to his house, she'd quickly agreed, not wanting the evening to end. She loved being with him, enjoyed his wit, loved listening to his low drawl, and man, was he easy on the eyes. But Shep made her feel good. She couldn't remember the last time she'd been so comfortable being with a man. She should stop thinking about what might happen and just enjoy his company.

Shep lit a fire and then offered her some wine. "I don't know much about wines, but I do like this Moscato d'asti. Slightly sweet." He held up a bottle for her to see.

"Sounds good."

He poured them each a glass and joined her on his comfy couch. She took a sip, enjoying the fruity flavor.

"Mmm, this is good. Not bitter."

"You like wine?"

"I'm more of a margarita girl. But I like this."

"I have very little alcohol in the house. I keep it on hand, but I normally drink tea or water."

"I've noticed you're not much of a drinker." The one time she'd seen Shep with a beer had been the night she'd gotten sloshed. He'd ordered shots, but she never saw him drink one.

"Never cared much for the stuff. I'm just as happy drinking water. Hydration."

"When the boys are gone, it's my chance to unwind. Sometimes Cassie and I go Mexican and I'll get a margarita. Mostly, I enjoy a glass of wine at home."

"Here's to not drinking alone."

"I'm all for that." She clinked his glass and then took a sip. Sitting by the fireplace in Shep's home, feeling the warmth from the flames, she was more relaxed than she'd been in a long while. The evening seemed perfect. Shep was perfect. And so easy to talk to. "When I was younger, my sister let me use her ID to get into clubs."

"You used a fake ID?"

"It wasn't fake. It just wasn't mine."

"That does make a difference," he said playfully. "Were you a wild teen?" His eyes glittered. Was it because he teased or was she reading more into his expression? Either way, being here felt cozy and right.

"Maybe."

"I can't imagine."

"Why?" she asked, shifting to face him.

"You seem so ... nice."

Nice?

If he wanted to discuss nice, Shep was the prime example. He'd been courteous, considerate ... *nice.*

When he'd bracketed her to his door, he'd shocked the shit out of her. Ever since that day, all she'd wanted was for him to kiss her again. A real, deep, gut-wrenching kiss. Was this man ever going to make a move?

"You're together," he continued. "Sensible. You're a mom."

"I wasn't always a mom." She remembered being young and liberated. A young woman with desires. She was older now, but she still had desires. "I was once a teenage girl. I wanted to see what the hoopla was about. I wouldn't say I was wild, but I went places with my friends. I drank some—what teen doesn't like to experiment? Mostly, I liked to dance. But I was a good kisser."

"You used your fake ID so you could kiss guys?"

"Didn't need to."

"Would you care to explain?" The flash in his eyes must have been her imagination. No way it could have been jealousy.

"We used to practice in my girlfriend's basement."

"We. As in, boys or girls?"

She smacked him on the arm.

"It's an honest question," he blurted in surprise. "You made it sound like you practiced with your girlfriends."

So much for being jealous.

"My *friend's* brother was two years older than me, and I had a crush on him. He took turns kissing all the girls." At the time, she'd been caught up in the new, exciting French kissing she'd learned. Young and stupid, she had wanted to experience everything.

"In your friend's basement."

She nodded.

"How old were you?"

"Thirteen, I guess."

"Which would have made him fifteen."

"Yeah. He nicknamed me Frenchie. Boy, I was proud of that title."

"I suppose that is in reference to French kissing?"

"Yep."

"All you did was kissing?" The tone of his voice suggested he was simply curious.

"Yeah. Then, he got a girlfriend. She was his age. When you're a teenager, age is a big deal. He started treating me like a kid."

"No more kissing?"

"I quit going back to their basement. Seeing him kiss her, well, it pissed me off. So, when I got older, I used my sister's ID to meet older guys."

"You used her ID because you wanted guys to think you were older?"

"That and to get into clubs. If my dad had caught me, he would have beat my butt. I got lots of practice."

"Kissing?"

"Yeah. I had no idea guys could kiss so different. Man, I found out."

"Lots of practice, huh?" His eyelids got all droopy.

"Lots," she replied with a sigh. "There's nothing better than a man who can kiss."

"Is that so?" His gaze lowered to her mouth. "Let's test that theory."

One of his hands grazed her neck, while those bright gray eyes stared intently into hers. She couldn't move. Couldn't breathe. Could only stare back. As if in a trance, she waited and then he drew her to him. As his mouth covered hers, she melted, slid into the kiss, slid into him.

A steel band slipped around her waist and crushed her to his chest. He kissed her with a hunger he'd obviously been holding back. Glorying in his taste, his passion, she matched his need. He groaned and pulled back just enough that his lips barely touched hers. "You're just like your cake and pudding creation. Sweet and mouthwatering."

She ran her fingers over his temple and through his short hair. She had wanted one of those kisses and he'd just melted her bones. The electrical charge still sizzled in her body.

He kissed her cheek, the corner of her mouth, then followed a trail down the vein in her neck. Her breathing grew heavy and she sighed with longing. She was swimming in a sea of passion. Wanting and craving and floating at the same time. His touch soothed, tingled, made her ache. Startled at the intense feelings, she burned with awareness, wanting more. Needing more.

He brought his mouth to hers again and she lost herself in it, in him, and the need to draw him closer. She clutched him tighter, their kiss growing more frantic. Suddenly he pulled back.

"Do you have any idea what you do to me?"

"I think I do," she whispered kissing the side of his mouth. Tammy wondered how he'd held out this long. How *she'd* held out this long.

His chest rumbled as a deep lustful moan vibrated up his throat. She dived into the heat, the energy they were creating. She was hungry. Hungry for sex. Her body had been denied for far too long.

CHAPTER 20

Tammy's smooth fingers swept along Shep's jaw, just before she tugged on his hair. Passionate Tammy. Adorable Tammy. He knew she'd be delectable, but he hadn't prepared for this woman to knock him on his axis. The barest taste and he was instantly hard.

The faint scent of chocolate teased his nose, the familiar fragrance that was *her* scent. One that would always belong to her. The tiniest whimper escaped as they ground their lips together. He devoured, slowly, torturously, taking his time. A slow glide of his tongue in her sinfully, delicious mouth and she responded with a suck. Arousal stabbed his chest. On the heels of delight, a fierce craving took over.

He wanted her to say his name in passion. He wanted her to plead and beg for his touch.

"You're beautiful," he murmured as he licked her neck. "It may be too soon, but I want you."

Her eyes lit up, making his pulse race. He was thirty-five and felt like a damned teen. Her hand dropped to his waist and she tugged harder, as if she was trying to erase any distance between them, while rolling her luscious breasts against him. It took all of his self-control not to grab her and hike her over to straddle his lap. He had to go slowly and learn exactly how much more she wanted.

He kissed her unhurriedly as his hand trailed over her collarbone and the fleshy top of her breasts, moving cautiously. She kissed him with a hunger to match the pulse beating wildly along the column of her neck.

"Do you have protection?"

For a split-second, he froze. He had to grasp his mind around the fact that she had taken the lead. Then he wondered how long it had been. He pulled back and saw she was embarrassed.

"You know what? I do." He rubbed his hands up and down her back, hoping to soothe any inhibitions she might have, and ease her discomfort.

"Good."

So much for him being in charge. Since they both had the same idea, there was no need for seduction. Still, foreplay was often the best part.

He kissed her again and felt the moment of her total surrender. Still, he wanted to hear her say it.

"Tell me you want me," he whispered.

"I want you. More than anything."

He stood, holding her hand and pulling her up beside him. Then he quickly bent down and swept her into his arms. She gasped.

"Shep. I'm too heavy for you. Put me down."

"Not a chance." Pride swelled in his chest. Since his promotion to captain, his active physical roll of fighting fires had been diminished. Being the one in charge, he assessed and commanded the crew, issuing orders and keeping abreast of the situation, although he still carried sixty-pound packs in the instance he needed to charge into a building. To stay in shape and keep his strength, he worked out at his home. In his barn, he'd attached ropes to high beams and a punching bag chained in one corner. So, hell yeah, he was ready to carry his woman.

His woman. He liked the sound of that. He was about to make her his. In every way.

Shep's scent flooded Tammy's senses. His abrupt action, carrying her up the wide stairway to his bedroom, was more arousing than anything she'd imagined. She'd seen the man was ripped, but now she felt the hard muscles beneath his clothing.

He gently placed her on the bed and sank down beside her. He smelled so good, felt so good, and when his hot gaze locked on hers, her insides quivered.

"If you want to stop at any time, it's okay."

The speed with which her body was ready for him astonished her. "Please Shep. Don't stop."

He cupped his hands around her face, diving his fingers in her hair, and kissed the tip of her nose. "My dearest woman, you are precious." He drew his tongue over her lip, drawing it between his teeth. She held her breath near to bursting. Nothing had ever felt so intoxicating. Never had she felt so desirable. Shep kissed her and caressed her as if he couldn't touch her enough.

She fell. Hard and fast. She wanted him. Wanted him with everything in her. Her hands on his chest, she twisted her fingers in his shirt.

"Do you mind if I help you get out of this dress?"

"Please," she whispered, without a coherent thought in her head.

He slid his fingers over her shoulder, slowly, provocatively, making her frenziedly aware of every inch of exposed skin. His fervent gaze scorched her flesh as he followed the movement. She had no idea being with a man could feel so sensuous.

He smiled, then together, they tugged at the confining material. She could tell her lacy red bra and panties caught him off guard. His eyes fastened on her breasts and he swallowed, hard. If she took off her bra, her girls would be all over the place. He seemed to sense her hesitation and leaned back, sliding a button through its hole on his shirt. Her nimble fingers took over the task and then he removed his pants.

She chewed on her tongue as Shep stood in his boxer briefs. Good Lord the man was bulging there as well. She shouldn't look, but damn it ... She couldn't help that she wanted everything this man had to give. Curious, she stared. He stood there, letting her. Giving her all the time she needed.

"Are you okay?"

She snapped her gaze to his. "I can't think. I can only feel."

He stepped to a drawer and took out a packet. She knew what it was and wondered if he kept a supply there, or if he'd bought them just for her. He caught her gaze. A lot of men wanted a skinny model and ignored a woman with meat on her bones. The way Shep's eyes devoured her, he liked what he saw.

His fingers lightly grasped her shoulders, pushing her back until her head rested on a pillow. His face and upper chest filled her vision, but all she saw was his eyes. His desire. His hunger. His adoration.

In that instant, she breathed in the raw masculinity of him. A feeling unlike any she'd ever known swarmed her body. A fierce longing threatened to consume her.

The kiss was deep, hungry. She didn't want gentle. He held himself on his elbows, but she wanted skin against skin.

Bending his head, he closed his lips over a nipple. The wetness of the fabric and the heat of his mouth made her shiver. As he continued his assault, she tugged on her bra straps, giving him a hint. He took it, making short work of removing the darn thing.

His mouth was back. Licking, fondling ... She shoved her hands into his hair, gripping restlessly. She arched and clamped her knees. Shep was slowly and maddeningly driving her crazy.

Cool air caressed her breasts as he moved down and slipped off her panties. She waited to see what he'd do next. He could do anything he wanted as long as he came back to her. He hooked his thumbs in the waistband of his boxers and with a yank, they were gone.

Fascinated, she stared. Glory God, he was magnificent. Her belly tingled with stabs of desire, and her woman's center ached. Her tongue darted out to run along her top lip, then she bit her bottom one.

"I'd let you touch me, but I don't think I would last."

Her gaze shot to his face and she noted the strain along his jaw. By his expression, he was hanging onto his control by a thread. The idea stirred her even more. She held her arms open in invitation and sighed as his skin heated hers.

She held him close as his hands wandered and fondled. The calloused fingers ran up her thighs, slowly, caressingly, setting her body on fire. The flat of his tongue licked her beaded nipple with one long stroke. Lightning ripped through her body. His hot breath created chills over her breasts and then he was suckling. His hands and lips were everywhere.

Then he touched her there, where she needed him to touch her. But it wasn't enough. It only fueled her desire. She needed more.

She whimpered.

"Want me to stop?"

"God no."

"Tell me what you want. How you want it."

"I don't know. I want this. I want you."

He touched her again, circling, stroking, sending her out of her mind. She thought she might die from the torture. She ran her hands over his skin, pressing hungry kisses on the side of his neck, fisting her hands in his cropped hair.

"Dear God," she moaned.

He thrust a finger and she opened her mouth to scream, yet no sound came out. Only a piercing quiet, with the scream lodged in her throat. Her orgasm was immediate, forcing its way across her belly and shooting down her legs. He gave her no time to recover before she felt him plunge.

She clung to him, her fingers digging into his back. One sensation after another fogged her mind.

He whispered something in her ear, that sounded like, "I can't hold back," but her brain was a mass of goo. The over-whelming emotions ran deep, her passion instilling only desire.

"I want it all," he growled. His silver eyes glittered as he stared down at her, watching, communicating, while he drove into her with long sure strokes. "I knew ... I knew you'd feel perfect."

Her heart fluttered, bursting with joy. He rocked, his thrusts growing faster, harder. Need speared her. She met him thrust for thrust. His urgency brought her quickly to the edge. Then, with a harsh grunt, he stilled, his body tense. He sucked in a sharp breath and then groaned long and low in his throat. She fell, and he fell with her. She gasped for air, her heart bursting with love. She'd never been so overwhelmed in her life.

She held him tight for a long time, while he struggled to regain his breath.

His forehead heavy on hers, he opened his eyes. What she saw made her melt all over again. All she could do was stare back and wonder if the expression on her face revealed what she was feeling at this moment.

"I didn't even know it was possible," she murmured.

"To have an orgasm?"

"No." He might be teasing, but she'd never been more serious. "To feel like this. To be wanted this much."

"So, I've taken care of any doubts?" his low voice rumbled. She loved the sound.

"No doubts. I will say this. When you set your mind to make love to a woman, you pull out all the stops."

He pressed his lips to hers so tenderly, she thought she might cry. Shep made her feel as if she was the only woman in the world. The only woman he wanted.

She trusted Shep. That frightened her.

"I'm too heavy for you."

"No, you're not." Her instinct made her clutch him, but she didn't want to appear a clinging, desperate female. Reluctantly, she let him go. He gathered her close, bringing her head to his chest. He rubbed her back, making her feel cherished. No words needed between them.

In such a short time, she'd come to care for him deeply. She'd fantasized for a while, but tonight, the depth of her feeling rocked her to her soul. She cuddled into his side, fighting back tears.

She'd gone and fallen in love with Shep.

Was he her soulmate? She'd heard the saying. Listened to others' claims. Believed it to be true until she'd married Steve. Then she thought her chance had passed. Now she knew what the term meant.

She was sure Shep cared for her. He'd made love to her as if he did love her. If she were a betting woman, she'd put her money on the chance that he did.

But then, hadn't she already gambled?

***

Tammy jerked awake. The sound of Shep's steady breathing eased her alarm, lulling her back into total relaxation. She was in his house, his bed. She wanted to snuggle and wondered if she could do that without waking him.

The sun's rays trickled in through the long glass pane above the double window. Had the sun ever shined so bright? This reminded her of her college years, a young, foolish girl who'd just found out what sex was all about. Then she'd married and thought her sex life complete. True, she had abstained these last two years, but she'd had no idea what she'd been missing. She glanced to the sleeping man beside her. It was not a dream.

Her lips lifted with affection as she recalled Shep's gentle touch and how he'd played her body like an instrument. A tingling of awareness grew anew. Her heart warmed just to be near him. To remember the evening, their lovemaking and realize she was in love. She had no poetic words to describe their night of raging passion. But she knew the way she felt—the way she was sure he felt—had to be the reason for her euphoric mood.

And, *oh my God*, the orgasms. She'd had them before, but definitely not like last night. The earth had moved. No doubt about that. She closed her eyes and smiled.

"Do I have anything to do with that?"

Her eyes flew open and she saw Shep staring at her.

"Uh, what?"

"That smile on your face."

Caught. Damn her blushing. When would it stop?

She rolled to her side, her smile growing bigger. "It sure is."

He wrapped his arms around her, pulling her in and she snuggled, just like she'd wanted. She inhaled his own special scent, all man. The hair on his chest tickled her breasts. After last night, she was more aware of her body. Shep had brought nerves to life she didn't know she had.

"How are you this morning?" he murmured, his lips in her hair.

"I'm fine," she answered, tracing his delectable tattoo. "How are you?"

"I'm asking if you're okay."

She lifted her head, meeting his gaze. "Why wouldn't I be?"

"Just checking to make sure you don't have regrets."

Was he nuts? "Do you?"

"I could never regret making love to the most beautiful woman in the world."

"Now I know you've lost your mind."

He frowned "I'm serious."

She snuggled back into his warmth. "I'm not beautiful."

"You are to me," he said, giving her a squeeze. "And yes, you are beautiful. Inside and out. Look at that blaze of fire you wear on your head."

My hair? "Since it's attached, I don't have a choice."

"You could change the color, but I'd be heartbroken if you did. And what about your perfect body?"

"Hardly perfect," she quietly argued.

"Hmm. Let me guess. Forty double D?"

"Try forty double E."

"I didn't know they made them that size."

She punched his arm. He cuddled her closer, sliding his hands down her back. "You have a tiny waist."

She laughed out loud. Maybe it seemed that way to him because of her chest size. "My waist is not tiny."

"Perfect for my hands to grasp you." He did. She giggled. "And then there are those curvy hips."

His fingers curved over her backside, making her glad she worked out. "I walk on the treadmill at least twice a week. I should do it three times."

"Must be why you have such toned thighs." He ran his hand down her leg.

"I better." Even though she'd grumbled, her efforts had paid off.

"You have a beautiful body. And flawless skin."

"I have freckles."

"Not many. Besides, they're cute."

"Cute?"

"Adorable." He kissed her nose.

She loved this playful side of Shep. She had an idea people didn't see it much. "Do you think compliments will get your way with me?"

"I sure hope so. Is it working?"

She nodded.

He placed his knuckle under her chin and lifted. "Then let me give you more."

"I don't need more compliments."

"Is that so?" His voice lowered. "Tell me what you do need."

"You," she said, sliding her hand up his splendid chest.

"I think I can manage that."

"Oh, you definitely have what it takes."

"In that case ..." His voice drifted off as he spread a trail of open-mouth kisses down her neck, his breath hot and scalding, triggering electrical charges zinging through her system. Shep had awakened a height of desire inside her that she had no idea she could reach. His soft caresses were rousing her again, bringing her passion roaring back to life.

She slid her hand down his belly and he groaned, the rumble reverberating along her body. His mouth opened on a growl and he sucked her tongue inside.

"Mmmm," she moaned, rolling deeper into him. God, she loved how he responded to her touch. She loved knowing she jacked him up. Her hand dipped lower and gripped his burgeoning erection, loving the feel of silk and steel on her fingertips. He took her mouth with urgency, then when he needed air, he broke the kiss, yet pulled on her lower lip with his teeth.

His moans drove her further, making her brazen. She stroked, caressed, even toyed with his balls. His body taut, his breathing grew harsh and he groaned like a man in pain. The more excited he got, the more she played.

"You're driving me crazy," he gasped, grasping her hand. "I want this to last. I feel like I've waited forever, and now that I have you, I want to hold you and touch you, and keep touching you."

He made good on his promise. He kissed and caressed and loved every inch of her body. When she thought she couldn't wait any longer, he quickly sheathed himself, and then plunged inside.

Pleasure exploded, launching a tidal wave of sensation through her veins. Every cell shattered with ecstasy. He rode the wave, and a few driving thrusts later, he fell over the edge with her.

She held him tight, unable to let go. Emotions came at her from every direction. A flood of feelings new to her. Passion beyond anything she'd ever experienced. Joy beyond anything she'd imagined. A deep, powerful love she had no idea was possible.

"You are so precious," he whispered.

Tears burned her eyes. Happiness seared her soul. Did he love her? He showed his feelings in so many ways. The arms that held her tight, the kisses that took her breath, the desperate way he made love, the words he'd just uttered ...

Whether Shep loved her or not, she would savor every delicious second she spent in his arms.

***

There was something about the open space late at night when the evening was not altogether quiet. The bristling breeze stirred Shep's senses, yet he was calmed by the tranquil dark as the shadows took over. Crickets sang their songs, leaves danced along the ground. It didn't get any better than this. Except, he was alone.

He'd never minded living alone. He had his dog and his job kept him busy. He liked coming home to the peaceful countryside. And on nights like tonight, the quiet serenity gave him plenty of time to think.

Of his future.

He leaned on the rail that ran along the edge of his porch. A full moon cast a halo over the forest of trees and draped the mountain's peak in shadow. He inhaled a satisfying breath, appreciating the expanse that belonged to him. All he needed was someone to share it with. And that someone could be Tammy.

Watching her boys playing in his backyard had given him ideas. The twins had obviously been happy romping around with his dog, and Hutch loved the attention. The smile on Tammy's face had been priceless. It warmed his heart and filled a void that had been empty for a long time. He imagined Tammy and her boys in his home. In his life. On a regular basis. A permanent one, if he could swing it.

Hutch lazily brushed his head against Shep's leg. He dropped his hand over the dog's head for a dutiful rub.

"Okay, fella. I guess we've been out here long enough."

He opened the door and stepped inside, the backwash from the fireplace lighting his way. Hutch's paws padded on the wood, following Shep through the kitchen. He drew fresh water and placed the bowl on the floor.

"Last drink of the night, fella."

He had his dog.

But he craved a woman.

Making his way to the bedroom, he stripped off his clothes, hung them on a chair, and then crawled into bed. For all the good it did. He lay awake thinking of fiery red hair draped over his pillow.

CHAPTER 21

Life was good. If Shep had to say so himself, he'd say great. The best it could be, if Tammy's ex would leave her alone.

The asshole had her wound tighter than a coiled spring ready to snap. The man called her every time Shep was with her, demanding to see the boys—which he didn't need to insist upon because she was already kissing his ass. Damn, it burned Shep up the way Tammy catered to her ex's every whim. The bastard was not going to drop the custody case, so she should stand her ground.

Shep didn't want to add to her burden, so he kept his mouth shut. Still, he fumed at the way Steve had her jumping at every tone on her phone. Tammy needed something good to occupy her mind for a bit. Shep decided a cookout was just the thing.

He invited the team, and other firefighters who could make it, to his home for a barbeque. There'd be enough people, food, and conversation to hold Tammy's attention. And he'd pocket her damn phone. If her ex called, the asshat could leave a message. If there was an emergency, he could leave a message. And Shep would check it out. Steve would not bother Tammy today.

Laredo and Cooper strolled up the walkway carrying a cooler.

"Hey, Cap," Laredo called. "Got the Bud on ice."

"Want one, Cap?" Cooper lifted the lid.

"Maybe later." Shep gestured to the bottle of water sitting beside the grill. Chicken and steak was on the menu today. For most of his barbeques, he cooked a hog on the roaster. He didn't want to overwhelm Tammy with a large crowd of people she didn't know. Not when she was already under stress.

Of course, Cassie and Mike would be here. Tammy had already met his team. As for the others, a few volunteers and their wives. Given Tammy's personality, she should fit right in. Elf had a boy two years old. Maybe his wife would want some pointers from Tammy.

As if conjuring up his dream, Tammy stepped onto the back porch. His entire world lit up every time he saw her. He'd never known such a feeling and he hoped it would never die out. Tammy's eyes found him and she smiled, setting his insides on fire.

There had been no repeat of the night she'd spent with him. If he'd known it was going to be so long before he would have her in his bed again, he might not have let her out. Damn, the woman was fine. Everything he wanted. Exactly the kind of woman he'd dreamed and hoped and prayed for.

He could feel a tightening and figured he'd better think of something else real quick. Wouldn't do to be sporting wood at a cookout.

She rose on her toes and he leaned down so she could place a kiss on his jaw. Damn, her lips were soft. He got a whiff of her scent, sugar and maybe strawberry. What he wouldn't give to toss her over his shoulder and take her upstairs.

"What can I do for you?" As always, Tammy offered to help.

"You've done enough. I need to keep an eye on the grill. If you just want to hang out and look pretty ..."

She smiled her sweet smile and he wanted badly to kiss her. "I'll mingle."

He watched her backside as she ambled over to the guys.

For weeks, Tammy's head had pounded with worry, and she'd chewed her fingernails down to the skin. So, when Shep told her about the cookout, she was excited. Desperate to grab any chance of normalcy, she'd figured the gathering would be a source for her to release some tension. She had looked forward to socializing with Shep's friends.

Cooper was bending over retrieving beers from a cooler, then handed one to Laredo. With their backs turned, Tammy slipped next to Laredo.

"Hello, handsome."

"Hola, Hermosa."

"What does that mean?" she asked.

"It's either sexy or sweetheart." Cooper piped up, then pointed a thumb at Laredo. "I'm learning from hanging around this guy."

From a sexy Latino? She could imagine Cooper was learning plenty. "You speak Spanish a lot?" she asked Laredo.

"When I'm around my family."

"Or he's hitting on a chick," Cooper added.

"Callate."

Cooper sniggered. "Think I'll wander over there."

"As I was saying, sometimes it comes out natural. At my mother's, it's faster and gets the point across. With all the shouting that goes on, it's easy to drift into the lingo."

"Shouting?"

"So many of us trying to talk at the same time. *Madre* would think something was wrong if we did not shout."

"So, you're from where? Spain? Mexico?"

"Forgive my manners. I'm holding a cold drink and you have none. How about a beer? We have a cooler full."

"Shep has a huge tub over there."

"Why leave my side, when you can stay?" Laredo's mouth curved up in a leering grin. His accent, his charm … Oh yeah. He was definitely Latino.

"I have no idea why I didn't think of that. Yes, thanks."

Laredo took an ice-cold bottle from the cooler, wiped the moisture off with his hand and unscrewed the top. "Here you go, *mi querida*."

"I've heard that word."

"It can mean many things, depending on how it is used. I merely said *my dear*."

She wasn't sure she believed him. She thought it meant lover. "Thank you."

"To answer your question, my mother is from Spain. I was born here."

"In Virginia?"

"Originally Florida. My family moved north, staying along the coastline."

"You're three hours from the coast." She took a sip of her beer.

Laredo shrugged. "What can I say? I drifted west."

"And your mother?"

"Virginia Beach, with my siblings."

"How many?"

"Two brothers and three sisters." He leaned toward her, hiking a brow. "You see why I needed my own space."

"Speaking of which, move along." Shep stepped up beside them. His possessiveness amused her and thrilled her.

"It's a *fiesta*," Laredo said.

"You are monopolizing Tammy's time."

Laredo's expression went from mock surprise to mock despair. "I would argue for you, *Hermosa,* but he is my captain."

She giggled.

"Go find your own girl."

Laredo staged an outrageous wink before giving in to Shep's command.

"Is everyone at Station Eight a flirt?" she asked as Laredo sauntered away.

"Just those three." He pointed to Laredo, Cooper, and then glanced around, looking for someone. "Guess Jared isn't here yet."

"I noticed you left yourself off that list."

"I'm not a flirt."

If anyone knew that, she did. Though she vaguely remembered the night at the *Pitt Stop*, she suspected he had kept a watchful eye, completely conscious of his every word, never stepping out of line. He'd had every opportunity to take advantage. Afterward, he'd still kept a respectable distance. She'd thought he would never ask her out. He'd taken forever and she'd begun to think he wasn't interested. If his brother wasn't a lawyer, maybe they would still be apart. She couldn't imagine that. Couldn't imagine not being with Shep.

"You don't need to convince me. I practically chased you."

He smiled. "You did, huh?"

"Better wipe that sloppy grin off your face, Cap. The rest of the team is watching." Jared had snuck up behind them.

"'Bout time you got here."

"Hey, I'm on time. Besides, I had to pick up my date." Jared turned his attention to her. "Hello, beautiful." Good Lord, he could melt butter. Then she noticed the woman at his side. "This is Sheila. Sheila, this is Tammy and Shep."

"Hello, Sheila. It's nice to meet you."

"Thank you, Tammy. You too." The woman had a pretty smile. Big boobs. Probably fake.

"Welcome to the cookout, Sheila," Shep said.

"Thank you."

"How about something to drink? There's a tub over there, Jared."

"I know where it is. This ain't my first rodeo."

"Hi, guys." Cassie slipped between Tammy and Jared.

"Hey, doll. You still hanging out with this big galoot?" Jared nodded to Mike, who stood right behind her.

"Who's your friend, Mr. Sunglasses."

Jared's brow popped over the top of his shades. "This is Sheila. Sheila, Cassie. And the big guy is Mike."

"Hi Sheila," Cassie said with a little wave. Sheila's fingers stiffly waved back. It was obvious the woman felt threatened by Cassie's beauty, and just as clear she didn't like it. Mike gave the blonde a nod.

"You like my Oakley's?" Jared asked Cassie.

"Mr. Sunglasses is the name Tammy and I gave you before we knew your name."

Jared lips lifted in his normal sexy grin. "I like it."

"Gave him when?" Mike asked Cassie.

"When all those fire trucks pulled into El Puerto's and a dozen men climbed out," Tammy replied before Cassie had a chance.

Mike grunted.

"Don't feel bad. She has one for you too."

Mike faced Cassie. "What is it?"

She leaned into his arm and squeezed a bicep. "Mr. Muscles."

He laughed out loud, Shep joining him.

"Looks like they pegged you right, buddy." Jared took Sheila's hand. "Come on. You can meet the rest of the guys."

As they wandered off, Tammy said aloud. "Well, what do you think?"

Shep glanced up. "What do you mean?"

"I saw you sizing her up."

He shrugged. "Jared's type."

A soft laugh escaped from her mouth.

"Men," Cassie muttered. "I'm ready for a cold beer."

"Help yourself. Right over there." Using a tong, Shep pointed to several coolers.

"I'll show you where," Mike said to Cassie, taking her elbow.

Tammy was happy to forget her worries and enjoy the moment. Being with Shep was ideal.

"Here comes Elf and his wife." Shep took her elbow. "Come on. I'll introduce you."

The party was in full swing by dusk. Food and drink were plentiful, and the constant twangs of country songs drifted across the big backyard into the meadow. She'd never seen such die-hard competition at a corn hole toss game. They were just as bad battling horseshoes. Jared and Laredo had encouraged the women to play, not leaving anyone out. Everyone had a good time, ate too much, then filled up on deserts. Tammy couldn't remember the last time she'd laughed so hard, or so much.

When the hour grew late, the whole bunch packed up to leave, but not before helping with clean up. Trash was gathered, dishes washed, and the leftover food carted away.

Now, only she and Shep remained.

"Would you like a glass of wine?"

"I think I'd rather have your hot chocolate."

"Coming right up."

Tammy perched on a stool. "Tell me about your younger days."

"How far back?" Shep took down a container and scooped cocoa into mugs.

"I told you about my teens, college, and when I got married. What were you like in high school?"

"Dad died in an accident, then Mom died two years later while us kids were in high school. With both parents gone, my brothers and I got tight. We took up for each other and allowed no one to interfere with the rest of us." Shep put water in the microwave and pushed the timer. "Eddie took the lead, and with three younger siblings, I figured I needed to step up, too. We worked our butts off to go to college."

He hesitated, and Tammy knew he was debating on what to say next. The microwave dinged and as he poured hot water, he started speaking again.

"I met a girl, got married way too young."

Tammy's throat went dry. She tried to absorb the bomb Shep had just dropped. Not once had she considered Shep's matrimonial state.

"Had no idea what I was doing. She wanted money. I wanted to be a firefighter. We fought a lot. Ended in divorce. I ditched college and went to fire academy."

Not once had he looked at her while he spoke. He kept his eyes on his task. She had wondered why he was still single. He acted like his marriage was no big deal. She couldn't bring herself to comment on it.

"You became a firefighter. Do you mind talking about your job?"

He handed her a mug. "Let's go out on deck." He grabbed a flannel shirt from a peg by the door. "Here, might be chilly with the sun gone down." He held it while she slipped her arms into the sleeves. His scent immediately enveloped her and she mentally cuddled into the fabric. He opened the door and then followed her through.

The evening had gone from dusk to black night. Earlier, the fireflies flashed their green glow, but now only the light from Shep's house swathed them in the darkness.

"As to your question, I don't mind at all, talking about my profession. What do you want to know?"

She settled onto a chair, carefully, so not to spill her hot cocoa. "I understand you must like your job or you wouldn't be doing it. After all, you made captain. You seem to get along well with your team."

"Firefighters spend hours together. The station is their home away from home. We're like family. Brothers. The guys know everything about each other, and they should because they depend on each other in life-threatening conditions."

She wanted to say they were all hot, and a bunch of flirts, but she was more focused on Shep. "Are you there every day?"

"Most days. I like to check on things. A full-time firefighter works rotation. Different stations have various schedules. Some work twenty-four hours on, forty-eight off. Other shifts rotate two days on, three days off. Some days I work more. We have several volunteers. A fire department couldn't work without volunteers."

"It's a dangerous profession."

"Yes, it is. A firefighter needs to keep his head in the game."

"Do you ever worry? Get scared?"

Holding his mug, he swallowed before answering. "The day a firefighter gets over-confident is the day he needs to hang up his helmet. If you're asking if I'm afraid, no. I concentrate on the job, the situation, what needs to be done, and I do it. There are always classes, continuous training. Structure designs constantly change and men need to be updated to prepare for the best possible rescue. I don't claim to know everything. All of us are still learning. If a firefighter thinks he knows all there is to know, then he's going to get his ass in a bind."

"I have faith in you." She wanted him to know that. The look he gave her made her glad she'd told him. He looked like she'd just given him the best thing ever.

"Thank you. That means a lot to me."

"You get a lot of 911 calls?"

"Everything from a house fire to a car accident or a heart attack. We're first response. Dispatch contacts us with vital information so we know what rig to send out. If we're not sure, we send everything."

"I don't know how you deal with that type of pressure every day."

He inhaled deeply and let out his breath. "Calls involving babies are the worst. We've had too many of those."

That was just heartbreaking. She didn't know what she'd do if something happened to her boys.

"Cassie said there was an incident at a training site and Mike is worried? Is it okay that she told me?"

"Good time to ask after you tell me she opened her mouth," Shep said with a grin. Tammy bit her lip and he quickly assured her. "Don't worry. He won't tell her any secrets, but we can't talk much about it because there's an ongoing investigation."

"Oh."

"How's your chocolate?"

Tammy wondered if that was Shep's way of changing the subject. She took a sip and swallowed. "Wonderful."

She relaxed back into her chair and stared out into the night, the sounds of nature at work. Crickets and other critters sang their songs as a whispering breeze carried the tunes over the fields. The moon's glow broke through the trees and lit the tops of the mountains. It was beautiful. A scene that could rob a person's breath or breathe life into a lonely soul.

Shep reached for her hand.

She needed that connection. His touch calmed her in a way she couldn't explain. Excited her by confirming this moment was real. He was real. And he wanted her. How did one accept something so blissful when she'd had no idea such a sentiment could exist. Love, sure. Many kinds of love. But a feeling this deep, she had trouble fathoming. She wanted to wallow in it, in him. She loved Shep so much. Holding his hand gave her the hope that he felt the same way. She couldn't explain the difference, only that it was. So different. She supposed she had loved her ex, but he'd never made her feel cherished. Shep made her feel so many things—glad to be a woman was only one of them.

"A penny for your thoughts."

She glanced at the man she decided belonged in her world. The man she wanted to share a life with her and her children.

"I'm happy," she whispered.

His fingers tightened. "I'm glad. I want you to be happy. As happy as you make me."

Her eyes burned.

"Now, don't go crying. I said happy."

"These could be happy tears."

"No tears. You want to sit in my lap?" He tugged, then waited to see if she'd come to him. She did.

He liked holding her, and she had to admit, she loved him doing it. His arms wrapped around her made everything right. Good. Perfect. She snuggled into his warmth.

"It's getting chilly. Want to go inside?"

"No. I'm fine right where I am."

"Mmmm. I agree," he said, rubbing a hand over her back. "A perfect evening."

"It was, wasn't it?"

"Mmm, hmm." The stubble on his jaw rubbed her temple.

"How did all of you manage to get an evening without any 911 calls?"

"Luck. We do have nights off now and again."

"I like spending time with you."

A few quiet moments passed before he replied. "I've thought about you for months. Of evenings, just like this."

"You have? I don't want to be a distraction to your job. I know you need to focus."

"You are a distraction. In the sense that I can't get you out of my head. I think about you all the time."

His words thrilled her, his low voice initiating tremors over her skin.

"As for my job, when a call comes in, there's no room for anything but the job. I won't risk the safety of my men. Or the people who depend on us to rescue them."

"You *are* a hero."

"Don't think of me that way. Too many people do. Firefighters may be considered heroes but to most of us, we're just doing our job. It is risky. We never know what might happen or what we might find. Fires are unpredictable. We just need to rely on our training."

She burrowed deeper into the man who meant so much to her. How had she fallen so fast?

"Does it bother you? My profession?" he asked.

"I think you're very brave. And wonderful."

He hesitated, and she knew he wanted to say something important.

"Some women can't handle the danger part."

"I'm not some women."

"You've made that very clear," he said, lifting her hand and placing a kiss in her palm.

She leaned back. "If you think your profession scares me, *duh*. You fight fires. Charge into a building when any sane person is running out. Do I think you're crazy? Yes. Do I think you're stupid? Of course, not." She shrugged. "Different strokes. Like you said, you're trained. I need to trust your training." She cupped his whiskered cheek. "I trust you."

"I'm glad to hear that." He slid a hand around the back of her neck and drew her in for a kiss. Light, not demanding. He ran his tongue over her lips, then kissed the corners of her mouth. He smoothed his lips over her cheek and buried his face in her neck.

"Shep," she whispered. "I care about you a lot. More than a lot." She felt the blood rush to her face. "I think you know how I feel about you."

"Mmmm." His lips vibrated on her skin, sending a hum shivering through her body. "I feel the same way. So you'll know, I'm in this for the long term."

She pulled back, echoing his words. "I'm glad to hear that." She smiled, her heart full of joy.

"I care about your boys, too. When they were here playing with Hutch, I couldn't help but think of them being here all the time."

"You did?"

"I love you, sweetheart."

"Oh, Shep." She threw her arms around his neck and kissed him with all the love in her heart. He held her tight and kissed her back, passionately, hungrily. They both were breathing heavy when they pulled apart.

"I want you in my life forever, woman. I'd like to wake up with you every morning. Make love to you every night."

"Yes. I want that too."

"Are you sure?"

"I love you."

One side of his mouth lifted. "I know."

"You know?"

"We have some heavy magnetism going on." He lifted her to her feet, rose, then scooped her into his arms. "I can't resist. What do you say we give in to this powerful force?"

CHAPTER 22

Tammy's boys, decked out in matching Avengers PJs, came tearing through the kitchen. Once again, Shep was struck at how exactly the twins looked alike. Except for a few more freckles on David's cheeks. And one of Christopher's eyes favored more toward brown than green. Just like his mom.

"Hey, Shep. Who do you think is the best? Hulk or Thor?" David pointed to the green character on his shirt.

"Thor's a god. He's the bestest." Christopher stood next to his brother with his little hands braced on his hips.

"Nuh, uh. Hulk is strongest," David shot back.

"Aren't they on the same team?" Shep interjected.

"Sure. They're the Avengers," David answered. "Which one do you like?"

"I don't know. I haven't seen the movie."

Both boys' eyes grew big and their jaws dropped open. "What?" they said in unison.

He hadn't taken the time to go. Who would he have gone with anyway? He'd heard the team in conversation with the young volunteers, so he knew who the boys were excited about.

"This is the Hulk." David pointed to the green face on his shirt.

"This is Thor," Christopher said, pointing to the character on his shirt.

"You like the Hulk?" David asked.

"Sure," Shep answered.

"But you said you like Thor," Christopher argued.

"No, he didn't," David shot back.

"He did too."

"Nuh, uh."

Christopher shoved David.

David shoved him back.

The two went at each other like wrestlers on the WWE circuit.

"Hey, there." Shep grabbed each kid and held them apart.

"What's going on in here?" Tammy's heels came clicking into the kitchen. "I could hear you two shouting."

"David said Hulk was the best."

"He is. Not stupid Thor."

"He's not stupid."

The two boys struggled to get free, making Shep tighten his hold.

"Stop it right now," Tammy said, glaring at her children. "When Kayleigh gets here I'm telling her to put you in separate rooms. Neither one of you will have anyone to play with."

"Aw, Mom." Both boys fussed.

"What's the matter with you? Fighting. You don't fight. Now, apologize to Shep and go to your room. I'll be in to say goodnight in a moment. When you hear the doorbell, you do not come out of your room. Am I clear?"

"Gee, Mom," Christopher began, but Tammy interrupted.

"Want me to add no TV?"

His mouth snapped shut.

"I'm sorry, Shep," David said with a pout.

"Me too." Christopher hung his head. Then the twins turned as one and padded down the hall.

"Wow. You're tough."

"They never fight." Tammy placed her purse on the counter top. She looked fine in a navy-blue skit and semi-colored top.

"I wouldn't worry too much," he told her. "Boys will be boys."

"Once in a while, when the twins don't get their way, I might receive a pout. But this ..." She shook her head.

"They're growing up. Competitive years are on the way." He should know, growing up with four brothers.

"Hmmm. The boys are smart and comprehend a lot for their age. However, I doubt their behavior has much to do with maturing. They've been spending more time away from me. I have no idea what Steve is allowing." Tammy exhaled a heavy sigh. "My sweet-natured boys, normally bristling with energy and friendly to everyone, are sulking and moping. And fighting."

Tammy had a point. Who knew what her ex was doing, or putting the boys up to? Either way, this custody business was working on her. And tonight was her big night. She should be looking forward to her evening.

At the cookout, Tammy had let go for a bit and enjoyed herself, exactly like he'd hoped. She'd interacted with everyone and had a good time. He was just glad she'd relaxed enough to enjoy herself.

After the cookout had been the part he liked to remember the most. A night where nothing had existed but the two of them. They'd merged their hearts, bodies, and souls. The woman had rocked him to his core. He loved the idea of planning a new life with her and her boys.

For the past weeks, they'd been together every chance they could, yet managed only once during that time to be intimate. Just seeing her, being close enough to breathe her air was a heady experience like no other. He looked forward to having this woman in his life every day. He had no idea he could love a woman so much.

If only he could kick Steve's ass the way he wanted. Eddie would take care of the custody end of things. Shep would take care of Tammy.

"Maybe the stress of the custody battle is affecting my children."

Shep turned his focus back to her. "They're kids. Six years old. They'll have many squabbles. Wait until they reach puberty."

"Perish the thought."

He stood and pulled her close, rubbing his hands up and down her arms. "You look beautiful. You'll outshine every other teacher there tonight."

"You haven't seen the women I work with."

"Doesn't matter," he said, slipping an arm around her waist and bringing her in for a kiss. The doorbell rang before their lips met.

Tammy giggled. "Just as well," she whispered. "Two pairs of eyes are peeking around the corner."

The woman must have eyes in the back of her head. Guess most moms did.

***

The applause was deafening. Tammy's speech had been superb. Shep could see why she'd been voted Teacher of the Year. The more time he spent with her the more remarkable she became. So many depths. He was finding he loved everything about her.

Tammy had a heart of gold. Tonight, she shined. The woman on stage deserved her award. If the applause was anything to go by, several people had the same opinion. It was obvious she was well liked. To be with her on such an important evening made his chest swell with pride.

The crowd stood as a blushing Tammy left the podium and returned to the table they shared with Cassie, Mike, and a few of her coworkers. Her gaze locked with his and he fought the urge to open his arms. Her face beamed with pleasure. Cassie hugged her, and then a few others did as well.

"Glad this is about over," Mike said tugging at his tie.

"I'm surprised. Not that Cassie dragged you here, but she managed to get you in a monkey suit." Shep figured Mike would do anything for Cassie. Those two were as thick as maple and syrup. He knew some of what Mike was feeling.

"Oh my gosh. I can't believe everyone is standing," Tammy said, taking her seat.

"That was quite a speech you gave. Congratulations," Shep whispered next to her ear.

"Thanks."

"Can we get out of here now?"

Cassie poked Mike. "Give her a chance to sit down."

"She is sitting down," Mike grumbled.

Cassie ignored him. "I wish we had champagne."

"I'll buy you a whole case if we can leave now."

Tammy giggled. Shep snorted.

"You two don't need to stick around. The superintendent will say a few thank yous, then we're outta here." Tammy waved a hand between Shep and her.

"Good." Mike made to rise and Cassie gripped his arm.

"One more minute," she said. Mike could deny Cassie nothing. The fool grinned and kissed her cheek.

Shep wondered if he'd be acting the same way with Tammy and knew there was no doubt.

The event came to a close, and Mike and Cassie made their getaway. Several people stopped by to give Tammy well wishes. Shep stood to the side, giving her plenty of space, yet close enough to be near.

Finally, the crowd thinned and Tammy picked up her purse. "I had no idea there would be a stampede. Sorry you had to wait."

"Don't apologize," he said taking her elbow. "I enjoy watching you glow."

"Glow?" As if on cue, she blushed.

"Yes. Glow. You're in your element."

"I don't like all of this attention."

"That's not what I mean. You love teaching. It shows. The other teachers are a testament to that fact. Standing in line to acknowledge and commend you. And I assume they voted for you."

"Someone sure did. We can go now."

"No hurry. Take your time."

"Are you kidding? I'm ready to get out of these heels."

Which made him think of getting her out of a few other things. Like her clothes.

"Hello, Tammy."

She whipped around with a fierce look for the owner of the voice. Her body tensed to the point Shep thought she might shake. A man with more gray than himself faced Tammy and Shep suspected the guy was Tammy's ex-husband. Shep immediately wanted to wipe the smirk off her ex's condescending face.

"Who's this?" the arrogant shithead asked Tammy while sizing up Shep.

"This is Shep, a firefighter for Staunton Augusta Fire and Rescue."

Shep held out a hand. Steve ignored it.

"Where'd she find you?"

Between the arrogant tilt of his head and his sharp words, Shep had accurately judged the guy an asshole. The idiot had no reservations embarrassing Tammy at an event spotlighting her. Maybe he should put out this fire before it started.

"We met when my squad gave a demonstration to the kindergarten class at Verona Elementary."

"She doesn't teach kindergarten."

Shep grappled with his rising ire. "Her boys were in the class."

"Those are my boys too," the ex snarled.

"When it's convenient," Tammy snapped.

Shep could see this getting out of hand, and Tammy did not need that.

"So, you're a volunteer fireman," Steve said derogatively. "What's your real job?"

Shep's pulse sped up another beat. Outward, he expressed no reaction of the emotion boiling inside. "I'm Captain of Station Eight."

A tinge of pink flushed the assholes cheeks and he turned his attention to Tammy.

"While you're flitting about, where are my boys?"

What was this jerk even doing here?

"*My* children are at home with a sitter. It's their bedtime. And my lawyer told me not to argue with you."

"I must be giving you too much money for *my children* if you hired a lawyer that fast."

"You barely give me enough to take care of *your children*."

"If you can't raise them, I can."

Shit. If they kept going at each other, someone was bound to start swinging. Shep slipped an arm around Tammy's waist and pulled her against his side, giving her comfort as well as marking his territory. Steve narrowed his eyes at the motion.

"You sleeping with him?" His voice chafed stiffer than his lips.

Shep's arm constricted. A vein flexed in his temple.

"If I am, it's none of your business," Tammy hissed.

"If you are, *it is* my business," Steve snarled. "My children live in your house. I'll not have them exposed to—"

"I *suggest* you lower your voice," Shep commanded in a quiet, menacing tone. One he'd used on numerous occasions when he intended to get his don't-fuck-with-me point across. "This is not the place."

Steve's eyes flew wide, then narrowed with harnessed fury. A few tense moments passed while he tried to judge whether or not Shep would follow through on his projected threat. *Yeah, read my body language asshole.*

Yielding the moment, Steve turned his haughty gaze on Tammy. "You'll be hearing from me."

"I'm sure I will."

Shep could pound the man into the ground for putting a damper on Tammy's evening. Two seconds earlier, she'd been ecstatic. Jubilant in winning her award.

Tammy slumped into a chair. Shep went down on his haunches in front of her.

"Are you all right?"

"I can take care of myself," she said on a shaky sigh. "I've been dealing with his crap for two years."

"Not exactly what I asked. Yes, you can take care of yourself very well. But you don't have to. Not anymore. Let me help you."

"You don't know how much I'd like to wash my hands of this mess and let you take care of everything. I'd like to be a kid without a care in the world, no responsibilities at all. Let someone else take care of me. But that's fantasy and I'm a realist. I have two children who depend on me."

"Let me help you. Not make you dependent on me, although I'd like nothing more than be a person in your life that you couldn't live without. But that's a discussion we can have later." He stood and pulled her up next to him. "As for Steve, I watched your face when he was mouthing off. I thought you were going to explode."

"I have so many things to say to that man, but I knew once I started, I'd end up screaming the place down. He's always known how to push my buttons."

"You gave as good as you got. And you kept your temper in check."

"Steve isn't interested in anything but his image. He wasn't about to make a scene."

"I, uh, interfered. Are you mad at me?"

"How can I be?" she said with a smile. "Actually, it was kind of nice. Jealousy or someone taking up for me is something I'm not used to. I like it. But he didn't."

Shep rubbed her arms. "Never mind him. Tonight is for you. Don't let him intrude."

"Too late."

"No, it's not. You can deal with him later. And I'll be with you." Shep slid an arm around her back, giving comfort and hoping to save the evening. "Where's that glorious smile I saw a moment ago?"

A corner of her mouth lifted and her eyes locked with his. Seconds lingered as they communicated in silence. The muscles in her shoulders eased, and he sensed her need to lean her head on his chest. If they weren't the center of attention, he'd sweep her into his arms and carry her away into the night.

"I've got this," he whispered. "I've got you."

"What would I do without you?"

He hoped she'd never have to find out.

CHAPTER 23

Shep knew what was coming, and dreaded it. Tammy's body language told him everything he needed to know.

When she'd called earlier, he heard the sadness in her voice. He'd driven to her house with the same speed he normally used when responding to a fire. Now he saw the pain in her eyes. Her fingers trembled, and she was jumpy, raw, vulnerable. Still, she kept her distance, not allowing him close.

"Shep. I uh, want to thank you for everything."

"Tammy—"

"I'm sorry. This isn't working out for us."

"What isn't working? I've enjoyed being with you and I'm pretty sure you've enjoyed being with me."

She twisted her hands and looked everywhere but at him. "I have to consider my boys."

Patience. Tammy was under a lot of strain from Steve. The skirmish at the award ceremony must have been harder than he'd realized.

"Anyone can see how you care for your children. I like Christopher and David. They're great kids."

"They have a father."

That hit him hard. "I know that."

"I can't see you anymore."

Even though he'd known she was leading up to this, hearing her say the words, hurt like fuck.

"What exactly are you saying?"

"You and me. We—" Her voice cracked. She took a deep breath. "We can't see each other anymore."

Steve. Her rat bastard husband had done this. "Tammy, you know how I feel about you."

"It doesn't matter. I've made up my mind."

More than likely, her ex had forced her hand.

Shep took a step closer. "No one is going to take you away from me."

"There is no one else," she said, stepping away from him. Then, she took a deep breath as if she needed to spit out her next words.

"This is my decision. I have too much going on in my life right now. I'm divorced with two children and I don't have room in my life for anyone else right now."

"Yes, you do. You need help. You need me."

"I've been taking care of myself for a long time without any-one's help. I don't need a man to take care of me."

The way she'd clung to him when they'd made love told him otherwise. "You've proven you're a strong woman. I'm only saying I want to help. I want to be with you."

"I still can't see you anymore. I have to do this. It's ... for the best. You have to leave. Don't come back." She was prattling. A sure sign of distress.

"Your damned ex-husband," he spat, clawing a hand through his short hair. "I will not stand by and watch that—"

"You have to leave," she shouted. But he heard the tremor in her voice. Any pressure from him and she just might shatter. She was barely keeping it together as it was.

He clenched his jaw in frustration, biting back his anger.

No doubt Steve had threatened Tammy with some new form of torture. She would never do this. Never rip out his guts unless her bastard husband was behind it.

"Is that what your heart wants?" He knew better. His heart had connected with hers. He'd learned more about this woman in the past weeks than she knew about herself. He could read every gesture, every emotion. He'd soaked her up like a sponge, and wanted to go on absorbing, for the rest of his life.

"I ... I want you to go. This is over. We are o—over—" She barely got the word out.

Tammy couldn't hide her feelings. Especially from him. He knew every expression, every shadow in her tortured eyes that revealed every thought in her head, no matter the lies that spewed from her lovely mouth.

The boys. Of course, Steve had threatened the boys. Christopher and David were Tammy's weakness and her ex had no qualm using them as a weapon.

"Steve is using me as leverage, isn't he? Threatening your children?"

"Oh, God," she burst out. Her head slumped and her shoulders shook. "He'll paint me as unfit. He'll accuse me of being in bed with you while the boys were in the next room."

"That's absurd."

"He'll do it. He's mean and doesn't fight fair. He'll drag us both through the mud."

Shep hated Steve. Hated what he'd done to Tammy. What he was forcing her to do.

And he couldn't do a damn thing about it.

Shep took a breath, then another. Tammy had enough on her shoulders. Her heart bled just like his own. He didn't give a shit about his reputation, but he would not put Tammy and their relationship in the spotlight of a messy custody battle. It was bad enough the bastard was threatening to take her children. Shep would not give the asshole more ammunition.

She blinked, trying to hold back her tears. Ripping his heart at the same time. He couldn't stand it. Couldn't stand here and watch her tear them both apart. It made him sick seeing her in such agony. He had to be strong. Do this for her.

He took a step forward and her hand shot out. "Don't touch me. If you do, I'll fall apart."

"No, you won't." He pulled her into his arms and held her close. Rubbing his hands over her back while she sobbed.

"I'm sorry." Her arms gripped his waist, her hands clutching at his shirt.

The only thing that mattered was Tammy. She didn't want him to go. He hated like hell to leave. But, if there was to be any peace between them, he had to do what was best. He had to say the words that might strangle him, knowing it was the only way. Her ass of a husband was still pulling her chain.

One last kiss.

He gave her a few minutes to exhaust her sobs, then pulled back and wiped the tears from her cheeks. "Don't be sorry. This is too much of a strain on you." Her pleading eyes nearly did him in. He had to be strong for the both of them.

"I'll leave."

"I don't want you to go," she sniffed.

"I know."

"But I don't want Steve to hurt you. He will."

"He won't." That's why Shep had to do what he must. For her. "You don't need to worry about me on top of everything else."

"Steve—"

Shep placed a finger over her quivering lips.

"Yeah." He fell into her eyes, drowning in her sorrow. No regrets. He loved her heart, body, and soul. "Remember one thing."

"What's that?" she whispered.

"You're not alone." He sucked in a deep breath, seeking the strength of mind for what came next. "I'll go. I won't be back. But I'll always be thinking about you."

"Wait, uh ... what do you mean you won't be back."

"You know it's for the best. I won't allow Steve to use me as a weapon against you."

"Oh, Shep," she cried, tears flowing freely, again. "After what I'm doing to you ..." She grasped his neck and pulled him to her, kissing him with everything in her soul.

He returned her yearning, plunging his tongue deep. Taking her. Branding her. A kiss she would always remember. Her breathing was ragged as he pulled back.

Placing a knuckle under her chin, he lifted her gaze to meet his. "As long as I'm in the picture, he won't let us be. I won't be a tool Steve can use against you."

The danger was real. Tammy needed her kids. Shep would never stand in the way of her children. For Tammy's sake, Steve had to be convinced their relationship had come to an end.

Over.

She buried her face in his chest.

Right now, he wanted to slam Steve's face into a brick wall, but he needed to step back. Let the court handle it. Eddie would castrate the bastard and Shep would be there to see it happen.

"Tammy." God. Was that gravelly voice his? "You're a strong woman. Eddie will take care of you. I promise."

"You're just going to leave?"

"Like you said, it's for the best." The pain in his chest could choke him. But the words he forced from his throat nearly destroyed him. Destroyed them both. He had to stay focused. Think of what Tammy needed more.

Her children.

"You were right. We need to end things. This is our last moment together."

"I was wrong," she pleaded. "I don't want to lose you."

"Nor I you." He shook his head, not believing things had come to this. "Your children are your life. You deserve to be happy. If it can't be with me, then—"

"Don't say it. I can't bear it."

"Yes, you can. For your boys." He watched the emotions whirling in her eyes. Pain, anguish, denial—the same ones rolling through his chest.

"I don't know what I'll do if I can't see you ...?" Her voice trailed away as he shook his head.

"Concentrate on now. The custody. Nothing else." With everything in him, he gently pushed her away. "I better go."

How he managed to walk out of that house he'd never know. He just put one foot in front of the other, and kept thinking one more step. Unmindful of his surroundings, he made his way to his Land Rover and drove home. Another thing he had no idea how he achieved. He supposed his subconscious had taken over. Avoiding other cars on the road, staying in the right lane.

He was not one to be careless. Yet he had been.

Face it. Life as he'd known it was over. No more Tammy. Steve could drag this out forever. Hopefully, word would get back to him quick and the bastard would back off. Only if he believed the breakup was real.

God, Shep hated doing that to her. His own heart had bled right along with hers. But if he'd given in and told her anything other than what he had, she would cling to clandestine meetings and sneaking around. Steve would find out. Better to break off completely. David and Christopher were priority.

Hutch was there to meet Shep as he entered his house. He headed to the refrigerator and took out a Coke, then continued on to the back porch. The soft padding of Hutch's feet let him know the dog followed. He dropped into his favorite chair, Hutch curled up by his side.

Just like before. Before Tammy.

Already, he missed her. Wished she was sitting on his porch with him, looking at the stars in the sky. Where before the twinkling specs of light brought him joy, they promptly hissed out his loneliness. Before Tammy, he'd cherished his evenings alone under a full moon or a starlit night. He supposed this could be the stage of his life he'd call "after Tammy".

A respite?

Permanent or temporary, he would suffer deeply during this interim.

Hutch raised his head and let out a whine. Even the dog noticed his somber mood.

Shep scratched his dog on the head. A half moan, half growl rumbled from Hutch's throat.

"I know, boy. Not much for company, am I? How would you like to spend time over at Macy's for a few days?"

The twelve-year-old girl loved Hutch and checked on him when Shep had to spend nights at the station. The only way he'd survive the next few days, weeks, would be to keep his mind busy. Staying at the firehouse twenty-four seven would not be allowed. But he could spend his time off helping with the investigation. Unofficially, of course.

There were too many questions. The explosion at the Wimer property. Someone stealing firefighter gear and dressing as one of their own. The person responsible had known firefighters could get hurt. Counted on it.

He wanted answers. Hooley was the investigator, but Shep had energy to burn.

Still, with detectives and a fire inspector on this case, what made him think he could find out more than Hooley or Chuck? Hooley said the guy could be anyone. The arsonist had left no trace or clue of his identity. A pro. Was the sniper downtown the same man? Was it all connected?

Chuck said this perp could be a killer. Shep could be headed into dangerous territory. His specialty was fire, not criminals.

The bullet to Mike's helmet may not have been an accident. A killer.

At this point, Shep didn't care. He had time on his hands and a fire in his belly.

Finding the culprit who had a vengeance with firefighters would not only occupy his mind but give him an outlet to exhaust his pain. A purpose. To go on. Find and put an end to a monster, while he fought the demon on his back.

***

"What the hell is wrong with you? You've always been the good Samaritan. Why would you throw your happiness away?"

"Knock it off, Eddie. I'm not in the mood." Shep retrieved two mugs and poured coffee into each of them. Finding his brother on his doorstep at the crack of dawn had surprised the shit out of him. "What are you doing here so early anyway?"

"If I could ever find you at home, I wouldn't have to resort to early morning tactics."

"Try using the phone."

Eddie pulled his cell from his pocket. "Oh, let me try that. Why lookie here. Six calls Thursday. Six more on Friday. Every hour Saturday. Laura threatened me Sunday. So here I am today. Why the hell didn't you call me back?"

"You didn't tell me anything I didn't already know."

"Then you did get my messages."

"All twenty-three of them."

Eddie raked his hands through his hair. A sure sign of his irritation.

"Will you sit down? Drink your coffee."

Eddie pulled out a stool. "Damn it, Shep. You didn't have to do this."

"I thought to make matters easier for all involved." Shep leaned a hip against the sink and sipped his hot brew. An image of Tammy's Keurig popped into his head. It seemed everything reminded him of her.

"You made it painless for her ass of a husband. Not for you or for her. Can't you see she loves you?" Eddie stopped ranting long enough to drink from his mug. "This is the best thing that's happened to you."

Shep wouldn't argue that. "I didn't have a choice."

"Like hell. I told you to wait. Don't give in to this bastard." Eddie smacked his hand on the counter.

Not much Shep could do about it at the moment. The mess with Tammy's husband was tearing her apart. Shep had done what he had to do. "It's what she wants."

"She wants you."

Not as much as he wanted her. "Under the circumstances—"

"Fuck the circumstances."

Eddie never swore. Shep hiked a brow in question. This custody case was getting to him.

"That's how frustrated I am. I can't believe you're so calm."

"Calm?" Shep placed his mug on the granite countertop before he crushed the thing with his bare hands. Every nerve tensed, every muscle flexed, ready to pop out of his skin. "You think I'm calm. I want to kill the bastard," he barked in anger. "Peel the hide off his skin. Walking away from Tammy was the hardest thing I've ever done."

"And the stupidest. It's not the case I'm disturbed about. I've had to battle dozens upon dozens of assholes like Steve Michael. What has me pissed is the barrier you put between you and Tammy. I've never seen you happier. You two love each other."

"She was being torn in two. Tammy is nothing without her kids. I will not come between her and her kids."

"She's not going to lose her kids."

Shep braced both hands flat on the countertop and leaned into his brother's space. "She better not."

"Are you threatening me? I'm not the one who deserves your anger."

"I know that!" he roared. Rage tackled every cell in his body. Resentment threatened to consume him. If he gave in to it, he'd lose himself. He whirled on the ball of his boot and paced. "It's all I can do not to face him and kill the son-of-a-bitch. He has a wife. But he won't let Tammy have a life of her own."

Yes, he'd ended his relationship with Tammy. Told her goodbye. Now he lived in a hell of his own making. Still, it was better than watching her suffer a second longer, struggling with her decision in telling him to go. Trying to be brave.

He stood at the window of his back door, staring out at the landscape. He scrubbed a hand over his face, attempting to wipe away the unforgettable scene. Tammy in agony. Tears in her eyes. Her breath lurching out in gulps. If only he—

He knew better than to dwell in what ifs. That's why he'd done what he had. Wanting to save her from herself, he'd ripped his own guts out. Trying to make things easier on her, he'd obliterated his own heart. Even though he knew he would never give up, the pain he'd caused her filled his gut with anguish. Now, he had to ride this out.

Eddie attempting to reason with him only made him more miserable. Shep spoke with his back to his brother.

"How could I ask her to make that choice? There was only one conclusion. I had to make the decision for her."

"No, you did not. All you had to do was wait."

"Don't you see? Waiting was killing her."

And me.

***

Shep's shoulders tensed the second he heard Alice's voice echo to his office on the second-floor landing.

Christ, I don't need this now.

With one foot in the doorway, he'd nearly stumbled right into view. He stepped back into his office and quietly closed the door, then flicked the lock.

A coward he was not. But dealing with the pushy woman today of all days, he did not have the patience. Or the stamina.

The break with Tammy had knocked him on his ass. He'd been unable to digest the decision, let alone come to terms with it. If he had to deal with Alice now, he just might tear into her and handle things badly. He didn't want to be cruel to the woman, but Alice showing up on the heels of Tammy's ex giving an ultimatum, Shep was loaded for a fight. Alice might be a nuisance, but she didn't deserve to be dumped on by circumstances beyond his control. Right now, he didn't give a good damn about anyone's feelings other than his own.

Better to have a locked door between them until his temper had some release. Hopefully on someone who deserved it. Like Steve—which was out of the question since Tammy would catch the fallout. Or the firebug—who they still hadn't found. You'd think a madman with a vengeance would take credit for his triumphs.

Shit. Shep couldn't hide behind a locked door. Alice would find him.

Three sharp raps reverberated on metal.

Shep flipped the lock and took a few breaths hoping to get his aggravation under control.

"Hey Cap."

"What the—" Shep caught himself. Damn it. These days he had less restraint over his emotions. Cooper snickered and Shep wanted to punch the smirk right of his young face.

"You gonna let me in or keep blocking the door?"

Shep glanced over the kid's shoulder and took a quick look down the corridor.

"She's gone."

He wasn't sure how Cooper had gotten rid of her, but Shep guessed he owed the kid. He walked to his desk, not quite believing Alice had gone.

"You can breathe," Cooper said, closing the door. "She's not here. It was a close one, though."

"What did you tell her?"

Cooper dropped into a chair before he answered. "That you were hiding in your office and she had to come back later."

"Son-of-a-bitch. She's coming back?"

Cooper belted out a laugh. "The look on your face. I never, uh ..."

Shep gave him a new look that clearly stated, 'keep talking nonsense and you'll have shit duty for a month.

"I've got your back, Cap. You're off the hook."

"Define 'off the hook'."

"You don't have to worry about Alice. I took care of her popping in here."

"As in temporarily or for good?"

"Geez, Cap. You don't want much, do you?"

Shep gave him another glare.

"All right." Cooper shot up straight. "I figure you don't need Alice messing up anything you might have going with Tammy. You said yourself, you might have to do something if Alice kept being a pest."

"What did you do?"

"I more or less explained you weren't available. Then I fed her tidbits sending her in another direction."

"What direction?"

"Mitchell, over at Station Three. He has a house, lives alone. Close to her age."

"Tell me you did not sic that woman on another firefighter."

"What's the harm? Got her out of your hair. Besides, if she wants a hot firefighter, he might be her man."

Shep groaned and scrubbed a hand over his face.

"Come on, Cap," Cooper cajoled, looking entirely too damn comfortable. "She can pester another station for a while. We have a new woman bringing us goodies."

Anguish struck him like a blow. Tammy would not be paying a visit to the station. Not anymore. Anger was the only emotion that saved him from the pain. He fisted his hands, wanting to throttle someone. Anyone.

"Shit ... uh ... Cap?" Cooper's smirking expression quickly fled his suddenly pale face. He knew he'd just stumbled into forbidden territory. "Uh, sorry Cap. I think I hear Mike calling me." Cooper leaped from the chair and sprinted out of Shep's office.

He wanted to yell. Howl his agony. The business with Tammy hurt like fire from hell. Somehow, he would manage. Somehow, he would survive. Somehow, he would get through the day.

One day at a time.

Somehow.

CHAPTER 24

Work today was brutal. One alarm after another kept the team on the road. First an accident on I81, two EMT squad calls, a fire in a hair salon—that was a comical sight—and a house fire on Old Greenville Road. By the time Station Eight arrived on the scene, there wasn't much left of the house. Ten-foot flames shot out from the roof while four stations battled the fire.

Kids. Left at home alone. Playing with a lighter.

Evidently, the oldest of four children had been babysitting her three siblings. She looked to be no older than twelve. Her two younger brothers found their dad's lighter and had been playing in the bedroom. The youngest of the four was a little girl. When he saw her, his heart clenched. Soot on her cheeks and a rat's nest in her hair. He wondered how much of her appearance was a result of the fire. It was obvious, the kids didn't have much. Both parents trying to make ends meet. But still ...

He just wanted to thank God the kids were okay.

By the time he got back to the firehouse, his mood had not improved. There was no time left to work on his pet project, finding the arsonist who set up the explosion at the training site. He was grumpy, fidgety, and battling his own temper.

Five weeks since he'd seen Tammy and it felt like months. He wasn't one damn step closer to any indication of who the perp might be. Focusing on the SOB who was targeting firefighters couldn't keep thoughts of Tammy at bay. He hated what her ex was doing to her.

Doing to them.

The guys had noticed. He'd been distracted. Driven. They did their jobs and asked no questions. But still delivered their raised eyebrows and knowing looks, which only irritated him more. They knew their asses would be in a sling if they got on his bad side. He could rip them a new one without much provocation these days.

Good thing shift was over.

He dragged his ass home for a shower but was too wired to go to bed. He knew he wouldn't sleep. If he was a drinking man, he'd kill a case of beer, right now. Since he'd rather drink coffee, and he couldn't drink hot chocolate without thinking of Tammy, he settled for iced tea instead.

Hutch padded into the kitchen and looked at his master, knowing something was wrong.

"I know, boy. Haven't been myself since I met that woman." He'd been flitting around like a teenager since he first kissed her. After the breakup, he'd been angry as a sore bear.

There had been nothing new from Hooley. Chuck had the team suspicious of every run. How the hell were they supposed to do their jobs effectively when every call could be a setup? Every run could be a ruse to target another firefighter? What kind of maniac called in an emergency then took potshots at the response crew?

The same kind who blew up buildings at a training site.

Shep frowned and the muscle in his cheek tightened, contemplating the two incidents.

He didn't give a good goddamn if the police didn't want his help. He wasn't about to sit on his ass twiddling his thumbs while a member of his team could be in danger. The arsonist had covered his tracks pretty well. If Hooley and Chuck didn't catch the bastard soon ...

Hutch brushed against his leg. Shep released a frustrating sigh.

"Yeah. I know. Been ignoring you, too. Come on. Let's take a stroll."

He drained his glass of tea and strode to the porch. The moon was bright tonight. Pitching a glow over the sky and a blush over the meadow and beyond. Often, he and Hutch would take walks at night without any problem of seeing. The stars or the moon would light their way.

The phone in his pocket buzzed. Eddie's name flashed in bright white. Shep's pulse took a dive. Either Eddie had news or he called to get on Shep's case again.

"Hey, bro."

"Are you still at the fire station?"

"No, I'm home. Hutch and I just taking a walk. You got some news?" Every day he hungered for any word of Tammy.

"Can't a brother just call to say hi?"

"Yes or no?"

"I'm working on it. Why don't you ask what you really want to know?"

Shep closed his eyes and released a sigh. "How's Tammy?"

"Why don't you ask her yourself?"

"Why don't you answer the damn question?"

"Ready to admit your mistake?"

Hell. He'd made a lot of them. At the time, Tammy needed him gone. He'd saved her the trouble of kicking him out. She didn't need that guilt on top of everything else she'd been going through.

"Ending things was not a mistake. Steve no longer has a threat."

"He has a threat all right."

"Has he done something?"

"Nothing new."

"At least he can't use me as leverage." What Shep would really like to do was rearrange the asshole's face.

"You took away his power, but Tammy is still suffering."

She wasn't the only one. But he hated knowing Tammy suffered at all. "Did you call to make me feel worse?"

"You don't need me for that," Eddie shot back. "You do a good job of the guilt trip on your own."

"If it makes you feel better, I'm agonizing in my own hell. I just want Tammy to be okay."

"She will be. She has me. She also has spunk."

That she did. Too bad all that fire and brimstone couldn't burn her ex to cinders.

An independent woman, with fire and passion and a zest for life. Then there was her passion in the bedroom. No matter what he did to fight the reoccurring images of their lovemaking, Tammy kept popping up in his mind. God, he missed her.

"Have you found your arsonist yet?"

Shit. He had other problems to deal with. He'd have to trust his brother to take care of Tammy.

"Not yet. Hooley and Chuck are working on it."

"Who?"

He wasn't thinking. "The fire inspector and a detective."

"Right. Well, get some rest man. You can't burn the candle at both ends."

Who the hell invented that saying?

"Kiss Laura and the kids for me." He shoved his phone back in his pocket and ambled down the steps.

He'd said he would not see Tammy again—but he'd lied. He ached with need. He went to bed at night wishing for what he couldn't have. Not until this miserable mess was over.

He needed to release his frustration. The team would blow off steam in the weight room, pumping iron or laying into the punching bag. To avoid more scrutiny, he'd stayed in his office, waiting for the end of shift, when he'd sooner go home and chop wood.

Or take walks with his dog.

***

Cassie narrowed her green eyes. "When you say fine, it means shitty."

Tammy shrugged. Her life was in chaos and she had no one to blame but herself.

"You're taking on more than one person can handle."

Her hackles rose in defense. "Other women teach. Other women bake cakes. Other women are divorced and raising children on their own."

"But you are doing all these things while your ex-husband is manipulating you. I don't like seeing you take crap from Steve."

"I'm not. I still remember what I went through with our divorce."

"You didn't learn anything. He's still pushing your buttons."

"I don't need you ganging up on me too. Bonnie and Vickie are both telling me what to do and fighting with each other over who I should listen to. I've been taking care of myself for years."

"I'm not ganging up on you. I just don't want you to kill yourself trying to do everything on your own. Let me help. Let Shep help."

She shoved her hair from her face. "Shep is no longer in the equation. It's my mess. Will you have some faith in me? I know what I'm doing." She jerked open a cabinet and snatched a pot.

"Where Steve is concerned, you need all the help you can get. What are you doing?"

"When I'm mad, I cook. It gets my mind off what's bothering me."

"Now you're going to exhaust yourself." Cassie took the pan from her.

Tammy jerked out another pot and slammed it on the counter, startling herself and Cassie. They both jumped.

"I'm sorry." Tammy propped her hands on the counter and hung her head.

"Look, honey, you've got me."

Shoving self-pity aside, she tucked a curl behind her ear. "You have a man now."

"You'd have one too if you hadn't sent him away."

What choice had she had? After Steve threatened to use Shep against her, slander them both. She chewed her lip.

"Now, I'm sorry," Cassie said, slipping onto a stool. "I'm only thinking of you."

"I am not going to cry. I refuse to cry." Tammy sniffed. "Okay, you're right. Steve threatened me. I tried ending things with Shep. I love that man. Telling him to leave was like slashing my heart from my chest with a pair of gardening shears. I couldn't stand it," she burst out. "I didn't even think about the consequences from Steve. I clung to Shep and begged him not to go."

Cassie reached across the table, placing her hand over Tammy's shaking one. "Oh, honey. You've got to stop torturing yourself."

The first tear glided over her cheek. Not a moment later another, then another. She had cried so much, how could there be any tears left? She stared into space, seeing nothing but the pain on Shep's face. The hurt in his eyes as words fell from his tight lips. Words she hadn't wanted to hear. Words she'd uttered only moments sooner.

"Tammy!"

Coming out of her daze, she swiped her cheek. "What?"

"Shep is a good guy. He won't desert you."

"No," she sniffed. "He said if I need something, he would do what he could to help. But he made it clear that we're no longer together." Her throat clogged.

"When this is all over—"

"Will it ever be over?" she muttered and grabbed a tissue.

"Of course, it will. When you get custody, Shep will be back."

"Even though I told him to leave, I never wanted him to go," she said, barely raising her voice. "It's been weeks." The only emotion she felt these days was sad. It took too much energy to show anything else.

Every time she thought about that day, the crack in her heart grew bigger. She'd wanted to die and if it weren't for her boys, she might have done just that. But life went on. She still hoped Shep would come back.

***

Steam hissed from hot pipes as Shep did a walk through. The fire trucks had arrived quickly, so most of the building was still intact. He stepped over fallen debris, the creaking boards under his boots sounding their strain. He heard an unusual sound, different from the busy echoes of an after a fire. He stopped to listen. Blocking out the firefighters, zeroing in on the source, he tried to identify the noise.

A whine? A yip?

Where was it coming from?

He shined the flashlight on the floor above him. Nothing.

Come on. Let me here you again.

He pushed the button on his mic. "Sound off your location."

"Mike. Ground floor."

"Jared. Out front with Laredo."

"Cooper here. In back."

"What's up, Cap?" Mike called back. "You find something?"

"I heard something. Out." No one was above him. It wasn't his imagination.

Shep made his way to the stairs. The quick response had kept the building from being engulfed in flames, so the stairwell had not suffered. No problem coming up to this level. The upper floor should be safe. He climbed the stairs, his senses on full alert, listening for the sound he'd heard earlier.

There it was again. He froze with one boot on the next step. Longer this time.

"Mike. You get that?"

"What, Cap? Only thing in here is charred wood and hissing steam."

"Rolling up the hose, Cap," Cooper's voice came next. "I'll do a perimeter check."

"Look up as you go. I'm on three. I swear I heard someone."

"Roger that."

Shep was about to break one of his own rules. Do not remove your helmet while still inside a smoldering structure. He glanced about. If he wanted to find that sound, he had to remove his helmet. Positioned on the top floor of the warehouse, he found the steps to the roof.

There. He heard it again.

Charging could be reckless, but his senses said he should hurry. He shoved his helmet back on his head and hastened up the last flight of stairs, cautiously pushing on the roof-top door. It opened easily.

Once outside, he tilted his head and listened.

"Help. Someone please help!"

With the roaring of the flames, the static from the radio and all the commotion, the piteous call for help had gone unnoticed. But he heard it now.

"Help." Even though the voice had lost strength, the distress remained evident.

"Cap. Someone's over the side," Cooper called over the radio.

Adrenaline pumped in Shep's system, sending him racing to the far corner. By the grace of God, a woman dangled off the side of the building. His heart lodged in his throat. A rusted-out fire escape that had once been attached to the old building hung sideways putting strain on the bolts connected to the other end. The woman gripped her forearms, an elbow locked through one bar, with a death-grip resembling a wrestler's chin lock. By the looks of things, the outdated metal, unable to bear her weight, had detached from the bricks. It wouldn't be long before the other hinges broke loose. He had to move fast.

"Fire department," he called down to her, praying the woman didn't fall apart now. "I'm here. Hold on."

"Thank God. Help me. I can't hold on much longer."

"Don't let go, now. You can do it. I'm right here."

For Christ's sake, hold on.

She closed her eyes, and for one heart-stopping moment he thought she might loosen her grip.

"Hold tight! Don't let go!"

Damn. No rope. Nothing to hook on to.

"Laredo! Get that ladder up here!"

"Where, Cap? Where are you?"

"Roof, east corner. I found a woman hanging over the side. Get the led out."

Shep tested the narrow ridge of brick, bracing his boot on the edge, searching for the best way to grab her. He needed rope. All he had was the straps holding his gear. That would have to do.

"Please hurry."

His fingers flew over the fasteners while he thought of how to calm the woman. He figured mere seconds, if she lasted that long.

"What's your name?"

"Sharon." Her voice weaker than a moment ago.

"Sharon. Don't let me down. It's very important you stay as still as you can. Don't wiggle. I'm here to save you." He kept talking, saying anything to keep her focused on him instead of the ground four floors down. "You have to make me look good. I can't do this without your help. I'm coming to get you. Don't let go."

He stretched as far as he could.

"What's ... your ... name?" At least she was talking. No signs of panic. That was a good sign.

"Shep."

"I'm afraid."

"Who wouldn't be? But you don't need to worry. I've got you." The straps were useless without an anchor. The fire escape could fall at any moment. If he could get them around her, at least he'd have something to grab. He edged a bit closer.

She looked at him then, with trust in her eyes. He would not lose her. A little more. "Here, Sharon. Let's see if I can get this strap around you."

Where the fuck was that ladder?

"No. I can't—"

Everything happened in slow motion. Her arm slipped from the bar. On pure reflex, Shep shot out and grabbed the arm above her head. He felt the jerk as her shoulder came out of socket. He had a good firm grip, but the jump caused him to lose his footing. He had no time to process. He'd managed to grasp the woman and now they both were falling to their doom.

He saw the shocked expression on Sharon's face, heard a grinding noise that had to be the iron ripping from the building. Instead of terror that his life might end, his mind filled with dismay that the woman would be with him when he hit the ground.

His neck snapped with a hellacious jolt, but he instinctively tightened his grip on Sharon. It took him a few harrying seconds to realize someone had him by his leg.

"Gotcha."

Mike.

Thank fuck.

***

Staunton Augusta Fire Department. How convenient. Quaint little town, smaller than what he was used to, anyway.

Seth watched the scene play out before him as men decked out in fire gear charged into the burning building. Watching the firefighters chase their tails was entertaining.

Take that, motherfucker.

Flames had raged on one level, but all too soon were out. All these helmets running around, he couldn't make out one fucker from the other.

Guess, he shouldn't complain. Hadn't that been the very thing that saved his own ass? The fireman's gear had worked perfectly to his benefit. Right in the middle of the action and he'd blended in as one of them.

A corner of his mouth lifted in a grin. Who cared which one it was? He'd get them all if that's what it took.

For his brother.

Bitterness wedged in his throat.

He'd have that son-of-a-bitch twisted in knots. He couldn't wait to see the look on the bastard's face when *his* brother fell.

CHAPTER 25

Tammy stared at the food in her refrigerator. Why did she keep cooking when she couldn't eat a bite? The boys loved chocolate cake and pudding. Normally she'd sample while baking. Sweets were her weakness. Over the years, making so many cakes and keeping snacks on hand for her boys, she'd never been able to resist temptation. Then when Steve left, she'd gorged herself on comfort food.

Lately, she didn't care if she ate. Sweets no longer looked appealing. In fact, her stomach rolled at the thought of food. Desserts could not take the place of the man she wanted.

She'd lost him. Lost Shep. She'd been wandering around her house in sweats, no make-up, and her hair going in every direction. In the past month, she'd had no appetite. She baked fewer cakes because she just didn't have the desire. If it weren't for David and Christopher, she would probably remain in bed. She didn't like pity parties, but it seemed she floated in a well of commiseration.

The boys were with their dad tonight. She had no one to impress. No one to sit with her while she watched chick flicks, sobbing her heart out. She eyed the wine bottle she'd purchased.

Where was her happy ending?

Where was the one man meant for her?

She'd had plenty of time to think. Entirely too much of it. Years of overeating, she'd been happy. Even after her divorce, she'd retained her forte. Actually, she'd grown stronger. Where was that strength now? She had to stop moping and sort out her tangled life.

Shep. She'd been so sure he was her future. He loved her, adored her even, and she loved him back with all her heart.

Dear God, the ache.

The doorbell rang, jerking her from her self-pity. She looked a mess. Maybe if she ignored whoever it was, they'd go away.

Ding dong. Ding dong. Ding dong.

Or maybe not. She trudged to the door and looked through the peephole she'd installed after Steve moved out.

Cassie.

With a heavy heart, Tammy opened the door. "There's no reason for you to be here. I told you on the phone, I'm handling this."

"Not very well, I see. Misery loves company." Cassie gave her a quick hug.

Tammy padded back to the couch, grabbed her blanket and curled up. Cassie and Mike were a perfect couple. Tammy didn't want to intrude on their time. Just because her relationship with Shep hadn't worked out, she didn't need to make Cassie give up her time with Mike.

"Why is it so dark in here?" Cassie asked as she turned on a lamp. "I was beginning to wonder if you were home. Where are the boys?"

"If you expect me to answer a ton of questions, you're going to be disappointed," she said miserably. "I'm not in the mood."

"Tammy, this isn't like you."

"What? Curled up on the couch with a blanket on a cold night?"

"Sitting in the dark alone. You don't look good, and you've lost weight. Are you eating?"

How could she eat when very little appealed to her? For years, she'd tried to lose weight. Finally, she'd done it. But this was no way to shed the pounds. In wretched misery and heartache.

I guess it's true what they say about a broken heart.

The suffering, the crushing pain in her chest, would kill any hunger.

"Tammy. I'm worried. You need to eat. You don't look well."

"I can't eat. I'm sick to my stomach over what I did to Shep."

"Worry, I can understand. But you're not one to mope and feel sorry for yourself."

"Steve made me miserable." She stared at the wall, recounting her thoughts. "I got rid of him and got my life back on track. Now he's trying to destroy me."

"Don't let him."

She blinked. Cassie was trying to make her feel better, but nothing would make the ache go away. "There's a bottle of wine on the counter. Open it if you like. All of my energy is going into the custody battle."

"Steve started this custody business before he knew about you and Shep. Using Shep to threaten you was just a ploy to scare you. You're giving into Steve by turning Shep away. Don't you see? Steve will fight you for those boys whether Shep is here or not."

Tammy agreed. Steve knew exactly how to make her do what he wanted. He liked having her under his thumb. She'd sworn she'd never be there again. And look at her. Cowering in her home. Wandering around in her darkened room. Missing the one man who made her feel worthy, who made her feel as if she could do anything.

She'd shoved him away.

When Shep walked out her door, she'd wanted to die. Unable to bear the pain, she'd cuddled into a ball and wallowed in grief.

Damn Steve.

Furious that Steve had made her sink so low, she turned her misery into anger. After a while, even that dwindled. All she could do was care for her children and trust Eddie had an ace up his sleeve. For, if Steve somehow managed to take David and Christopher ...

She'd lost Shep. She would truly die if she lost her twins.

"At least Steve won't be able to use Shep as a weapon," she mumbled.

"Can you hear yourself? God, I want to shake you. You've already given up. Where is that snarky spirit? You're entitled to a life of your own. Steve is married."

Yes. Married. With a home. Two parents. The perfect couple. That's what he'd be selling the judge. She was a single mom. With a lover.

Not anymore. She wondered if Steve had thought of the consequence of Shep leaving. If Steve had kept his mouth shut, he would have had leverage. Getting rid of Shep also meant Steve losing the tool he needed for his influence in court. Had his intention been merely to threaten, and make her jump through hoops the way she used to?

"Tammy. Did you hear me?"

"Yes. I heard you. I am entitled to a life. But, Shep is gone. He was just a ..."

What? What was he?

Nothing now.

"What? Shep is what? A man who loves you? He's crazy about you."

"He's gone, Cassie. I told you. Shep and I are over."

Cassie leaped from the couch and began to pace. "How do I get through to you? You're letting Steve control your decisions. You love Shep. You need Shep. Why the hell don't you tell him?"

"It doesn't matter anymore."

Cassie halted her pacing and whirled, shouting, "It does matter!"

"You weren't here. You didn't see Shep's face. You didn't hear him, or look into his eyes as I tore my world apart."

"Steve is the one tearing your world apart, and you're letting him."

Unable to hold herself together any longer, Tammy finally broke down. Her shoulders shook as sobs rocked her body.

"Ah, honey." Cassie's arms enfolded Tammy and hugged her tight. "Things will get better. I promise."

"How? I pushed"—sniff—"Shep away." Tammy swiped the tears from her cheeks. "I tried to change my mind, change his mind. I told him I ... I was sorry." She grabbed a tissue and blew her nose. "I've never seen a man look like that," she continued as she crushed her tissue. "I hurt him. Bad. But he was so damn understanding I wanted to scream. He thinks Steve will always be a problem between us."

"He said that?"

"More or less," Tammy nodded. "I just figured after the trial, he'd be back." It had been weeks. She had to accept it. "Shep won't be back."

He was broken.

I did that.

Me.

***

"How's it going, bro?"

Shep swallowed the retort on his tongue, knowing Eddie was asking out of concern. Shep felt like hell, and he suspected his brother knew that.

"Like you'd expect," he answered with a heavy heart.

"How's the investigation going?"

Same shit. Nothing new, which was frustrating as hell. "Haven't learned a damned thing."

"No clue who is targeting firefighters?"

"None. Or why." Every time he thought about some asshole setting traps for his guys—any firefighter—he seethed. What kind of maniac wanted to harm men who were only trying to help?

"You think this guy might be a firebug, and not with a purpose or anything as deep seeded as vengeance?"

"I wish I knew." Shep scrubbed a hand over his face. He'd found no clues behind the threats against firefighters and every road explored had come to a dead end. Add to the setbacks his fear for Tammy losing custody, he'd been on edge. He needed a clear mind to do his job. There was no room for screw-ups. "It's exasperating, the not knowing. Little things happen and the first thought is, 'could it be this guy?' The son-of-a-bitch is influencing our every move. It'd be a hell of a lot easier if we could respond using our customary instincts instead of worrying about whether or not a perp is behind every 911 call. We don't know if we're rushing out to save someone or running into an ambush."

"Well, maybe I can take your mind off this madman for a while."

That got his attention. Shep hoped like hell it meant good news for Tammy. "What's up?"

"I need you to do something for me."

"Is Tammy all right?"

"Why don't you call her and ask her?"

Damn it. They'd had this discussion. "You know why."

"You and your damn misplaced principles," Eddie snorted. "You didn't have to break things off with—"

"Hindsight," Shep interrupted. "You were asking me for a favor?" On top of everything else, he didn't need grief from his brother.

"To answer your question, how the hell do you think she is? Miserable. But that's about to change."

"You better be giving me some good news pretty damn quick."

"Impatient. Did I call the right brother?"

"Eddie," Shep growled.

"The favor? I want you to come to court."

He hadn't expected that. "Did Tammy ask for me?"

"Does it matter?"

"Cut the lawyer shit, will you?"

"Habit. No, she did not ask for you. But you need to be there."

He wanted to be there. Desperately. If only to feast his eyes on Tammy. Make sure she was okay.

"It's easier for her if I'm not. You know her ex will use me as a conduit against her."

"It's over, bro. I've got him."

The coiled spring snapped. He'd been fretting for weeks, working himself into a state of exhaustion.

Had he heard Eddie right? Was this whole custody mess coming to an end?

"Say again?"

"Things are falling into place. I want you in that courtroom. You need to be there when the shit hits the fan."

"You're saying—"

"Tammy is not going to lose her kids."

Shep shot out of his chair, the grip on his phone making his fingers cramp. "You sure about this?"

"Just be there. She's going to need you."

Disbelief hovered like a dark cloud. Needing to believe so badly, he hesitated with doubt. But this was Eddie. The best at what he did.

Shep's chest eased and a flood of gladness rose from within. If Eddie pulled this off, his fee would be worth whatever Shep had to pay.

The last time he'd seen Tammy, she'd been in agony. Him too. Trying to make things easier on her, he'd obliterated his own heart. Would she welcome him back? Would she understand that he'd done what he had to?

God, he wanted to see her. Everything in him demanded he dash to her house, now. He'd never been one to rush without thought. He'd always considered the consequences.

Eddie said *tomorrow*. Be in the courtroom. Be there for Tammy.

Shep only hoped it wasn't too late.

CHAPTER 26

People filled the courtroom. Some waiting their turn, some had nothing better to do than watch the proceedings. Shep slipped in, unnoticed. Eddie and Tammy sat at a table in front with their heads together. As luck would have it, Shep found a seat just before the judge entered.

Tammy leaned back and Shep tightened his jaw. What he saw stunned him. She looked haggard. Dark shadows circled her eyes. Her beautiful eyes. She'd lost weight and her pale expression resembled a woman without hope.

My God. He hadn't seen her for weeks. What the hell had happened to her? Guilt stabbed his gut. Although, in his defense, Tammy had tried to send him away first. He needed to hold onto the fact that he'd left for her own good. To take away the power Steve had attempted to use against her. Shep refused to be used as a pawn to manipulate Tammy. Breaking things off had taken away Steve's leverage. But seeing the result crushed Shep.

He prayed Eddie was right and this battle would end today. He couldn't bear to be away from Tammy another day.

Steve's lawyer had finished his part, so it was Eddie's turn to call the next witness. Shep waited in anticipation as a man took the witness box. He was sworn in and then Eddie took the floor.

"Would you please state your name for the court?"

"Maynard Barry."

"Thank you, Mr. Barry. What is your profession?"

"I'm retired from White Way Creamery."

"We all look forward to the day we can enjoy retirement. My wife thinks I work too hard and that day will never come." Oh, his brother was smooth. "Tell me, Mr. Barry, how long were you at White Way?"

"Twenty-five years. I started when I was twenty-two years old. Right after I got out of the Army."

"A respected military member. Thank you for your service, Mr. Barry. Would you please tell the court what you do in your spare time?"

"I like keeping busy, so I help out at the Scout Hut. My boys were boy scouts. Each of them earned their Eagle."

"That's an honorable accomplishment. Please continue."

"My boys are grown and gone, but I love working with kids. I'm the Cub Scoutmaster of Troup #231."

"Arc Christopher and David Michael members of your troop?"

"Yes sir, they are."

"Will you tell the court, Mr. Barry, when you first met me?"

"Yes." The scoutmaster shifted, but Shep didn't think it was from nerves. "Last week on Tuesday, you came to the scout hut."

"Would you enlighten the court of our conversation?"

"I have a pretty good memory, but I don't know if I can repeat it word for word."

"That's all right, Mr. Barry. A summary will do. Please give us your understanding of the conversation."

"You asked me if I knew Christopher and David's parents. Then you asked me if I would be willing to be a character reference for Mrs. Michael. I don't butt my nose in other people's business, but I told you I'd rather see her with those boys than their father, and you asked me why."

"Objection, Your Honor." Steve's counsel stood, buttoning his suit coat. "The witness has no authority or professional background to make such a suggestion as to the placement of the Michael children."

"Your Honor, the witness is merely expressing an opinion," Eddie responded. "A statement made during a private discussion. Which I have asked him to repeat to the best of his recollection."

"Overruled. I'd like to hear the testimony of this witness. Mr. Shepherd, you may continue."

"Thank you, Your Honor." Eddie turned back to his witness. "Mr. Barry. I did ask you why. Would you please tell the court your response?"

"Well, there were a few times the new Mrs. Michael, the boys' stepmom, came to pick up Christopher and David. Now these boys are six years old. They need to be helped along, if you know what I mean."

"What do you mean, Mr. Barry?"

"Well, boys like to explore and run around. Inside the hut and on the grounds, we keep a close eye on them. Especially the younger ones. You can't let them out of your sight for a minute. When the stepmom picks up Christopher and David, she doesn't really pay attention to them."

"Objection," the opposing counsel called out. "What are the qualifications of this witness in deciding how much attention any parent should pay to their own children?"

"Mr. Santos. Please sit down. This is a custody case. I want to hear everything anyone has to say regarding these children." The judge gave a nod to Eddie. "The witness may continue."

"Please proceed, Mr. Barry."

"I don't mean dote on them and such. Let me just tell you this one particular instance. Mrs. Michael, the new Mrs. Michael—that is the stepmom—is always on her phone. Texting and such like you see young people do. She talks at you, if you know what I mean. She doesn't look at you, eye to eye, when she speaks. On this particular day, she said she was here, I mean at the hut, to pick up the Michael twins, and then she walks back to her car, expecting them to follow on their own. These kids are six."

The scoutmaster glanced to the judge. Shep waited, anxious as hell to find out what happened.

"Well, they're trying to open the back door and climb inside while she goes around to the driver's door and gets in, leaving the kids on their own. The boys are struggling with the door and I thought David would fall out trying to get the door shut. When I saw she wasn't bothered, I walked over to the car—it was an Escalade—and buckled the kids in. Didn't know if she even saw me."

"What did Mrs. Michael do while you were assisting the twins?"

"Messing with her phone. She didn't say thank you, kiss my a—uh, excuse me." His face turned red. A few people in the back laughed. "I'm sorry, your Honor. I sorta got carried away."

The judge nodded as if he understood, or accepted the apology.

"It just made me so darned mad. She wasn't even going to buckle those kids in."

"Was this a one-time occurrence, or did this happen more than once?"

"Usually there is another leader out front when parents come to pick up their children. The only other time I saw her, there was a man with her."

"Did you know this man?"

"No. I'd never seen him before."

"Thank you, Mr. Barry. Your witness, counselor." Eddie was in his element in the courtroom. Sophisticated, polished, smart, and gracious—with an underlying air of a predator.

Satisfaction and pride filled Shep as he watched his brother. He was damn glad Eddie had called and even more relieved after this testimony. Eddie must have something else up his sleeve.

Shep was more interested in the look on Steve's face than listening to his attorney's cross-examination. Tammy's ex looked pissed. His wife looked like she'd been sucker-punched. Maybe she was cheating on Steve. Wouldn't that be a hoot?

Their heads together, Eddie patted Tammy's hand. Shep wished he could comfort her. Wrap his arms around her and tell her everything was going to be all right. Better yet, take her away from this God-awful mess. To his house. Close to his heart.

"Yes, your Honor." Eddie's voice brought Shep's attention back to the front. "I'd like to call Harold Fultz as my next witness."

A man in a short coat and carrying a little notebook took the stand and was sworn in. Shep didn't recognize the guy. He wondered if this was the man who'd been with Steve's wife when she'd picked up the boys.

"Mr. Fultz, would you please tell the court what you do for a living?"

"I'm a private detective."

Oh shit.

"Would you please tell us about your most recent case?"

"I was hired to follow Mrs. Michael."

"Who hired you, Mr. Fultz?"

"Mr. Michael, her husband."

Shep hadn't seen that one coming. By the gasps in the courtroom, neither had anyone else. The sound of surprised spectators rumbled like thunder. Dammit. He'd hired a PD to follow Tammy. Good thing Shep had kept his distance.

"Mr. Fultz, let me clear this up so there is no misunderstanding. Would you point to the gentleman who hired you and say his name?"

"Yes. Right there." Fultz pointed to Steve. "Mr. Michael."

"Since there are two Mrs. Michaels in the courtroom, would you please point to the woman you were hired to follow and say her name?"

"Yes. Right there." He pointed to Steve's current wife. "Mrs. Michael."

Not Tammy.

The spectators gasped again, followed by many murmurs.

Who were all these people?

"You've pointed to Mrs. Michael, Mr. Michael's current wife?"

"Yes."

The bleached blonde's mouth hung open. This was getting good.

"Did Mr. Michael say why he wanted you to follow his wife?"

"Objection. Hearsay," Steve's attorney shouted.

"Overruled. This is a professional witness."

"Thank you, your Honor," Eddie told the judge, then turned to his witness. "Would you please answer the question?"

"Mr. Michael thought his wife was cheating on him. He hired me to find out."

Several moments passed. Every person had to be on the edge of their seat. Shep forced himself to sit still.

"Did you find out—"

"Objection!"

"I rephrase the question. Did you report your findings to Mr. Michael?"

"Yes, I did."

"Did you report that Mrs. Michael was in fact cheating on her husband with another man?"

"No. I did not."

"You did not." Eddie repeated, then placed his finger under his chin as if puzzled. "Mr. Fultz, what exactly did you find out during your investigation?"

"The man Mr. Michael thought his wife was cheating with turned out to be her brother."

Fuck.

Right when things were getting good. Had Eddie known that before he asked? Hell. What a shock. Tammy couldn't take any more.

"I see." Eddie showed no expression. Had he been surprised like the rest of them? No. Eddie seemed as cool as a cucumber. "Her brother. So, the man Mrs. Michael had been keeping company with was her brother?"

"That's correct."

"Why did Mr. Michael—strike that. Why do you *suppose* Mr. Michael thought she was cheating?"

"She'd been meeting her brother in secret."

"In secret. Hmm." Eddie hesitated. He sure knew how to draw out the suspense. "If this person was Mrs. Michael's brother, don't you think it strange she would keep their meetings a secret? Don't answer that. Did you find out why Mrs. Michael was hiding these meetings from her husband?"

"I did," the witness replied with a nod.

Shep couldn't look away from the nail-biting scene.

"Did you give this information to Mr. Michael?"

"I did."

"What did Mr. Michael have to say?"

"He told me to keep my mouth shut."

"If Mrs. Michael meeting with her brother was innocent, why would Mr. Michael tell you to keep your mouth shut?"

"Objection."

"Overruled!"

"Because it wasn't innocent at all. She was helping her brother deal drugs."

Groans, grumbles, and mutters exploded in the courtroom. Where only a moment ago, Shep could have heard a pin drop, now chaos erupted. It took a few shouts and some whacking of the judge's gavel to settle things down.

"Mr. Fultz, do you have proof that Mrs. Michael was involved with trafficking drugs?"

"Yes sir, I do."

"Why have we not heard about this before now?"

"It happened yesterday."

"You notified Mr. Michael of his wife's actions yesterday?"

"Yes, I did. I also notified the authorities."

From where Shep sat, he could see Steve clenching his fists. The wife looked ready to bolt. Shep couldn't wait to hear what was coming next.

"Mr. Fultz, I must ask you again. Did you explain your findings to Mr. Michael in a way that he understood his wife was participating in a crime?"

"I made sure there was no doubt."

"Why is that?"

"I believe in justice. When I take on a case, I do a little background research on my clients. Just enough to know if they are upstanding citizens. I don't take on cases where a person has a grudge or is out to ruin another person's life." He hesitated as if making his point clear.

"Please continue, Mr. Fultz."

"I found Mr. Michael had a previous wife and two children. Further research showed Mr. Michael in a custody suit. When Mr. Michael told me to keep my mouth shut, I figured he had his reasons, being the woman was his wife. But since children are involved, I thought it my duty to come forward. The court should be aware of all the facts."

The current Mrs. Michael jumped up, quickly scurrying to the end of the aisle. Two officers blocked her path. The woman clawed and screeched like a hellcat, creating a pretty chaotic scene. Tammy stared at her ex. He argued with his attorney. The whole damn place was in an uproar.

If Shep hadn't been so relieved, the commotion might have been entertaining. Counsel argued, and then the judge slammed his hammer a final time, ruling his decision. Shep was out of his seat without wasting another second. Making his way around Eddie, he caught a smiling, crying Tammy hurdling into his arms. God, she felt good. He'd had no idea how Tammy would react when she saw him. The last time he'd seen her, he'd been pretty emotional.

"Can you believe it? Oh, my God. I never imagined ..."

"Congratulations, Sweetheart," Shep whispered in her ear. "It's over."

She leaned back, tears streaming down her beautiful cheeks. "It is, isn't it?"

Shep used his thumbs to brush the crystal drops away. "Yes. It is." God, he wanted to kiss her so bad. To hell with her ex-husband, but he wouldn't embarrass her in a room full of people who already had seen quite a show. Even if the focus was on Steve and his wife.

A hard slap landed on his back. "Glad you made it, bro."

"Thanks for calling. I wouldn't have missed this for anything."

"I'm so glad you're here," Tammy muttered.

"See. You should listen to your big brother. I'll always be older and wiser. And better looking," Eddie said with a wink at Tammy.

"You've got the older part right," Shep said. "I think I see a few wrinkles. And is that more gray hair I see?"

Tammy gave Eddie a hug. "Thank you. Thank you. Thank you. How on earth did you find out? Why didn't you tell me?"

"I couldn't risk you saying something to your ex. Besides, Harold called me last night. I only needed a few more hours, in court."

"You knew when you called me?" Shep asked.

"Sorry, buddy. It had to play out the way it did."

"I was shocked."

"So were a lot of other people. Including the two who tried to hide what they were doing." Eddie chuckled. He faced Tammy. "The kids are yours," he said squeezing her shoulder. "You don't ever have to worry about Steve again."

"Are you sure?"

"He tried to cover up a crime. He's looking at jail time."

"Oh. I never meant for him to go to jail."

"You had nothing to do with that. His wife was in over her head and Steve tried to cover it up."

"Come on. Let's get out of here." Shep took Tammy's hand in his and tugged. He'd been without this woman entirely too long. He wasn't letting another moment pass without telling her how he felt.

"You two go celebrate," Eddie said as he closed his briefcase.

"Aren't you coming with us?" Tammy asked.

"I'm going to make sure the documents award you full legal and physical custody."

"Thank you so much. I don't know what I would have done ..." She choked up. Shep put his arm around her and held her next to his heart.

"We're out of here, bro."

"Later."

Shep herded Tammy out of the courtroom, then out of the building, not taking the time to see where her ex had gone. He wanted to get Tammy as far away from Steve as possible.

The sun hit Shep in the eyes and he reached on top of his head for his shades, which weren't there.

Tammy glanced at him, puzzled.

"I had to leave my shades in the truck."

"Where are you parked?"

"Around back." He laced his fingers with hers, liking what the gesture signified. Him linked to her. Their hands joined together. Hopefully more.

He tucked her in on the passenger side then hopped into the driver's seat. Unable to deny himself another moment, he reached for her, took her in his arms and placed the kiss on her he'd desperately wanted to do since seeing her in that courtroom. She grasped his head, molding her mouth to his, giving him back everything he tried to convey in the kiss.

After a few passionate, mind guzzling seconds, he finally released her. Their breaths mingled and her chest heaved against his. Damn, she was beautiful, looking all mussed with that longing expression.

"Don't look at me like that or we'll never make it out of the parking lot."

Tammy giggled. A provocative sound that went straight to his dick. With a growl, he reached above her for the seatbelt and latched it into place.

"Let's get you home."

Chapter 27

A year ago, he'd been ignorant of a love so deep it could paralyze him. Today, Shep experienced a love so fierce it consumed every bone in his body. And he wouldn't have it any other way.

The sun glinted off Tammy's red hair and winked at the pale lashes encompassing her beautiful eyes. A few wisps of hair fluttered as the slight breeze wafted over the back deck of Shep's home. His chest swelled with adoration, and a yearning to keep her forever.

He'd be nothing without the woman by his side.

Squeals of laughter soared in the air as two little boys chased and fell and played with Hutch. A sight Shep treasured. He adored Tammy's twins and promised to cherish them for as long as she would let him.

The day had started as a gruesome burden. Thanks to Eddie, Tammy now could be at ease. Worry had filled her life for so long, he wanted to shield her from ever experiencing such a thing again. With his life, he would shield her, protect her from harm. Slay her dragons.

"What are you thinking?" Her gentle voice tweaked the longing in his chest.

"How beautiful you are." He loved it when she blushed. She didn't like it, said it embarrassed her, but she glowed with radiance. Her vivacity being one of the things that had attracted him. "I love having you here at my home. You look so peaceful. Happy. I haven't seen your smile in so long."

"I had little to smile about. I was so stressed."

"I know," he said gently. He understood what she'd been going through. "I only wish I could have been with you these last weeks."

"I'm sorry I made things so difficult for you. I pushed you away because I was scared. You're such a considerate man. You made the decision for me. I know your intention was to make things easier for me, but it didn't. It nearly killed me."

"It was tough on us both."

"Thank you, for not giving up on me."

"Never," he said squeezing her fingers.

"I'm so glad it's over, so glad you came back."

"Where else would I be? Anything worth having isn't easy to get."

Her eyes bore into his. "I love you. I never want you to leave me again."

"I won't. Even if you want me to."

"I'll never want that. I didn't want it this time. Steve had me so twisted and torn, I didn't know what to do. You did what you thought was best for me. I love you even more for it."

"Know this." He covered her hand with both of his and met her eyes, letting her see everything in his heart. "I want you forever. Nothing will ever change that. All I want or need is you."

"Well, it looks like you got me. And two kids to boot."

"I'll take it." He lifted her hand and kissed her knuckles, all the while holding her lovely gaze.

"You look like you have something else on your mind," she said softly.

That he'd die without her? That he thanked God his brother had saved them?

"How much I owe my brother for giving you back to me."

She wrinkled her brow and sat up. "Nonsense. He had little to do with it."

"Woman, how can you sit there and say that? He wrapped Steve up, nice and neat, and gave you what you cherished."

"Eddie took care of *Steve*," she whispered, not wanting the boys to hear their father's name. "He settled the custody issue. But you are mistaken if you think your brother is the reason I am here with you."

Shep's heart danced double time. Feisty Tammy. His Tammy, her love shining in her eyes for him to see. For the world to see. God, he loved this woman.

"Do you know how beautiful you look when you get all fired up?"

She gave him a sexy smile. "Wait till later."

He groaned. "Now you're torturing me."

"Promising," she purred.

Just like that, he had an erection.

"Careful, my love. I don't need your youngsters asking about the tent in my pants."

She laughed. He could listen to the erotic sound the rest of his life.

Family. His family.

"I'm glad you and the boys are here."

"They like you." She turned to watch the frolicking in the backyard. "And they like Hutch."

"I figure they like him more."

"Maybe. He's a dog. Kids love animals, and mine are no different."

Shep settled back against his chair, rubbing his thumb over Tammy's knuckles, unwilling to let her go. "I'm thinking of getting horses."

"Shut up!"

"What? Why?"

"Not really. It's what someone says when they are astonished."

"You told me to shut up."

"Never mind." She waved a hand.

"Women." He shook his head.

"Are you seriously thinking about purchasing horses?"

Yeah, he was. He'd been thinking about lots of animals and lots of kids.

One thing at a time.

"I don't have any because of my schedule. I'm gone most of the time. I think it would be nice to have some livestock. Kids should be around animals. I've got the space."

"How much land do you own?"

"Round eighty acres." Eighty-three to be exact. He might check into expanding.

"Really? Horses," Tammy breathed. "The boys would go nuts." Suddenly she lost her smile and her body grew taut. "Shep."

He wondered what in the world was going through her mind. He didn't want to ever see her apprehensive again. "What is it? I'll fix it, whatever it is."

"A horse is huge. His back is pretty far from the ground."

He signed with relief. He hoped he could fix any future problems as easy as this one.

"Don't worry. We can start with ponies."

"You're going to spoil them. You're spoiling me."

He tugged her hand and pulled her onto his lap. This was where she belonged. He rubbed his thumb over the back of her knuckles, relishing the feel of her soft skin. Savoring the way her curves fit against him, and how she made him feel. He'd waited long enough. It was time.

"Tammy. I want you here with me. I want you and your boys in my life permanently."

"Shep," she choked. "I ..."

"You what?"

"Me *and* my boys?"

"How could you ask? Of course, you and Christopher and David. Those two tykes already have my heart."

She sniffed.

"Don't cry. They'll be up here thinking I did something to their mother."

She swallowed and got herself together. Then she looked at him with tenderness and a love so intense his legs would have buckled if he'd been standing. He caressed her face, his thumb smoothing over her soft cheek.

"Do you have any idea how much I love you?"

"That's not helping. I'm trying not to cry."

Shep rose from his chair with Tammy in his arms and swung her around.

"What are you doing?" She sputtered with laughter. His intent to lighten the mood had worked.

"Mom. What ya'll doin'?" Christopher bounded up the steps. David and Hutch right behind him.

"Can we play?"

Shep sat, holding Tammy on his lap. "Your mom wants to be tickled. Let's tickle her."

The boys laughed and screamed and poked her in the sides.

Life was good.
And it was about to get a whole lot better.

EPILOGUE

Look at her, all stiff and snotty.

Her routine hadn't changed for the past three weeks. She drove to work every day at the same time, taking the same route, and every night she went home the same way. Even the gas station and supermarket she'd stopped at were on her path.

Predictable as the sun setting each evening.

Seth bet he could bang the starch out of her backside. She'd like it, too. Just what the nosy bitch deserved.

After weeks of constant surveillance, Seth was ready to make his move. He'd followed her to the hospital parking lot and then into the building. When she took the elevator, he took the stairs. It wouldn't do for her to recognize him.

He wished he knew how much the bitch had heard and if she'd said anything to anyone.

At the top of the stairwell, he slid through a door and peeked around a corner, watching the movement behind the counter at the nurses' station. One woman stared at a computer, another was on the phone. A doctor slapped a folder on the tall counter, then leaned on his elbows, flirting with the woman sitting be-hind it.

Prick. Seth bet before the night was over, the fancy doctor would have her knees up around his ears. Seth didn't give a shit. The only one he cared about was the blonde bitch he'd followed to this floor. The one who'd overheard him when he was on the phone with Carl. She should have minded her own business and not listened in on his private conversation. He was on the fucking phone.

Patience was a virtue. Wasn't that what he'd been told? All he had to do was wait. And he had. Carefully planning for months.

He didn't like loose ends. This bitch was a loose end.

The nurses on duty went about their business.

The snotty blonde strode down the hall and went into a patient's room. Just like clockwork.

Perfect.

Seth hurried down the stairwell and marched outside. He double-checked to make sure she'd parked her car in the same space she always did.

Carl stood at the back of the pickup, smoking a cigarette. When he saw Seth, he tossed it on the pavement and ground it with his boot.

"She there?"

"Yeah. All clear."

Carl got what he needed and slipped behind the row of cars. The guy was so smooth, even Seth had trouble seeing him.

Ten minutes later, Carl opened the passenger door and hopped in. He gave a nod the job was done. Seth cranked the engine.

Goodnight, bitch.

The End of Book 2: Shep.
Be sure to read on for a sneak peek of Book 3: Jared!

THANK YOU

Thank you for reading my story. I hope you enjoyed reading it as much as I loved writing it.
And, if you did, would you consider leaving a review online? It really would mean the world to me.

Thank you!
Samanthya

Passions soar and desires burn hot, yet each is afraid to surrender to love. 5 Men - 5 full length books. Together, the hero and heroine overcome their inner conflict to achieve love completely unaware there is a more dangerous peril—one man's revenge.

Jared was used to getting what he wanted and he wants the enticing nurse who makes him burn hotter than some of the fires his team puts out. But he finds himself caught up in the disappearance of her friend and their search lands them in a hot situation —the danger to his heart could be more perilous than the villain pursuing Station #8.

Jessica has worked hard for her career as a nurse and her life seems full, until she meets the rugged firefighter who takes up entirely too much time in her head. Then her co-worker's car explodes, she disappears, and the hot man in uniform has made it his mission to keep Jessica safe. But who will keep her safe from him?

***Keep Reading for an Excerpt from
Jared: The Firefighters of Station #8 – Book 3***

JARED

CHAPTER 1

"911 Dispatch. What is the address of your emergency?"

"Is this the fire man?" a little girls voice came across the line.

"What's your name?"

"Tiffany."

"Hi Tiffany, my name is Terri. How old are you?"

"Five."

"Is your mom or dad there?"

"No."

"Are you alone?"

"No. My brother is here. He kicked me in the balls."

"Are you hurt?"

The little girl started crying. "It's Charlie. He's stuck in the tree," she said between sobs. "Can you get him down?"

"Tiffany, honey. Don't cry. I'm sure your brother is all right and we'll get to him as quickly as possible."

"Not him. It's Charlie. He's up in the tree. Aiden chased him up there. When I shoved him, he kicked me in the balls."

"Who's Charlie?"

"My cat. He's scared."

"Sweetheart, he'll be okay."

"You gotta come. I need a fire man to get him down."

"The firefighters are busy putting out fires. When Charlie is ready, he'll come down."

The pitiful voice cried harder. "He's scared. I am too."

"Are you hurt? Did Aiden hurt you?"

"No, but I had to run away. My other brother tried to take the phone from me."

"Tiffany. Don't run away. Where are you now?"

"Hiding in the bush."

"Are you at your house?"

"Yes."

"Where is your mom?"

"She's gone."

"Where is your dad?"

"He's in the miliferry."

"Oh. How old is your brother?"

"Aiden is four. I'm older and he should listen to me."

"How old is your other brother?"

"Tanner is seven. He thinks he's the boss."

"Tiffany, is there any other adult at the house? Maybe a neighbor or family member?"

"No."

***

There were few days when Jared Collins had a chance to unwind. Today, the hours stretched long into a hot summer afternoon, and the guys were sitting in the firehouse bay shooting the breeze. Now and again, dispatch received some entertaining calls, and it looked like this just happened to be one of those times. The fire department did not respond to 'my cat is in a tree' calls.

"Are you kidding, Cap? Dispatch doesn't send us calls to get a cat out of a tree." Jared was surprised the captain was even considering it.

Other than the arsonist who had every firefighter looking over their shoulders, things around the station had been quiet for the past couple of days, and the captain did not make up stories. As for Jared, he liked taking a breather, especially after the hellish inferno from the other night. Station Eight had received a call at two in the morning, reporting a hotel on fire. The first thing he'd thought of was how big the building was and how many people were asleep inside. Thank God, it had been in the process of renovations and the place was empty. Sounded to him a lot like arson, making him wonder about the firebug currently on everyone's mind. The training site explosion had been explained, but they had no idea who the culprit might be.

Hooley, the fire inspector, came by last week to give them an update, but no news as to the identity of the person who'd stolen the equipment from Station Nine. No one recognized the imposter dressed in the firefighter's uniform from the film recorded at the training site.

Jared had been drawn back into the incident of that dreadful day, reliving the horrific explosion as it blew up on the screen when Hooley showed them the film. Every gruesome detail.

We have no idea of motive. He could have chosen a firehouse randomly or he might have a beef with a certain individual. We don't know if he is targeting fire departments in general or firefighters, so you need to be on guard.

Jared blinked. A cat in a tree was just what he needed to get his mind off some nut-job out there targeting firefighters.

"Don't have nothing else to do," Laredo, a member of the team, said in a lazy tone while tossing a finger-exercise ball in the air. "Why don't we check it out?"

"If you're bored, go wash the quint." Jared couldn't imagine why Laredo wasn't already doing that. He kept the thing shined the way a man took care of his muscle car. The paint glimmered, and anyone could see their reflection in the bumper.

"That's not the best part of the call," Shep continued. "The child on the phone was a girl. She said her brother kicked her in the balls."

Jared jerked his head to see if the captain was yanking them around. Laredo snatched the rubber ball out of the air and wrenched upright, dropping his feet to the cement floor.

"Did I hear you right. You did say a *girl* was on the phone."

"Yep," Shep gave a nod. "No lie. She said her brother kicked her in the balls."

Laredo hooted in laughter. "I've got to meet this kid's mother."

"What about the father?" Jared questioned, trying to curb his own amusement.

"What man would tell his daughter she has *cojones*? Got to be the mom."

"Or she got it from her brother," Jared tossed back with a grin. Boys would tell girls anything.

"You're about to get your wish," Shep continued. "I'm sending you two out to check on this. Dispatch never got a parent on the phone. The kid said she was five years old."

That news grabbed Jared's attention. Children calling 911 could mean a number of things, and if there was no parent, no adult able to come to the phone, that could mean someone was hurt. He now understood why Shep wanted them to check it out. He glanced to Laredo.

"I'm one step ahead of you, dude." Laredo jumped to his feet. "I'll grab my gear."

"We'll take the squad, just in case we do find an injured person."

"Go ahead and take the quint," the Captain ordered. "You've got a kit if you need medical supplies."

Each truck was equipped with a certain amount of medical emergency equipment and bandages. The captain made sure of that years ago when a shaky bridge collapsed after only one rig managed to cross. The quint got separated from the rescue squad and men had been injured on both sides.

"If there is no emergency, you can get the kid's cat out of the tree," Shep added. "Kids love firetrucks. If this girl thinks she has balls, she's probably a tom boy. She'll get just as much a kick out of the ladder truck as any boy."

"You got it, Cap." With a big grin, Laredo headed to the quint.

"Wait till the rest of the guys hear about this?" Jared mumbled. He and Laredo were headed to a non-working call. No threat of a fire, but a little girl whose cat was stuck up in a tree. First time he'd been on this type of rescue. He just hoped they didn't find a real emergency.

When in doubt – send everyone out.

Someone had to respond.

***

Who knew when Jessica agreed to watch her sister's kids that she'd regret her decision within twenty-four hours? After dealing with her niece and nephews, she may never have children of her own. She shoved at the strand of hair that had escaped from her ponytail and exhaled a deep breath.

They weren't that bad. But they did keep her in the role of referee. And Tiffany was just as bad as her brothers.

"Rough morning?"

Jess glanced over to find the neighbor leaning casually against the gate. Connie had two kids of her own, but they were twelve and fourteen. She looked great. How did she do it?

"Those three will make me old before my time," Jess said as she strolled over to the backyard fence.

"The boys will be home from basketball practice soon. I'll tell them to take the kids off your hands and give you a break."

"Raven has only been gone two days. I'm ready to call her and beg her to come home."

Connie laughed, the tinkling sound echoing through the back yard.

"Honestly, I don't know how either one of you do it. Her kids are a handful. I know she needed a break. And look at you. You look so calm and, you're smiling. You survived your kids' hellion years."

"Siblings always bicker. Just don't let them run over you. And don't call your sister. If you need help, call me."

"Thanks."

"Come on over for some coffee. You look like you could use the extra caffeine." Connie opened the gate and motioned for Jess to follow her. Coffee sounded good. Jess would need the caffeine to keep up with the rugrats.

As soon as Jess stepped into Connie's kitchen she smelled the coffee bean aroma. She plopped down onto a chair at the kitchen table and propped her head on her hand, her mouth already salivating. She'd picked up the habit from her dad. He always had a pot of coffee on and when she wanted a cup of her dad's coffee, she immediately added milk and sugar to cover the bitter taste. But her dad told her if she was going to drink coffee, not to mess it up with sugar and stuff. She still added milk. She just couldn't drink it black.

"Do you take vitamins or do you have an energy drink stashed in the cupboard?"

"I make sure I get thirty minutes of uninterrupted me time every day. Rick helps."

Connie and her husband seemed like the perfect couple. Rick was handsome and the boys looked just like him. Jess had noticed he had a good rapport with his kids. She'd seen him playing basketball in their driveway and now wondered if that was when Connie got her *thirty minutes* of uninterrupted time.

"Cream or sugar?"

"Just some milk, please."

As Connie opened the refrigerator, Jess pulled her cup closer. Steam swirled in the air and again she inhaled the pleasing scent. She could already feel the tension ease from her shoulders.

A giggle had her snapping her eyes open. "If the smell of coffee puts that look on your face, I can't wait till you taste it."

"Coffee is the brew of the gods," Jess said shrugging her shoulders. "I love my java." She poured a generous blob of milk, then blew across the top as if that would cool the hot liquid.

Connie sat down beside her. "So. Are you doing okay?"

"Sure. It's great, actually. I love those kids. They're just a handful. I know why my sister needed to get away."

"She loves them fiercely. She fretted over the decision to go, but this was her chance to be with Chad."

"I don't know how she does that either. Being in the military, he's gone so much. I can't even begin to imagine the worry she has to deal with when he goes to Afghanistan."

"That's why it was important for her to meet him. They'll have a week together before he leaves. Did you know she talked it over with me? She felt guilty leaving the children. I'm glad you could help her out."

"Are you kidding? I'm happy to help. She certainly has nothing to feel guilty for. I'd do it more often if she'd let me know what's going on. She's so independent."

"She's a military wife. She's learned to take care of herself."

Jess thought about that. Raven was two years older and already had three children. She and Chad met when Raven was twenty-one and they'd been together ever since. Even growing up, Jess remembered her sister being strong and independent. Jess couldn't help but wonder if she would find a love like her sister had with Chad. Like the devotion she saw between Connie and Rick.

A wailing sound drifted in from outside.

"Do you hear sirens? They seem awfully close."

Jess tilted her head and listened. "Yes, they do." The piercing sound and a sharp horn grew louder.

"It sounds like it is coming down our street," Connie said as she rose and headed to the living room. She stepped to the big picture window and drew back a curtain. "I see a red fire truck. Oh my God."

"What?" Jessica asked, hurrying up behind her.

"They're stopping in front of Raven's house."

**Order your copy of Jared: The Firefighters of Station #8
Scan the QR code below!**

About the Author

Samanthya Wyatt writes sizzling hot romance with suspense. Intensely emotional characters with a deep passionate love for friends, family, and most importantly—between the hero and heroine. Although her first love is historical romance, this award-winning author also writes contemporary romance under the pen name S. R. Wyatt. Additionally, she has written a book of one family's struggle based on true life events.

Samanthya left her accounting career and married a military man traveling and making her home in the United States and abroad. She now lives in the Shenandoah Valley. On a sunny day, you can find her and her husband driving on the Blue Ridge Parkway or going to car shows in their 1969 Mustang convertible. She loves long walks, and a book to read on a sandy beach. Starbucks is her favorite drink and she likes hearing from her fans.

She invites you to lay the worries of the world off your shoulders and get lost in the pages of a romance, where you embark on a journey with the hero and heroine, become involved in a dream, plunge into a world of fantasy, and live an adventure your heart can share.

To find out more about Samanthya Wyatt and her books, please visit her website: https://samanthyawyattauthor.com/